The Frontier Gambler's Lady

"Colorado Reborn"

~ *A Stand-Alone Novel* ~

A Christian Western Romance Novel

by

Chloe Carley

Copyright© 2018 by Chloe Carley

All Rights Reserved.

ISBN: 9781718155077

This book may not be reproduced or transmitted in any form without the written permission of the publisher.

In no way is it legal to reproduce, duplicate, or transmit any part of this document in either electronic means or in printed format. Recording of this publication is strictly prohibited and any storage of this document is not allowed unless with written permission from the publisher

Table of Contents

Influence my next story	Pg 5
Chapter One	Pg 10
Chapter Two	Pg 19
Chapter Three	Pg 25
Chapter Four	Pg 30
Chapter Five	Pg 39
Chapter Six	Pg 46
Chapter Seven	Pg 50
Chapter Eight	Pg 58
Chapter Nine	Pg 62
Chapter Ten	Pg 69
Chapter Eleven	Pg 73
Chapter Twelve	Pg 78
Chapter Thirteen	Pg 83
Chapter Fourteen	Pg 88
Chapter Fifteen	Pg 93
Chapter Sixteen	Pg 98
Chapter Seventeen	Pg 104
Chapter Eighteen	Pg 109
Chapter Nineteen	Pg 114
Chapter Twenty	Pg 119
Chapter Twenty-One	Pg 132

Chapter Twenty-Two	Pg 139
Chapter Twenty-Three	Pg 144
Chapter Twenty-Four	Pg 152
Chapter Twenty-Five	Pg 157
Chapter Twenty-Six	Pg 164
Chapter Twenty-Seven	Pg 170
Chapter Twenty-Eight	Pg 175
Chapter Twenty-Nine	Pg 179
Chapter Thirty	Pg 185
Chapter Thirty-One	Pg 191
Chapter Thirty-Two	Pg 196
Chapter Thirty-Three	Pg 201
Chapter Thirty-Four	Pg 205
Chapter Thirty-Five	Pg 210
Chapter Thirty-Six	Pg 217
Chapter Thirty-Seven	Pg 225
Chapter Thirty-Eight	Pg 233
Chapter Thirty-Nine	Pg 237
Chapter Forty	Pg 246
Chapter Forty-One	Pg 253
Chapter Forty-Two	Pg 259
Chapter Forty-Three	Pg 265
Chapter Forty-Four	Pg 271
Chapter Forty-Five	Pg 278

Chapter Forty-Six	Pg 283
Chapter Forty-Seven	Pg 288
Chapter Forty-Eight	Pg 294
Chapter Forty-Nine	Pg 301
Chapter Fifty	Pg 308
Chapter Fifty-One	Pg 313
Chapter Fifty-Two	Pg 322
Chapter Fifty-Three	Pg 330
Chapter Fifty-Four	Pg 335
Chapter Fifty-Five	Pg 341
Chapter Fifty-Six	Pg 346
Chapter Fifty-Seven	Pg 351
Chapter Fifty-Eight	Pg 357
Chapter Fifty-Nine	Pg 362
Chapter Sixty	Pg 367
Chapter Sixty-One	Pg 372
Chapter Sixty-Two	Pg 380
Epilogue	Pg 384
Thank You!	Pg 395

Influence my next story

The core soul of the book you just bought was influenced by thousands of readers who became part of my "family" before you! The title, the cover, the essence of the book as a whole was affected by them!

I personally want to thank them for their support on my journey! I devote this book to them!

If you are not a member, **click this link to join**: https://chloecarley.com/ccbbsd

After you sign-up, you will receive as a BONUS my Full-Length Novella, "Boston Bride Salvation! With more than 140+ positive GoodReads reviews it's a safe choice, you don't want to miss:

FREE EXCLUSIVE GIFT
(available only to my subscribers)

Visit my webpage to get the FREE BONUS:
https://chloecarley.com/ccbbsd

PERSONAL WORD
from Chloe Carley

"Once upon a time..."

...my best childhood nights had started with this wonderful phrase!

Ever since I can remember, I loved a good story!

All started thanks to my beloved grandfather! He used to read to my sister and me, stories of mighty princes and horrifying dragons! Even now, sometimes I miss those cold winters in front of the fireplace in my hometown, Texas!

My best stories though were the ones from the Bible! Such is the spiritual connection that a cozy warm pass through my body every time I hear a biblical story!

My childhood memories were not all roses, but I always knew that the strongest shelter would be always there for me! It was Him!

Years passed by, and little-Chloe grown up reading all kind of stories! It was no surprise that I had this urge to write my own stories, and share them with the word!

If I have a God's purpose on Earth, I think it is to spread His love and wisdom, through my stories!

Now, it is your time to **read my STAND-ALONE Novel "The Frontier Gambler's Lady"**!

Brightest Blessings,

Chloe Carley

Chapter One

*Somewhere on the Mississippi River
1880*

"*Whoo-ooooooooooooo!*"

The steam whistle on the *Natchez Queen* sounded a long, low moan as she churned north up the Mississippi River. The paddle wheeler's proud smoke stacks were sharply outlined against the moon-silvered river, and the golden light in her windows, and the faint music drifting out over the water, advertised that there was a party going on inside.

The brand-new paddle wheeler had been roundly criticized by some northern newspapers as "vulgar", "tasteless", "void of any redeeming qualities" and "pandering to the lower elements."

But in New Orleans, where she was built, her gambling saloons were considered the last word in elegance, what with their red velvet curtains, rococo wallpaper, fringed chairs, and elaborate poker tables.

No matter that her abundantly opulent décor had been likened by some to "a French Quarter bordello." Or that her employees' red jackets and smart white trousers had been reviled as "a vulgar mockery of military uniforms."

The *Natchez Queen's* poker parlours had been a

smashing success from the day they opened.

And while there was a certain amount of truth to the criticism that her patrons were "the sort of bottom feeding gamblers, slicks, and con men who always frequent such low places," their detractors might have been surprised to learn that there was still one virtue the riverboat's sporting brotherhood absolutely upheld:

Fair play.

***

A dark, bearded gent pressed his cards against his chest, took a puff of his cigar, and blew smoke up to the ceiling. He nodded towards the dealer. "Three cards, please."

Doc Dailey watched as the player pulled the dealt card in and his blue eyes narrowed. This time he was sure of it: the man had cards up his sleeve.

His hand shot out, and in a split-second he clamped the player's wrist against the table as he pulled a high card out of his cuff.

Doc nodded his blond head toward it and announced: "He's pulling cards out of his sleeve."

The man tried to yank his hand back, but Doc's grip held his wrist like a vise, and the half-drawn Ace of Diamonds remained clearly visible. The other players straightened up, and their narrowed eyes moved from the man's hand to his face.

"Why you cheating son of a—"

"What do you take us for?"

Two of them pushed their chairs back and reached

inside their vests, and things might have gone sharply south if a smiling young woman hadn't placed herself smoothly between them and the ashen-faced cheater.

"Why, what's going on, gentlemen?" she enquired, turning from one to another laughingly. "This is supposed to be a friendly game."

One of the players gestured towards the guilty man with an engraved pistol. "That sidewinder's a mechanic! He's pulling cards out of his shirt!"

Another waved her away. "Step aside, Kate! Only one way to deal with a cheat!"

"Cheat?" she turned to look down at the terrified player. "That's a serious accusation. Are you sure?"

"Doc caught him red-handed."

Kate put up her hands in a calming gesture. "Gentlemen, please put away your pistols. I'll fetch Judge, and he'll deal with it, never fear." She turned away, and then looked back over her shoulder.

"*Please* sit down."

Kate's mild tone, and the wry amusement in her eyes, had their effect. The two men grumbled but returned their pistols to their vests and sat down again.

Doc watched in admiration as Kate's iridescent green gown swayed gently out of the room. Officially, Kate Dubois was the hostess of the *Natchez Queen*, but unofficially, the auburn-haired beauty acted as the 'cooler,' the calm hand and smiling feminine face that kept the play more or less civilized, and that drew male patrons to the riverboat's gambling saloon by the wagon loads.

Doc took a pull from his own cigar. Kate was the best

poker player he'd ever seen, as well as a dealer for the *Natchez Queen*, and he'd never caught her cheating. He still hadn't decided if that was because she was truly honest, or if she was a sharp—and just very, *very* good at it.

It had become an increasingly intriguing question for him in the last few months, since he and Kate had embarked on a secret love affair. Kate hadn't wanted Judge to know that she was seeing one of the saloon's patrons, and he had bowed to her wishes.

It was always wise to be discreet.

Especially when a man as powerful as Judge had his eye on the same lady.

Doc blew a lazy smoke ring over the table, recalling their last midnight tryst, in the darkened sanctuary of a New Orleans church. It was practically the only place they could meet without fear of being seen by someone they knew.

Kate had turned to him, worry clouding her beautiful green eyes. Moonlight slanting through the stained-glass windows had painted her hair rose pink and red.

"He scares me, Doc. He throws things when he gets mad. He screams at everybody on the staff but me, but I almost wish he did scream at me. He scares me more when he smiles.

"And—he all but told me that I'd better sleep with him if I want to keep my job."

Fury had surged up in Doc's chest, but it would've been pointless to burden Kate with his rage. He pulled her close, and his arms closed around her. He rested his cheek on her hair.

"Leave then and come with me. I'm going out west after this cruise, where the gambling's wild and wide open. Where no one man controls all the play."

He looked down into her face. "Come with me, Kate."

She met his eye and smiled. "All right," she murmured, and traced his lips with a light forefinger. "When are you leaving?"

"The *Queen*'s due to arrive in St. Louis at midnight, day after tomorrow. We can leave together, as soon as the boat docks, and then take the train out to Denver."

He gave her a slow, lingering kiss. "Then Judge can throw as big a fit as he likes," he whispered and was gratified to see Kate's worried look melt into a smile.

"He can throw furniture, and scream, and even toss a few of his employees overboard."

He teased a soft, reluctant sputter from those beautiful lips, and they laughed together, and then kissed again.

Doc took a flat-faced gold ring off his finger and put it to her lips. "Give me some luck, Kate," he teased and smiled to see her give the ring a tiny kiss.

"I can't lose now," he said with a smile and put it back on his hand. "And I'll never take it off."

***

Doc blinked back his memories, reached down into his pocket, and opened a tiny box. A diamond ring winked at him from its velvet cushion, and he smiled and closed it up again.

By midnight, he and Kate would be on their way.

The parlour door opened abruptly, and Judge Carter blew in, with Kate right behind him. Judge was a little shy of average height and stocky, a bad-tempered man with red hair, grey eyes, and a square jaw. He was mildly handsome and was unremarkable except for his angry expression.

But when Judge opened his mouth, the voice of a dragon jumped out. That deep, gravelly voice never failed to startle those who heard it for the first time, and Doc noticed that at least three men nearby flinched visibly.

"What's the trouble here?" Judge growled.

Doc nodded toward the player. "I caught him pulling cards."

Judge's eyes challenged his. "Are you sure?"

The other men at the table answered for him. They half-stood and pointed angrily at the guilty man.

"We all saw it!"

"Doc caught him with the card half drawn!"

"What kind of a place are you running?"

A perfunctory smile creased Judge's face. He held up his hands. "Now, now, gentleman," he replied, "this saloon has no control over the actions of its patrons. But we have a strict rule on this vessel. No cheating!"

Doc was tempted to roll his eyes but maintained an expression of lazy interest as Judge snapped his fingers, and two big men appeared and dragged the unhappy man away. The rule on the *Natchez Queen*, and one that was strictly enforced, was that all known cheaters were tossed unceremoniously into the Mississippi.

Judge turned to face him, and Doc drawled: "I want a new deck and a new dealer."

Judge waved towards Kate. "How about Kate? Is that all right with you gentlemen?"

They all nodded, and Doc watched as Kate smiled and settled in. Judge leaned over, placed an unopened deck of cards on the table, and whispered in Kate's ear before leaving.

Anger whisked up in Doc's heart like sparks. Judge never missed an opportunity to show every man in the room that he was laying claim to Kate.

Whether she liked it, or *not*.

His eyes bored into Judge's back as he walked out of the room, but he consoled himself with the thought that after midnight it wouldn't matter what Judge wanted.

Kate had made her choice. She was coming with him.

He lowered his eyes to see Kate dimple at him as she opened the pack of cards. "Well, gentlemen, are you ready to continue the game?" She cut and shuffled the cards expertly, and they rippled between her hands like running water. "Deuces are low, aces are high, and jokers are wild."

She paused with the deck in her hands. She questioned the table with her eyes. "Who'll start?"

A bearded man to Doc's right nodded towards her. "It was my turn." He took his cards and studied them intently.

***

To Doc's amusement, Lady Luck smiled on him that

night. In fact, she became increasingly more affectionate as the evening wore on: and by eleven thirty, a crowd of men had gathered around his table to watch as a fantastic sum of money teetered in the balance. Five tall piles of chips were stacked neatly on the table in front of him.

He had won almost ten thousand dollars—a record for that saloon, and a personal best for him.

The dark man was the only player who still had money enough to stay in the game with him. "One card, please."

Kate slid a single card across the table, and the man stared at it impassively. But Doc saw a vein in his neck throb as he pressed his cards to his chest.

The man looked up at him, smiled, and pushed all his chips to the centre of the table. "I stand pat."

Doc tilted his cigar up, studied his own hand, and pushed all his chips forward.

"I call."

A collective gasp, and then incredulous laughter, greeted his words as the spectators watched breathlessly.

The dark man spread his cards on the table.

"King of Hearts, King of Clubs, King of Spades. Ten of Clubs, Ten of Spades. A full house."

There was a roar of laughter, and Kate's eyes flicked to Doc's. Doc shook his head and smiled.

Every eye in the room turned towards him, and a hush fell on the crowd as he laid his cards on the table, one by one.

"Ten of Diamonds. Jack of Diamonds. Queen of Diamonds. King of Diamonds."

A gasp and amazed laughter greeted him, and Doc looked into Kate's eyes as he threw the last card down.

"Ace of Diamonds. A royal flush!"

The room erupted into chaos, and the dark man threw his hands up into the air, laughed, and shrugged. He extended his hand across the table, and Doc shook it.

"Lady Luck was certainly with you tonight," the man told him.

"You're a heck of a poker player, sir," Doc told him.

Doc turned to Kate. Her eyes were shining, and she smiled as she said: "Well, that's all for tonight! Mr Dailey, you may redeem your winnings at the teller counter. Congratulations on a game well played, sir!"

Kate rose from the table and retired from the room in a whisper of cologne and a hush of silk. Doc made his way through the congratulatory crowd and set the overflowing rack of chips on the teller counter.

But the teller on the other side of the grille looked less than happy. He took one look at the number of chips, and their colour, and smiled apologetically. "Wait just a minute, sir," he mumbled. "I'll be right back."

There was a murmur of confusion among the spectators who had followed him to the window and muttering and speculation as they waited for the teller to return.

After a few minutes, Judge Carter appeared, with the teller trailing after him. "Well, congratulations, Mr Dailey," he said tightly. "Your win tonight—twenty-five thousand dollars!—is a record breaking sum. Unprecedented, for any of my saloons!"

Laughter rippled across the crowd, but it changed quickly into indignant muttering when Judge added:

"I'm afraid the bank can't pay out the entire amount."

Doc straightened. "I beg your pardon?"

Judge flushed red and put up his hands for calm. "The *Natchez Queen* has never seen a winning sum quite so large!" he maintained. "But I will arrange to pay the full amount when we dock in St. Louis."

Doc gazed at him coolly. "I'm afraid that won't do," he drawled. "I have come for my winnings, and I expect to receive them all, as promised, at the cessation of play."

"That's right!" a man at his elbow shouted, and the crowd buzzed angrily.

"A bank that won't pay off! What kind of gambling hall is this?" another cried.

Judge glared, but the crowd was with Doc and against him.

"If the house pays out this entire amount tonight, it will have no cash to cover any other wagers until we dock in St. Louis!" he explained, but he was shouted down and finally had to motion to the teller, and the crowd cheered as the man began to count out twenty-five thousand dollars in crisp new bills.

When the amount was complete, and the cash neatly bundled and transferred to Doc's elegant leather valise, the crowd cheered again, and someone cried: "Make way for Doc Dailey—the man who broke the bank on the *Natchez Queen!*"

Chapter Two

Judge Carter slammed the door of his private office, then kicked it. He'd never been so humiliated in all his life, and he would've given another twenty five thousand dollars to be able to ram his fist right into Doc Dailey's sparkling white teeth.

Doc had cleaned out the bank.

The whole *bank*.

It was *impossible*.

He glared out the window of his office. The *Queen* had just docked, and the yellow lights of St. Louis glowed in the night.

A soft knock made him turn his head.

"What is it?"

The door opened, and a very large gentlemen appeared in it, hat in hand.

"Well?"

"We waited outside his stateroom, just like you told us, Judge," the man told him. "But he never came out. So we jimmied the door and went inside. There was nobody there, and his things was gone."

"Have you searched the ship?"

"Yessir. Bow to stern. There's no sign of him."

Judge cursed under his breath and glared out the window. The blazing torches on the dock illuminated a handful of passengers as they walked down the gangplank. A row of hackney cabs waited for them, ready to whisk these rich visitors off to St. Louis hotels, bars, or saloons.

Judge studied the passengers, and his fury at Doc Dailey was momentarily replaced by a slap of unpleasant surprise. One of the passengers leaving the boat was—he moved closer to the window—Kate Dubois, he was sure of it.

Judge frowned. Kate hadn't said anything to him about taking a day trip into St. Louis.

There was a uniformed riverboat employee walking behind her, a red-jacketed porter carrying several bags. A tall, broad-shouldered porter, carrying two carpet bags and a small leather valise.

He watched as a cab rolled up, and Kate climbed in. The porter handed up the bags and then jumped in beside her. The cabman whipped up the horse, and the rig clattered off.

Judge's mouth dropped open; then fury roared up from the lowest depths of his soul.

It was impossible to break the bank of the *Natchez Queen*.

Unless you had a partner on the inside.

"Quick!" he cried to the staring man, "run down to the dock, all of you, and catch that cab! Kate and Doc Dailey have robbed us—and they're getting away!"

The man gaped at him for a split-second, and then scrambled off to give chase. Judge swore furiously and scrabbled in his desk for his pistol. Once he had it in hand, he ran out of the office with murder throbbing in his every vein.

He burst out onto the top deck and shoved his way through the line at the gangplank. "Get out of my way!" he shouted and made the gangplank jump as he ran across it.

He waved furiously at a cabman and jumped up into the seat. "Did you see where that woman went—the one who just left with the porter?"

The man half turned. "They went up towards the hotel row," he answered, in a tone of mild surprise.

"Follow her," Judge barked, "as fast as you can! I'll pay you a hundred dollars if we catch them!"

The cabbie whipped up the horse, and the hackney lurched sharply. Judge leaned forward, his eyes searching the gaslit streets. Even at midnight, there were still rigs on the main road through town, and he scanned them hungrily.

"Do you see them?" he asked the cabbie. "Where did they go?"

The cabbie nodded forward. "I think she's in the first rig there," he answered, "the one pulling up to the Hotel St. Louis."

Judge leaned out of the cab and braced one foot on its metal step. He steadied his arm on the top of the cab and fired six shots towards the rig from his revolver.

"Hey!" the cabbie shouted. "Are you crazy?"

Judge shouted: "Keep driving! If you slow down, I'll make you sorry!"

The cabman shrank away but kept driving, and when they neared the hotel, Judge jumped out and ran up to the rig parked at the hotel entrance.

"I'm going to kill you!" he roared and yanked the shadowed man around by the shoulder. But to his confusion, the man who turned to face him wasn't Doc Dailey.

The man was six feet tall, looked like a miner, and wasn't very happy to be threatened with murder.

"The devil you say!" he roared and fetched Judge a blow across the jaw that made him see stars, and then—nothing.

***

Judge woke hours later to a splitting headache. He moaned and curled up in a ball of misery.

A dry voice asked: "Mr Carter, are you awake?"

He opened his eyes and looked up. The light hurt his eyes, but he could just make out the face of a shrewd-looking older man.

"Who are you?" he groaned.

"I'm Harwell T. Pierce, attorney-at-law," the man replied briskly. "The court has appointed me your defence lawyer."

Judge opened both his eyes. "What?"

He looked past the man, and to his outrage, he was in a jail cell.

"Why?"

The man's eyebrows rose slightly. "You don't remember what happened last night?"

Judge shook his head. "No."

The man folded his hands primly across his knees. "You shot at a miner and his pregnant wife outside the Hotel St. Louis and threatened to kill them both," he replied. "You also destroyed the hotel's $500 custom window and a Chinese vase of great antiquity in the window of the shop next door. You also threatened to shoot a cabman."

The older man pinched his lips together. "You're lucky you're not facing a murder charge, Mr Carter," he sniffed.

"Get out," Judge mumbled.

"I beg your pardon?"

Judge raised his head, and the look in his eyes made the attorney straighten in alarm. "I said get out. And tell the sheriff that I said I want him to bring me the chief officer on the *Natchez Queen*."

"Very well," the man replied tightly, and rose. "But I hope you can afford a very skillful lawyer, Mr Carter.

"Because the judge here has no love for riverboat riff raff!"

But Judge deigned no further reply. The memory of the last 24 hours was returning to him, and rage boiled up so hot inside him that he could barely see.

Doc Dailey had struck him like a lightning bolt. That slick pretty boy had robbed him of $25,000, his pride, and—Kate.

All in one night.

But one thing was certain: Doc's day was coming. When he got bailed out of jail, he was going to put a bounty on Doc's head so high that Doc wouldn't be able to show his face in any gambling hall, anywhere on earth.

Or live anywhere, except under a rock.

Doc might've taken his money, but he was going to make good and sure that he never enjoyed one red cent of it.

And as for Kate—he licked his lips painfully—she was going to be sorry too.

She was going to regret running away from him. She was going to regret throwing Judge Carter aside for some wily New Orleans dandy.

Kate was finished, too. She just didn't know it yet. But she'd find out.

They were both going to find out.

Judge rammed his fist into the wall, and then rammed it into the wall again.

Chapter Three

"Happy days."

Doc smiled and touched his champagne glass to Kate's with a faint *ting*, but instead of drinking, they both leaned over the dinner table and kissed softly.

They were snugly ensconced in Doc's luxurious private compartment, enjoying the last bites of a celebratory dinner. The remains of Lobster Newburg, red potatoes with butter and fresh dill, spring peas and pearl onions, and a tomato aspic covered the elegant table. Outside, Missouri farmland flowed by as the train made its way west.

Doc caressed Kate's silky hair. "Tell me, darling—was it Lady Luck who kissed me at the poker table tonight, or was it you?"

Kate pursed her lips and looked down almost primly. "Why, I'm surprised at you, Doc," she demurred. "I would *never*."

Doc smiled and lifted an eyebrow, but his lady love refused to say more, and so he decided to believe her claim of innocence. He reached into his pocket for the little box he'd been hiding.

"This is for you," he told her, and set the gift carefully on the table in front of her.

She looked up sharply, but he only smiled:

"Open it."

Kate put down her glass and smiled at him uncertainly. She picked up the little box and lifted the lid to discover a magnificent three-carat diamond ring nestled on the black velvet cushion. The stone winked and glittered with a thousand white sparks.

Kate's startled eyes flew to his. "Oh, Doc!"

"Do you like it?"

Kate slipped the diamond ring onto her finger. It flashed there like the North Star as she turned her hand.

"Like it! Why—I don't know what to say!" she gasped.

"Well, that's easy," he murmured. "Say yes, Kate."

Doc reached out and took her warm hand in his, but to his surprise, Kate's mouth crumpled up. He'd never seen her cry before. He laughed and rubbed her fingers with his thumb.

"Why, it's nothing to cry about!"

Kate shook her head wordlessly and was overcome, and so he waited patiently for her to recover her composure.

"You know, you're just full of surprises tonight," he teased. "I didn't take you for a sentimental girl."

"Oh, Doc!" she cried, and he laughed again and got up and sat down on the seat next to her. She threw her arms around him and buried her face in his vest.

He put his lips to her ear. "Can I take that for a yes?" he whispered, and she laughed.

Kate lifted her face to his, and her green eyes shone

like stars. She caressed his cheek with her hand and smiled.

"*Yes*," she breathed, and kissed him. Doc closed his eyes and abandoned himself to the luxurious, silken pleasure of Kate's kisses. His arms curled around her, and hers around him, and in short order they forgot about everything except one another.

He wasn't sure how much later the train pulled into Kansas City station. It might have been five minutes, or five hours, but Kate had that effect on him.

At any rate, he remembered that the porter had walked past in the hall outside, crying: "Kansas City! Kansas City station!"

There was a soft knock at the door, and Doc disentangled himself from Kate's embrace. "Yes?"

"Would you like me to clear away your dishes, sir?"

"Yes, you can come in."

The porter opened the door, and the two of them had looked away and adjusted their hair as he cleared the dining table.

"What time is it?"

The porter looked at his watch. "Almost midnight, sir."

He had turned to Kate then. "You'd better go back to your compartment and get some sleep," he told her. "I'll see you at breakfast."

They had kissed again, and Kate had returned, slowly and reluctantly, to her own compartment next door.

The porter cleared the table, folded it back up against the wall, and unlocked and pulled down his bed.

"Have a nice evening, sir." He smiled and left.

Doc stretched and pulled the curtain down over his window. He changed into a pair of linen pajamas, sat down on the bunk, and retired for the night.

***

Doc was generally not an early riser and had gotten to bed late, and so when he woke up the next day, Doc found that it was a bit past breakfast. But he'd purchased two tickets to Denver, and that was still two days away, so he could afford to be leisurely.

He got up and performed his morning toilette, read the paper that had been left outside his door, and ate a pleasant breakfast.

Then he dressed with more than his usual care, stuck the flower from his breakfast tray into his buttonhole, and sallied forth to greet Kate.

But when he knocked on the door of her compartment, there was no answer.

"Kate?"

Doc stopped a passing porter and frowned: "Excuse me. Have you seen the lady in Compartment 2A this morning?"

The man nodded. "Oh yes, sir. She got off at Kansas City."

Doc flinched as if he'd been punched in the stomach. He stared at the porter, and the man, seeing he was speechless, added: "She got off right after she left your room, sir."

Doc frowned. "Are—you *quite* sure it was the same lady? Brunette, green eyes, in her twenties?"

"Oh yes, sir. The lady who had dinner with you last night."

Doc watched the man as he walked away, feeling suddenly detached from his body. He drifted back into his compartment, closed the door behind him, and sat down.

He stared at his hands for a while, and then, just as a formality, reached under his bunk for the leather valise.

Of course, it was gone, but he'd had an absurd need to check, just the same.

Doc took a deep, painful breath, because his chest ached, but after a while, his cracked heart eased a bit, and his gambler insouciance returned.

In love, as in cards, you won some, and you lost some.

He reached inside his jacket, pulled out a slender cigar, and lit it. He inhaled deeply and blew a contemplative smoke ring.

Kate had robbed him, the little minx. He inhaled again and shook his head. He just hated that.

Because it was going to be a real shock to her when she opened the bag and found two bundles, instead of twenty-five. He'd given her the inadvertent gift of a little more than two thousand dollars. Doc blew another smoke ring.

Well, he told himself, *at least it'll get her back to New Orleans in style.*

Chapter **Four**

Tyler Martel lit the cigarette between his lips and shook out the match. Then he blew a spout of smoke towards the ceiling.

"Well?"

Judge Carter was glaring at him from behind his fancy mahogany desk, but despite Judge's arrogance and wealth, he was the one holding all the cards, and he knew it.

Judge needed a bounty hunter, and bad. He'd been cheated by a swindler, he said, but *he'd* been the one thrown in jail last night.

Judge had neglected to mention that he'd lost a whopping $25,000, but that story was all over town.

Tyler almost laughed at the man across the desk. The little banty rooster was pert-near dancing with rage. He wanted revenge so bad that he didn't care how he got it. Or how much money it cost him.

"I've been told that you're the best," Judge growled. His gravelly voice sounded almost bearlike in its guttural resentment.

"That's right. I always get my man. Or woman as the

case may be."

Judge frowned and lowered his eyes. "Right now, I'm only interested in a man. Have you ever heard of Doc Dailey?"

Tyler searched his memory. "The name rings a bell. Can't place it right now."

Judge snorted angrily. "He's a con man, a gambler, and a thief!"

Tyler grinned and tilted his cigarette towards the ceiling. He could always tell when a man had lost a girl to another fellow.

When he'd lost *real* bad.

A jilted lover glowed with rage. His pride had been crushed and hate burned in him like fire. He wouldn't stop until he saw the other man crawling on the ground.

Or dead.

"What do you want with this Dailey fellow?"

Judge's eyes snapped up to his. "I want him dead!"

Tyler tilted his head. "Dead'll cost you extra."

"How much extra?"

Tyler raised his eyes to the ceiling and pretended to deliberate. "Say … ten thousand dollars."

"Ten thousand!"

"Take it or leave it."

Judge's chest swelled visibly, and his face went red, but Tyler knew he'd knuckle under, in the end.

They all did. Because no one got better results than him, and they knew it.

Judge's grey eyes were cold and grim as a winter sky. "All right, ten thousand. But only on delivery. And I want proof."

Tyler shrugged. "I don't do any job without ten per cent down." He blew a spout of smoke into Judge's face. "And I'd be a little more polite if I was you. I've never been caught, Mr Carter."

Judge rang a bell on his desk, and a man appeared in the doorway of the office.

"Go down to the cashier and tell him I said to count out $1,000," he barked. "Then give it to this man."

"Yes, Mr Carter."

Tyler leaned against the wall and smoked in silence until the employee came back and counted the money out into his hand. Tyler grinned, stuffed the money into his pocket, and moved toward the door, but Judge's voice stopped him on the threshold.

"One more thing I hope you remember, Mr Martel."

He turned to scan the man's face indifferently.

"I've never been caught, *either*."

But Tyler only laughed and held his eye boldly until he walked out of Judge Carter's opulent office. For a man who was supposed to be smart, Judge Carter was powerful trusting.

He could see why the girl had thrown him over. Judge had a puny imagination.

He'd called the best bounty hunter in the nation and told him that he was offering $10,000 for Doc Dailey's death.

He plainly hadn't asked himself why the best bounty hunter in the nation would settle for $10,000 when he could have $25,000 all to himself if he found Dailey quick enough.

Tyler sauntered through the richly carpeted halls of the *Natchez Queen*. The riverboat was still tied up in the St. Louis dock, a red and white reminder of the scandalous crimes that its employees had committed in the town, and all of St. Louis was buzzing with it.

Tyler walked down to the dock and then up the street leading into town. He passed Hotel Row and the restaurants and bars that catered to the riverboat's well-heeled tourists. A couple smart enough to steal $25,000 would be smart enough to skip town.

Tyler pulled his slouch hat low over his brow. He was dressed like a dock worker, in a baggy jacket, and patched britches. He'd stuffed a wad of chewing tobacco into one cheek, and his teeth were brown with it.

He hadn't shaved that morning, and he had a dirty

stubble shadow on his chin.

He was no dandy, but he was correctly dressed for where he was going. He followed the seedy back streets to the seamier side of town, to the dark bars and questionable, low-rent hotels that lined the river. There the working poor of St. Louis gathered to drink and gamble—and talk.

And the tales they had to tell were always more profitable to him than the idle gossip of well-to-do citizens. The men who worked on the river knew about thieves and flim flam men, about whores and hobos, about cutthroats and occasionally, dead bodies.

They were notoriously wary of strangers; and so he had dressed the part of a dock worker, in the expectation that they'd take him for a man like them, away from home on business, or pleasure, for a day or two.

If he kept quiet and listened, he was confident that the local gossip would show him where to pick up Doc's trail.

It took him less time than he imagined. The town was still afire with gossip about the madman from the riverboat, and the sordid story he told about having been cheated at cards by a sly New Orleans gambler and his shady female accomplice.

Tyler shuffled into the nearest of many plank board buildings on the waterfront, *The Rusty Wheel*. He drifted in, bellied up to the bar, and nursed a glass of whisky in silence.

He stayed there an hour without result, and so he paid his tab and moved on to the next place.

By nine o' clock, he'd worked his way almost down to the end of the street

A painted sign hung over the door of the last bar. It portrayed a smiling woman with the words: *Naughty Nellie's.*

The interior was barely lit, and it took his eyes a few minutes to adjust to the low light and the layer of tobacco smoke hanging just under the ceiling. Tyler adjusted the wad of tobacco in his cheek and sent a stream of tobacco juice into a spittoon next to the bar.

He leaned up against the rough counter, and the bartender grumbled: "What'll you have?"

Tyler fished in his pocket for a coin and pushed it towards the man. "Whisky."

He took the glass the man offered and nursed it in frowning silence, there at the bar. At first, he got suspicious looks from the other patrons, but when he said nothing, they all gradually went back to their own conversations.

But he could tell they were wary of him. He had to find a table and work his way through half a bottle of rotgut whisky before the men around him relaxed enough to start talking naturally again.

At first, it was gripes about their jobs, and then gripes about their bosses, and then they spent a half-hour griping about local politics.

He was just about to give up on them and push on to another place when one of them murmured:

"Did you hear about the robbery on board the riverboat? It was a man and woman, and they got away with $25,000 dollars, they say," one wrinkled greybeard mumbled.

"My brother-in-law works on the riverboat, and he was there that night," another replied, in a low voice. "He said the woman was the dealer. The two of them were working together. No wonder the dandy won!"

"I heerd the dandy got the first dealer throwed out," his neighbour growled. "And that was when his woman volunteered to deal! They're slick ones, you have to give 'em that."

"Reckon how they got away?"

Tyler put the glass to his lips and made sure to stare away from them, out the grimy window.

"Can't say," the greybeard muttered. "The two of 'em was dressed fancy: should've stuck out like a sore thumb."

"Nobody at the hotel ever heard of 'em," the second man replied.

"What would you do if you just stole that much money?" a man in the back put in. "Get out of town as fast as you could, that's what. I say they took the train."

"*Shah*, Bill—everybody done thought of that. And if

they'd gone to the train station, they'd-a been caught the first night."

"Not if they got there just before it left. They's lots of trains that go in and out of that station, all hours of the day and night. They could switch trains, too."

"Eh, that's crazy."

"No it ain't," another man added. "Stockyard Dan was here last night, and he said the same thing. Dan says that he saw 'em both."

"The hobo?"

"That's right. He said he was walking out to the train to catch a ride and saw a pretty woman, dressed up fancy, and a man in a porter uniform. He said the man threw their bags up on the caboose, helped the lady up, and climbed up hisself just as it was starting to move out of the station. He said it hadn't been gone five minutes before a bunch of men came running into the station after them, but they was too late."

"How'd ol' Dan know it was them?"

"He didn't. Just said it looked like 'em."

"What train were they on?"

"The Kansas Pacific, he said."

"Aw, you can't pay no attention to what Dan says. He's drunk more than he's sober."

"Ten dollars says he's right!"

The other men laughed. "How'd you ever know if you was right? They're gone now. Probly no one'll ever hear from them again."

"Twenty-five thousand dollars," the greybeard sighed, and they all sank into a gloomy silence.

But Tyler drained his glass. Doc and the girl were headed west. And there were only two major gambling towns on the Kansas Pacific line: Kansas City and Denver.

He'd find them in one or the other.

Tyler pushed his chair back with a scrape and slouched out into the night.

Chapter Five

Kate Dubois stared at herself in the mirror and fiddled with her gleaming auburn hair. Her eyes were still alight with the excitement of how narrowly she and Doc had made the train and escaped Judge, a few nights before.

She pursed her lips and smiled, imagining Judge's face when he'd realized that she was gone. She saw Judge go beet red, swell up like a frog, and explode.

Kate sputtered with soft laughter, pulled a tiny jar of French pomade out of her bag, and smoothed it over her lips with her fingertip. It tasted faintly of oranges, and Doc liked it.

Her compartment was only a few doors down from his, and he'd ordered dinner for the two of them to celebrate his big win.

Kate also cherished the secret hope that they'd have something else to celebrate, soon.

A soft knock at the door made her smile and turn. When she opened the narrow door, Doc stood outside. He was holding two champagne glasses, and he offered one to her.

She took it, and a sip from its bubbling lip. "*Mmmm*."

"Dinner's ready, darlin'.'"

Kate smiled at him over the rim of her glass. "I'll be right down. Just give me a minute."

Doc nodded and smiled, and she closed the door and took another sip of champagne. She opened a little bottle of rose water, poured a tiny bit into her palms, and brushed her hands lightly over her hair, arms, and skirts.

She sighed at her reflection in the toilette mirror and pinched her cheeks until they glowed.

Another soft knock made her smile and hurry to open the door. "Doc, I—"

She got a split-second to register the sight of a dark man in a long duster before she was slammed up against the wall of her compartment with his hand clamped around her throat.

He kicked the door shut behind him and leered into her face as she clawed at his hands.

"Now I'm only going to say this one time," he breathed into her face. "I know who you are, and I know who that man with you is." He reached under his long coat and pulled out a sawed-off shotgun.

"You're going to go in there, get that money from him and bring it back to me. I'll give you until midnight. But if you're not back by then, I'll come to his door and blow you both right through the wall of the car.

"Do you understand me?"

She rolled terrified eyes to his and nodded. The crushing pressure on her throat lifted, and she slid down the wall, gasping for air.

He stood there, looking down at her, as she grabbed a chair, pulled herself up, and gathered her composure. She glanced back at him over her shoulder, and he lifted the gun towards her.

She swept out into the hallway and shut the door behind her with a *snap*, heart pounding.

Kate leaned against the wall and closed her eyes. If she told Doc now, maybe they could get away before the man …

But the door to her compartment opened, and the man stood there glaring at her as if he'd read her mind. She hurried down the hall and knocked on Doc's door as the man watched.

The door opened, and a smiling Doc made a welcoming gesture. "Well Kate, what a pleasant surprise!" he teased as she stepped inside. He closed the door behind her.

"I see you forgot your champagne glass. Have mine. I'll get another one."

Kate lowered herself into a seat at the elegant table in Doc's compartment. It had been set with fine linen and silver and was covered with dozens of dainty things to eat, but she'd never felt less like dining in her life. She closed her eyes, thinking of that grim looking man, standing just outside with a shotgun.

If she told Doc, there was no knowing what would happen. Doc was unpredictable—liable to do anything. Kate closed her eyes, summoned up her best poker face, and prayed that when she returned with the money, the man waiting outside would be content to take it and go.

She glanced around the room. To her relief, Doc had left the leather valise on the floor next to the bench she was sitting on. If she distracted Doc, she might be able to put her foot out, hook the handle with the toe of her little boot, and pull it under the table.

If she could get Doc out of the room just once more, she could tie the laces of her left boot tight around the handle and walk the little valise out of the room underneath the skirts of her gown.

Anger flashed up in her heart when she thought about Doc being robbed of what was rightfully his, but there was nothing she could do about it.

They could always win more money, but there was only one Doc.

Doc returned and sat down across the table, and Kate forced herself to chat, smile, and have dinner with him as usual. But her brain was churning to come up with something that would get him out of the room long enough for her to get the valise.

Until midnight, the man had said.

But she had no guarantee that he wouldn't kill them

both, even if she gave him the money. She glanced up quickly at Doc and wondered if she told him what happened, he might be able to come up with something to save them.

But there was only so much that even Doc could do. They were trapped in a train compartment, and the man with the shotgun was blocking the only way in or out.

Doc took her hand, and she snapped back to the present. He was smiling and presented her a little box.

"This is for you," he said softly. "Open it."

Kate blinked back tears and reached for the box with a trembling hand. Of all the times for Doc to propose!

And when she opened the box, the glorious diamond ring inside made her gasp—and then cry. Because she was thinking that if the worst happened, at least she'd die knowing that Doc loved her enough to make her his wife.

But she didn't want that night to be the best night *and* the last night of their lives.

She dried her tears, smiled, and allowed Doc to soothe her as she turned her hand back and forth and watched white sparks fly from the diamond's heart.

"Oh, Doc, it's beautiful," she breathed, and he leaned over to kiss her.

It should have been a perfect and magical kiss, but all she could think of was how to get the valise without

Doc seeing her.

"Doc," she said suddenly, "look! We're out of champagne!"

Doc laughed and lifted the empty bottle. "Well, now that won't do! I'll go and ask the porter to bring us another bottle."

He rose and walked out of the compartment, and as soon as the door closed behind him, she leaned down, grabbed the valise, and feverishly untied her left boot lace and knotted it tight around the handle. She had just finished and had straightened up again when Doc reappeared with the bottle. He opened it with a loud *pop* that made her jump, and then poured out two glasses full.

Sometime later, the porter passed by outside, calling "Kansas City! Kansas City station!"

To her relief, Doc suggested that they call it a night, and so she kissed him tenderly, rose carefully to her feet, and walked out slowly and carefully.

But when she reached the other compartment, the man opened the door, grabbed her arm, and yanked her inside.

"Where's the money?"

She leaned over, lifted her skirt, and went to untie the laces, but to her horror, the man crouched down and ripped the bag free with a knife.

He bent down to look inside the valise, and she saw

her chance. She hiked her skirts up to her knees and boot-kicked him in the temple as hard as she could.

She dashed out the door, almost knocking another woman down outside, and when she turned the corner at the end of the hall, she stumbled down the steps and out onto the depot platform in Kansas City.

She didn't look back to see if the man was chasing her. She just ran until she was worn out and alone in the meadow back of the train depot.

She crouched down behind a bush and strained her eyes for any sign of pursuit, and when she saw the dark man come stumbling out of the train and running frantically up and down the train platform, she put a trembling hand to her mouth. He confronted woman after woman, and their screams quickly brought help. Soon her attacker was struggling with three other men.

Kate saw them take him down on the depot platform, and then drag him away.

But to her despair, a shrill whistle sounded immediately after, and she watched the Kansas Pacific slowly pull out of the station. The train bore the unsuspecting Doc away and left her behind, as she stood watching.

Chapter Six

Thunder rumbled in the sky overhead, and Doc pulled up the collar of his jacket as he descended from the train in Denver's Union Station. He walked across the big, busy platform like a sleepwalker and wondered where Kate was at that moment.

On a train speeding back to New Orleans, most likely, though with considerably less money than she had no doubt hoped. Doc shook his head, and had to laugh a little in spite of himself.

It really was clever of her, to take advantage of the fact that he'd demanded a new dealer. To slide right in there, and take control of the whole poker game, knowing that he was going to win a lot of money, that she was going to ride away with him after, and then ride away alone, a little after that.

Kate was quick, he had to give it to her.

And lucky for him, that force of habit had made him careful with his money.

He walked out of the station and onto the street as big raindrops began to patter down. He hailed a cab, and it soon deposited him on the doorstep of the most luxurious boarding house in town.

The first thing he did, after he was comfortably ensconced, was to order a fine and very expensive bottle of Kentucky bourbon to help drown Kate's memory.

He settled down into a plush chair overlooking the street below, and began to work his way through the bottle. But at some point in the evening—long after sunset, and toward the bottom of the bottle—he looked up suddenly to see a man in a black duster standing in the room with him. At first he hadn't been sure whether it was a trick of the liquor, or if it was real, but when the man had lifted a sawed off shotgun from the long folds of his coat, and pointed it at his head, the matter had been settled for him.

The man's hair was long and black and greasy. He was unshaven and—Doc twitched his nose—unwashed. But the intruder had a ponderous gun, and he grinned:

"Well hello, Mr. Doc Dailey! I hear you stole twenty five thousand dollars. Get that sack of money and come with me."

He blinked, and looked down into his glass doubtfully; but the man yanked him to his feet, and he was compelled to get the satchel full of money.

The man marched him down the back stairs and out behind the boarding house. The sun had set, and it was a cool, moonless night. It was pitch dark except for a few distant street lamps and the yellow lights in the boarding house windows. The man kept the barrel of the gun pressed into his back and pushed him down the alley behind the boarding house, and then left into another alley, and then right into a third.

"Well, now, won't your old friend Judge be surprised," the man drawled, "when I ship your coffin back to New Orleans! Course, we'll have to say that you didn't have his money on you, at the time."

The man jammed the gun into his spine again. "I

guess you thought you was pretty smart, didn't you, to put just $2,000 in that bag? But nobody cheats Tyler Martel!

"And nobody boot kicks me in the head and gets away with it. I don't care if it is a woman! I made that pretty little lady pay for it, when I took her off the train in Kansas City! Don't look for her, slick. She won't be coming back!"

In that split-second Doc turned on the man. His right hand shoved the shotgun barrel aside, and the other shot the grinning man like a lightning bolt, right between the eyes. Martel's hand jerked, his eyes rolled up, and he staggered backward a few paces before both he and his shotgun fell harmlessly onto the ground.

Doc returned the gun to his vest pocket and looked around warily. The crack of the pistol echoed loudly in the empty alley, and it wouldn't be long before people were drawn to the sound. Doc leaned over the man, grabbed his valise, and walked away.

But he had a hard time for awhile. Rage and grief blurred his eyes, and it took him a little while to get his bearings.

The terrible thought that he'd dishonored Kate's memory burned in his chest. He'd really believed that his sweetheart had cheated him, when all the time—

Doc shook his head bitterly and walked doggedly back to Union Station. And when he settled into a train compartment at last, he swore to whatever God might be listening that he was going to settle that score with Judge one day, if it killed him.

Kate had been kidnapped right out from under his nose, and was dead at the hands of a monster; and

Doc felt shame, grief, and rage all the way to the desolate little train station in Wolf Table. Shame that he hadn't been able to protect her; fathomless grief; and rage toward that animal lying dead in the alley.

The only emotion left in him, after the others burned their way through his heart, was a deep desire to go high up into the mountains, and see no human face, and hear no human voice, until his pain eased.

Chapter Seven

Somewhere in the wilderness above Wolf Table, Colorado
Ten years later

Doc Dailey moaned in his sleep, and his eyelids fluttered open. At first, he wasn't sure where he was. The ceiling was made of rough planks, instead of the intricately-worked tin ceiling of a riverboat stateroom.

He glanced around in confusion. Three walls of his bedroom were made of logs, and the fourth wall was missing. It opened onto a large common room.

He was in a cabin in the woods, though his sleep-clouded brain couldn't remember why. It took awhile for him to recall the reason he'd come to this desolate shack high on a mountain in Colorado.

He'd buried himself in the wilderness to escape the new bounty hunters that Judge Carter had no doubt sent after him.

But mostly, he'd come here to recover from Kate's death.

Doc pulled his hand across his face, and to his shock, his smooth-shaven chin was covered in a bristling beard that covered not just the lower half of his face, but the upper part of his chest, as well.

He sat up and called sleepily: "Kate!"

A girl's bored voice answered him from the loft overhead. "You're having the dream again, Pa."

Doc frowned, and slowly his sleepy brain retrieved the last ten years. That was right, he'd changed his name. He wasn't Doc Dailey, at least not anymore. He fell back on the pillow.

He was Gideon McCall, brush-bearded mountain man, the father of Daisy McCall.

"Oh."

Daisy's upside down head and short, sandy hair appeared in the air just below the ceiling. "Who's Kate?"

"Never mind." He yawned and threw the blanket off, though it was very early morning, and still cold.

"That's what you always say," Daisy grumbled, and her head disappeared.

"I'm going to start breakfast," Doc mumbled. "It's almost time to get up anyway. Go out to the hen house and get some eggs for us, will you?" He stumbled into the common area that served as a kitchen, dining room, and living room. There was a cast iron stove pushed up against one wall, and he glanced into the wood box.

"Did you split those logs like I told you?" he yawned. "I don't see any wood in this box."

"Aw, I went hunting yesterday with Clay," his 16-year-old daughter grumbled, and pulled on a pair of breeches under her big nightshirt. "We almost got caught by Old Crunchy, too. Made me forget all about splittin' wood!"

Doc's sleepy brain woke up with a start.

"Were you teasing that bear again?" he replied sharply. "How many times must I tell you not to stir that monster up?"

"Clay says that his people used to hunt bear all the time, and with nothing more than a bow and some arrows."

"Clay's people told him a big pack," Doc retorted. "Or Clay made it up himself. And neither one of you is a Pawnee brave, so stay away from that bear. I mean it!"

Daisy slid down the rough ladder and plopped down on the floor to put on a pair of moccasins. "Clay's people were a power," she told him, her eyes wide. "You know what he told me? He said that not long ago, they could've captured me and offered me up as a human sacrifice to the gods, 'cause they captured young girls from other tribes and kept 'em six months, and fed 'em good and fattened 'em up like a Thanksgiving turkey. But when the time came, in the Spring, they'd tie the girl up on a frame of willow reeds and shoot her dead with arrows—*zip zip zip*!

"Clay said that was to make sure they'd get rain and good crops and hunting."

Doc frowned and tried to banish the hideous mental image. "I hope the Pawnee have abandoned human sacrifice?"

"Yeah," Daisy replied in a downcast tone. "The government made 'em stop. And they're all in Oklahoma now, anyway. But I would've given five dollars to see it. It would've made the skin crawl on the back of your neck!"

Doc stared at her. His ethics were tepid at best, but it struck him forcefully that it was wrong for his daughter to think of human sacrifice as a spectator event.

It gave him the vague sense that he had failed as a parent.

"You should be ashamed to say that you'd like to see another girl get shot with arrows!" he exclaimed. "I'm—er—disappointed in you."

Daisy looked up guilelessly. "Oh, Clay says that they took it in stride. Warn't nothin' hateful about it. Just insurance, and everybody knew that, goin' in."

"I doubt the girl thought of it as insurance," Doc retorted and massaged the little space in between his eyes. "Go on, now, and get the eggs. And some split wood for the fire."

"All right, all right."

Doc watched her go, and when she'd gone, he leaned against the cold iron of the stove and closed his eyes.

His dream, and his past life, were still heavy on him. They felt more real than this strange cabin, and the girl, and his new self. He picked up a small, cracked piece of mirror off a shelf and surveyed himself in it. His smooth, barbered hair had grown out bushy and long and wild, like so much straw. His carefully-trimmed moustache had bloomed out to cover his whole upper lip, and his beard was huge.

The man looking back at him was Gideon McCall, the bearded prospector and mountain man he'd created ten years ago and had played ever since.

Although he'd never intended to be Gideon for so long, or to live in a cabin in the back of beyond for ten whole years.

But then, a lot of things had happened that he never

intended.

Gideon walked to the window and watched Daisy as she lifted an axe and effortlessly split a log into two pieces. She was sixteen now, almost a young woman.

But she looked, thought, and acted just like some scruffy backwoods boy.

That was his fault, too, for raising her on the side of a mountain and hiding her away from the rest of the world. Daisy hadn't had a mother figure in her life, or known any other girls in years.

And the feeling was growing on him, that he was going to have to change his ways at last, if Daisy was going to have a chance to grow up.

***

He sighed and let the rough burlap curtain fall back into place. Had the avalanche been ten years ago? It still seemed like yesterday to him.

He'd just arrived on the mountain and was still getting used to the silence of the forest and the work of keeping up a cabin. Nothing about living in the wilderness had come naturally to him, and he dropped off that night to dreams of Kate and the *Natchez Queen*.

He'd awakened in the middle of the night to a deep rumbling that tilted the world and threw him right out of his bed and onto the cabin floor. It was an earthquake, but the cause hardly mattered when the ground was sliding back and forth.

He could hear pines tearing and cracking outside, and the fearsome *thump* of the huge trunks smashing onto the ground all around.

Then everything went still for a few minutes. He lay sprawled on the floor of the cabin, heart pounding in the silence, and then another, more terrifying sound rumbled on the mountain above him, faint at first, but building fast.

It was the rush of tons of rock, dirt, and trees sliding irresistibly down the mountain.

An *avalanche*.

He'd scrambled outside just in time to see a river of dirt roll through the trees a few hundred feet from the cabin door. It flattened everything in its path and carried felled trees and boulders far down the mountain as he watched in horror.

There was another cabin a mile or so below his. It belonged to a young family with three children, and it was right in the path of the slide. He'd thrown on his pants and shoes and gone running down the mountain as fast as he dared, jumping over rocks and felled trees. He'd fallen a dozen times, but he scrambled up and kept on running.

But by the time he got to where the cabin had stood, there was nothing to show that it had ever been there. He'd only found it because he remembered a big boulder lying in the yard, but the river of dirt had burst through the cabin and covered it twelve feet deep.

He'd clawed at it with his hands, dug hard, and called out, but there was no answer. He was just about to give up when he uncovered a hand in the dirt.

It had been Daisy's hand.

So he dug her out. She'd been unconscious, but still alive, and he'd laid her down on the grass and gone back to digging, in case there was anybody else.

But Daisy was the only one he ever found, and in the end, he'd given up and taken her back to his cabin. He knew nothing about medicine, despite his nickname, and that first night, all he could do was watch and wait to see if the little six-year-old girl lived or died.

But after a while, she'd opened her eyes and cried out, and he'd given her a little milk, and some food.

And when she asked, he'd had to tell her that her folks and her brothers and sisters were gone.

She'd curled up into a little ball and cried herself to sleep, and he hadn't known what to do or what to say. He wasn't the fatherly type, and he had no experience with children.

But the next morning, he made breakfast for her and went out to do his chores, and she was still there when he came back.

And gradually, he'd gotten used to her.

Over time, he'd gone from thinking of Daisy as somebody else's child, to *almost* his child, to *certainly* his child.

He rubbed his hairy chin. He wasn't the best father in the world; he knew that, and he hadn't chosen to become one. But he'd done the best he knew for Daisy, up until now.

He glanced out the window and saw Daisy pull back and throw the axe. The sharp blade sank deep into a tree trunk and stuck fast. Daisy clapped her hands clean and picked up an armful of the split kindling.

Gideon shook his head. One thing was clear: they

couldn't go on living the way they'd been. It was past time for him to take Daisy into town.

He was a gambler, after all, and for Daisy's sake, he was just going to have to take his chances.

Chapter Eight

"Bree-ee-hawww."

Gideon strapped the saddlebags on top of the wretched mule that was their only transportation and stifled the urge to kick it, rather than to lead it, down the mountain. Ezekiel, as Daisy had named him, surely had to be the ugliest, most stubborn, and most irritable mule to ever trouble the world.

Gideon conjured the memory of his beautiful Tennessee Walker, Galahad. He'd won that high-stepping beauty off a Kentucky planter in a poker game. Galahad had been the best horse he'd ever owned and had won a couple of blue ribbons back home in New Orleans. He'd even ...

A sharp, crushing pain in his hand pulled him rudely back to the present. He cursed savagely and yanked his hand away from Ezekiel's teeth.

"Ha—he got you again!" Daisy laughed. "You know better than to take your eye off that mule, Pa!"

"I'm going to sell him when we get to town," he vowed and sucked his hand resentfully. "The little ba—"

"You wouldn't sell Ezekiel!" Daisy cried and threw her arms around the mule's neck. "He's not mean. He's just playful!"

The mule, sensing praise, lifted its head, rolled its eyes, and pulled its lips back from its teeth.

"There!" Daisy laughed. "Look at him grin!"

Gideon grabbed the mule's halter. "Laugh away, you little devil," he grumbled, "but when we get to town, I'm selling you to a glue factory!" He yanked the halter hard, and the mule followed reluctantly as they made their way down the mountain and into town.

It was a beautiful spring day, with a bright blue sky, cool breeze, and green meadow grass. There was no road down the mountain, just footpaths that Doc, solitary travelers, and animals had worn into the earth, and the view from where they stood was impressive. Huge firs and aspens sighed in the breeze, birds trilled from every branch, and flowers spangled the grass.

"It's been a while since we've been down to Wolf Table," Daisy mused as they walked. "Almost a year. Reckon anything interesting has happened down there?"

"No," Gideon sighed, and then, conscious of Daisy's feelings, amended: "Or at least, I haven't heard yet."

"Clay was down there last month, and he said they've got two restaurants now, and a hotel!"

Gideon raised his brows and pulled his mouth to one side. "We're getting up in the world," he muttered.

But Daisy laughed and clapped her hands. "Well, speak of the devil!" she cried and tugged at Gideon's sleeve and pointed to a spot in the bushes up ahead. "Come out from there, Clay! Did you think you was foolin' us?"

Gideon turned his head in time to see Daisy's best friend Clay emerge from the underbrush beside the trail, smiling sheepishly. "I was gonna scare you," he confessed. "But you got the eyes of a hawk!"

Gideon stifled a sigh. Clay was their nearest neighbour, and Daisy's best friend, but the boy worried him. It was going to be hard to convince Daisy to learn how to be a young lady if her Pawnee friend was at her elbow every day, urging her to go hunting or fishing.

Or bear hunting.

Gideon frowned at the tall, raven-haired teen. "Daisy tells me you two went hunting Old Crunchy," he said, in what he hoped was a disapproving tone. "I don't want her anywhere near that bear, Clay. If I hear of you tempting her with that monster again, it'll be the last time I let the two of you go hunting together!"

Clay glanced at him apologetically. "Sorry, Gideon. But you know how Daisy loves to hunt. Reminds me of a cat."

"That's no excuse," he replied severely. "There's no way either one of you, or both of you together, could bring down that Grizzly. He stands almost nine feet tall. If he opened that mouth of his, I'd wager he could kill the two of you with his breath alone!"

Clay got a faraway look in his eye, and Gideon added tartly: "And I don't care how many Grizzlies the Pawnee brought down with their bows. Daisy isn't going anywhere near that bear, and that's final!"

"Aw, Pa!" Daisy cried, but Gideon gave her a stern look, and to his relief, she closed her mouth.

"You're getting to the age where you should be thinking about other things," Gideon added carefully. "A well-brought-up young lady doesn't chase after wild animals. She concentrates on—learning about more seemly things, and—making new friends."

"I don't have no objection to making friends," Daisy told him, and bit the end off a sweet gum twig. "And I'm up for anything going, ain't I, Clay?"

Clay nodded. "Daisy's game," he agreed, and Gideon glanced at him through suddenly narrowed eyes. But the boy wore an innocent look, and Gideon slowly relaxed.

He knew that Clay still thought of Daisy mostly as a boy, and he was thankful for that. But his luck wasn't going to last forever, and he worried about it. Daisy was unfashionably tan, her hair was lopped off short and bleached blonde by the sun, and she dressed in baggy boy's clothes. But she was pretty, and her figure was good and getting better every day.

Sooner or later, Clay was going to notice.

Gideon glanced at the boy again. Clay, or Shadow Foot, as his mother had named him, was a tall, handsome 17-year-old with jet black hair, a square jaw, and a fit body.

But Clay was half-white and half-Pawnee. He was also an orphan whose father had just died, and he was surviving in his father's cabin only because he knew how to hunt and fish.

If Daisy ever fell in love with Clay, she was going to have a hard life, and so Gideon had determined to do his best to head that off, if he could.

Chapter
Nine

They arrived a little after noon. It was a bright, sunny day, and Wolf Table looked almost like a toy village as they gazed down on it from the slopes above town.

There were about two dozen plank board buildings on the main street, mostly mercantiles and cafes, though Wolf Table also boasted a blacksmith and gun shop, a post office, a doctor's office, and an undertaker.

"Wolf Table has sure enough got bigger," Daisy observed and moved the sweet gum stick to one corner of her mouth. "Look at all the folks on the street! Must be a dozen at least, and it ain't even Saturday!"

They reached the main street at last, and Gideon led them down the dirt road to Hiram Heller's, the largest general goods store in town.

Gideon tied the mule to a hitching post and looked down at them. "Now I'm going into the mercantile to get some things," he instructed. "I want the two of you to stay here with Ezekiel and wait for me. I should be back soon."

Daisy pulled her mouth to one side and nodded, but as soon as Gideon was gone, she told Clay, "No use to sit out here. He'll be in there for hours."

Clay frowned. "But he just said—"

"Aw, you can't pay attention to what Gideon says."

Daisy shrugged. "He'll go in there and find somebody who wants to play cards, and they'll be in there all day. Come on!"

Clay glanced at the mule. "But what about Ezekiel? Ain't we supposed to be guarding him?"

Daisy laughed. "You heard what Pa said about the mule, didn't you? He won't care if somebody steals him. And I feel sorry for the fool who tries. That mule will bite his hand off. Come on!"

Clay shrugged and followed Daisy down the street. They walked along with their hands in their pockets, looking at the merchandise in the store windows, and sizing up the people who passed by. There were middle-aged women in poke bonnets and broadcloth gowns, little girls in gingham dresses and pinafores, and boys in white shirts and britches held up by suspenders.

The men wore big hats and buttoned-up shirts and jeans if they were cowboys, and all the men looked like they were in a hurry: riding off to someplace important, or buying goods, or talking business. Daisy and Clay leaned up against the wall of a mercantile store and watched them as they went by.

After about an hour, this palled on them, and Daisy jogged Clay in the ribs. "I got some money from selling pelts last year. What say we go and buy some candy and cigarettes and go out behind the store and light up? I wanna learn how to smoke."

"Ain't nothing hard about it." Clay shrugged. "You just breathe in and out. It'll make you sick the first time, though. And you're a girl. Ain't never heard of a girl smoking."

Daisy's eye kindled. "What's me being a girl got to do

with anything?"

"Nothing, I guess. It's just I never saw a girl do it before."

"Well, come on. You're about to."

Daisy dug in her pants pocket, pulled out a dime, and walked into the mercantile. It was a deep, narrow building with long counters on each wall: one for food, and the other for dry goods and ready-made furniture.

Daisy took it in, located the owner, and walked up to the counter on the left-hand wall.

"Afternoon," she told him.

"Good afternoon, young fella." The man smiled. "What can I get for you?"

Daisy looked around. "I'd like some liquorice whips, a bag of hard candy, and cigarette tobacco and papers. As much as I can get, for a dime." She slid the coin across the counter, and the man palmed it.

"Well, let's see." He scratched his head and pulled a paper bag out of a drawer. "You can get a bundle of whips, like so," he told her, displaying a sample, "and a quarter pound of hard candies, all types, one pack of cigarette paper, and a small bag of tobacco. That sound about right?"

Daisy nodded. "Sounds all right to me."

The man smiled again; then his eye lighted on Clay, as he lounged near the front door. He stiffened and nodded towards him.

"This stuff is for *you*, ain't it, boy?" he asked tightly, and Daisy frowned and nodded.

"Well, it's all right then," the man grumbled, and gathered up her order.

Daisy frowned at him in confusion, took the paper bag, and walked out.

"What's wrong with him?" she wondered aloud and glanced back over her shoulder. "Acts like somebody spit in his coffee." She brightened and handed Clay a liquorice whip. "Try these. They're a power. I think I like 'em better than peppermints."

Clay looked at her, and then back at the store. "No thanks."

"What's wrong with you? I thought you liked candy."

"I'm not hungry."

"Suit yourself." Daisy bit the end off the liquorice strip and chewed. "Now I got the makings, I'm gonna smoke a cigarette. Show me how to roll it up."

Clay sighed and held out his hand. Daisy placed the bag of tobacco and the packet in it, and he sat down cross-legged on the ground and sprinkled a little tobacco onto one of the papers.

He folded the edges, licked them, and then rolled the paper into a twist. He reached in his back pocket for a match.

"Here." He handed Daisy the cigarette, and she put it into her mouth and stuck her chin out. Clay lit the end of the cigarette, and Daisy inhaled deeply.

Clay watched her in amusement as she held her breath in increasing discomfort. She looked down, and set her chin, and pursed her lips: but soon she choked:

"*Gah*! That's the awfulest tastin' stuff I ever put in my mouth! I thought I was strong, but I can't stomach that. Can't figure why folk love it so. It's nasty!"

Clay swiped the cigarette out of her mouth and took a pull.

"Oh, stop showin' off, Clay," Daisy grumbled. "I could do that too, if I wanted. Just don't want to, that's all."

Clay grinned. "That's what you always say when I can do something you can't."

He looked up suddenly and jogged Daisy in the ribs. He took the cigarette out of his mouth and nodded towards the road. "Hey, look there!" he exclaimed, as a shiny buggy rolled up to a store and pulled to a stop. "That looks like Jem McClary and his son Jeremy!"

Daisy shrugged. "So? Who are they?"

"Why, they're with the Circle T, up in Indian Rock," Clay breathed and watched with wide brown eyes as a blond man and a blond boy climbed out of the rig. "Biggest ranch in this part of the state!"

"Oh, you and your ranches," Daisy scoffed. "What's so special about havin' a lot of cows, I'd like to know."

"What's special?" Clay echoed, still watching the two newcomers. "Cows are money! That fella there is one of the richest men outside of Denver. You oughta ask Gideon to take you to see the Circle T sometime. It's huge!"

Daisy waved him away. "I ain't lost nothing in Indian Rock to make me wanna go back there."

As they talked, two boys of their own age approached, hands in pockets. The first was a tall redheaded boy, and the second was dark. Daisy squinted up at them.

"Howdy."

The redheaded boy nodded towards Clay, sitting cross-legged on the ground. "Is he a friend of yours?"

Daisy frowned. "That's an awful funny way to say hello," she answered, clapped her hands together, and stood up. She put her hands on her hips and stared the boy down. "But since you asked—he sure is. He's my best friend, matter of fact."

Clay put the bag of tobacco on the ground and stood up beside her, and his expression was dark.

The boy pulled his mouth down and nodded. "Then you're a dirty Injun lover!" he replied, and spat on Daisy's shoes.

Daisy scowled and put her hands on her hips. "Them's fightin' words, buster," she warned him.

The boy half-turned towards his friend and smiled: "They sure are. Put up your dukes!"

Clay put a hand on Daisy's arm and stepped out in front of her. "I'll fight you, any time you like," he said grimly.

The boy turned back and suddenly threw his fist at Clay's head. Clay ducked under the punch and rammed his head and shoulder into the boy's chest, and they both fell down and rolled on the ground, fists flying.

The other boy circled around them, shouting. "Come on Leroy, get him!"

He pulled back and kicked Clay, and Daisy took a running start, jumped on his back, and ripped two handfuls of hair right out of his head.

The boy screamed and threw her off. She rolled on the ground, jumped up, and kicked him so strategically that he doubled up, howling, and when the redheaded boy shook free of Clay and took to his heels, both Clay and Daisy chased him down the whole length of the street.

Gideon came out of the mercantile just in time to see the two of them flying after the redheaded boy. He jumped a fence to get away, and Clay jumped it a split-second after in pursuit, and then Daisy stopped to scoop a rock off the ground and lobbed it after him.

"You come back any time you want some more!" she shouted furiously, and Gideon frowned and cried severely:

"Daisy McCall! Come back here this instant, young lady!"

But Daisy had already clambered over the fence and plunged into the underbrush to give chase.

Gideon stood on the sidewalk outside the store, face burning, and was mortified to see a blond man and his son on the sidewalk a few doors down, mouths hanging open.

The boy turned to his father in awe and exclaimed: "Did you hear that! That was a *girl*, Pa!"

"I'd hate to see her mother," the older man drawled, and shook his head.

Chapter
Ten

"That boy was heavier than you. He was taller; he was stronger. You're just lucky he ran away!"

Gideon glared at his sheepish daughter. Daisy had weeds in her hair from ploughing through three meadows and a hill covered in briars and vines; her face was scraped where the redheaded boy swung at her and mostly missed; her pants leg was torn ragged by briars, and dirt was ground into the knees.

"Aw, Gideon," she grumbled. "I know his type a mile off. He's like a rooster—all crow. Clay beat him like a drum. Didn't you, Clay?"

Clay glanced at her and smiled. He had the beginnings of a black eye and a split lip, but the glow of victory shone in his eyes.

"And besides, was I gonna sit there and let him badmouth my best friend? I was not," Daisy added indignantly. "You would've popped him yourself, Pa, if you'd heard what he said."

Gideon stared at her. "A young lady does not brawl in the street!" he replied severely. "I was wrong to raise you all alone, up in the wilderness. I see that now. We've been cut off from civilization too long. Well, it ends today. I'm going to buy a little house in town, and we're going to move to Wolf Table and start living like normal people!"

Daisy's mouth fell open. "But Gideon!"

"I'll be sending you to school as soon as we settle in," Gideon added. "You're behind the other children your age, but you're a bright girl, and if you work hard, I'm sure you can catch up."

"But Gideon—what about the claim you're working? You're all the time saying that there's gold in it. That it just needs a little more work!"

Gideon glanced at her and cleared his throat. "Never mind that now," he answered. "The important thing is that we're going to stop living like hermits and rejoin the rest of the human race!"

"But if we move down here, I won't be able to see Clay no more," Daisy objected. "Or hunt, or fish! I'll be miserable, and so will you!"

Gideon looked away. "I will not be miserable," he replied. "And you won't be either, you'll see. Don't argue any more, Daisy. My mind is made up!"

He stalked down the sidewalk. "We're going to check in at the hotel, and you're going to wash that mud and dirt off, and then we'll have dinner. Clay, you're welcome to join us if you like."

Daisy turned to look at Clay. "Coming with us, Clay?"

Clay shook his head. "No. I'm going back up the mountain. See you, Dase."

Daisy frowned and watched her tall friend cross the road, walk out behind the buildings, and make his slow way back up into the foothills.

She shook her head. "Clay's too proud. What's one little dinner, between friends? But he won't take nothing from nobody."

"Clay is a young man," Gideon told her. "And young men have pride."

"What, more than anybody else, you mean?" Daisy asked.

Gideon glanced at her. "Yes, more than anybody else. Especially when young ladies are nearby."

Daisy frowned. "I can't figure it. Clay ain't prickly in the general way. Must've been them lunkheads, wantin' to fight him, that's got him acting strange."

Gideon looked at her and decided to try again.

"Daisy, Clay is getting to the age when it becomes important to him what girls think, and especially what they think of *him*. No man wants a girl to think of him as—needing help, in any way. He's got too much pride."

Daisy's frown deepened. "Well, that's a stupid thing to think. Seein' as how they warn't any girls around to see what happened today, except for me. I don't give a rip either way, and Clay knows it."

"Never mind," Gideon replied with a sigh, and they walked back to retrieve Ezekiel and to check into the hotel.

***

The only hotel in Wolf Table had the virtue of being fairly new and mostly empty, it being a weekday, and Gideon had no trouble finding rooms. The man at the counter seemed overjoyed at the prospect of two new guests, and he smiled at them with all his teeth.

"Well, well! Welcome to Wolf Table, Mister ...?"

"McCall," Gideon replied. "Gideon McCall. This is my

daughter, Daisy."

Gideon noticed, with surprise, that the man didn't blink. "What brings you to our town if you don't mind my asking, Mr McCall?"

"I'm looking to buy a house," Gideon told him blandly. "We're going to be staying at your hotel while we look. I'd like two rooms, preferably side by side."

The man pulled two keys down off a peg board on the wall behind him. "Coming up," he said with a smile. "Please follow me."

Gideon followed and coughed: "Does this hotel have a bath?"

The man half turned as they climbed the stairs. "Oh yes! Brand new porcelain model, with soap and clean towels thrown in! Baths are a quarter extra, though."

"You can add them to my bill," Gideon told him and glanced back at Daisy. "We're going to require several."

Chapter Eleven

"Aw Gideon!"

Daisy shuffled into the hotel bathroom and turned a pitiful look towards her parent, but Gideon was unmoved.

"Go ahead and take a bath while the water's hot. I want you to scrub with that soap and washcloth, too! If you come out dirty, I'll make you take another!"

The door closed behind him with a *snap*, and Daisy cursed under her breath and flopped down onto a bench beside the bathtub to take off her shoes. Something had sure put a burr up Gideon's britches, and while she wished she knew what it was, it didn't matter in the end.

They was moving to Wolf Table, right downtown, and her life was never going to be good again. No more hunting, no more fishing.

School.

Daisy groaned and pulled her hands over her face. She'd rather be hung than to have to sit in a chair all day and have some old skinny teacher badger her, or God forbid, ask her questions.

She'd have to read, too, and she was no good at that. And the thought of having to do *math* made her almost desperate.

She peeled off her clothes and stuck a toe into the steaming water.

"*Ow*! Gideon, this water is hotter than he—"

His voice answered from the hall. "Good. Get in and take your bath!"

Daisy pulled her mouth down and slowly inched her way down into the fluffy soap suds. She sat there, frowning, and reached for the soap and washcloth.

There wasn't any help for it. Gideon had said that if she didn't take a bath, she wasn't getting any dinner, and she was hungry.

She took a deep breath, closed her eyes, and dunked her head under the water. She came up spluttering and rubbed the bar of soap over her hair.

"Wisht I knew what I done to make you so mad!" she yelled.

"I'm not mad," Gideon replied. "I'll be taking one next. I won't go to dinner scruffy and dirty, and neither will you."

"I'd rather eat over a fire in the woods," Daisy called. "If you gotta slick up every time before going to dinner in town, it's more trouble than it's worth!"

By five o'clock that evening, the two of them had bathed and dressed and were ready to patronize one of the town's two dining establishments. Having been told by the man at the hotel that Mrs O'Malley's was the better of the two, they sallied forth; Gideon with an expression of pleasure, and Daisy with a dissatisfied frown.

Mrs O'Malley's proved to be a clapboard storefront café with about six tables, a long counter, and a heavy scent of frying meat hanging in the air.

Gideon paused at the entrance, and his bushy moustache twitched, but Daisy revived.

"Something sure smells good!" she exclaimed, and the middle-aged woman who came walking out to greet them smiled.

"Welcome to my place," she said. "Table for two?"

Gideon nodded, and the woman led them to a big table next to the plate glass window in the front. From that vantage point, they could see the whole of Wolf Table's main street, from one end to the other.

"Tonight we have country fried steak or fried chicken," their hostess told them. "You can have two sides: mashed potatoes, green beans, corn, or rice."

"I'll have the steak and the mashed potatoes and green beans," Gideon replied. The woman turned to Daisy, but Daisy's eyes were riveted to a spot on the floor a few dozen feet away.

"Gideon, look there!" she cried and leaned out to peer around the table. "Have you ever seen such a rat as that outsized rascal?—he's a bold one, the big monster!"

Mrs O'Malley's horrified eyes followed Daisy's and fastened on the offending rodent. She put a hand to her mouth.

"*Oh!*" she gasped.

Daisy looked up and assured her, "Don't worry lady, I'll get him!"

Every head in the restaurant turned as Daisy grabbed the heavy salt shaker off the table, pulled back, and smoked it. They saw the shaker hit the rat and heard the tearing shriek as the rodent was knocked over on its back, dead.

"Ha!" Daisy cried, "I knew I could do it! Stone cold dead, and with one shot, too!"

The woman made a strangled sound, snatched up the menus, and ran to the kitchen, her face burning. Gideon sighed deeply and took a sip of water before saying:

"Come on. We're leaving."

Daisy frowned. "Leaving? Why? We just got here!"

"We're going to be eating at the other restaurant. From now on," Gideon replied wearily.

"But—"

"I'll explain it to you later."

***

They walked down to the sidewalk to the competing establishment, Mrs Hartwell's, and were given another window seat that fronted mostly on the woods bordering the town; Gideon settled in wearily.

He shook out his napkin, placed it in his lap; and watched in frowning silence as Daisy stuck hers in her shirt front.

Gideon leaned forward. "You put it on your lap," he whispered, and Daisy sighed, yanked the napkin free, and put it on her lap.

When their dinner arrived, Daisy watched in greedy silence as the hostess set the plates down in front of them, and as soon as her back was turned, she hunched over the plate and began shoveling mashed potatoes into her mouth.

Gideon scowled. "Daisy, I see that I am going to have to teach you proper table manners."

Two blue eyes looked up at him innocently.

"First of all, sit up."

Daisy looked around, chewed the mouthful of potatoes, and straightened up.

"Now watch as I use my knife and fork."

Gideon neatly cut a piece off his steak and put it into his mouth.

Daisy frowned and settled into her chair. She stabbed her beef patty with her fork, sawed off one end with her knife, and crammed the piece into her mouth.

She glared at him, chewing defiantly.

"Now you're just being difficult."

Chapter
Twelve

By eight o'clock, Daisy and Gideon had eaten their dinner and returned to the hotel, though they didn't retire right away. They stayed in the fancy parlour downstairs and performed the nightly ritual that they'd upheld ever since she'd come to live with Gideon.

They broke out a pack of cards and played until midnight.

"Just one game tonight, Dase," Gideon told her. "I'm a little worn out."

"Don't talk like an old man, Gideon," she teased him and shuffled the deck. "How about gin rummy?"

"All right," he sighed, and pulled his hands over his face. "We'll play our first hand in our new home. I'll shine up my lucky ring tonight. It'll give us good fortune while we're living here."

Daisy sputtered. Gideon never took that gold ring off his finger, and whenever they did something new, he rubbed it on his arm and claimed that it'd give them good luck.

"What is there about rubbing that ring on your arm that makes good things happen, Gideon? Sounds awful superstitious to me."

Gideon raised his brows. "This ring has always brought me good luck," he said with a smile. "Works every time. It'll make good things happen, you'll see."

"If you say so."

She dealt the cards and settled back into her chair. "I'll go first," she told him, but when Gideon took his hand, she was surprised to see the smile fade off his face.

"On second thought—I think I'll turn in early tonight, Dase," he mumbled, and set his cards down on the table.

"Ain't feeling sick, are you, Gideon? Was it the food?"

He waved her away. "No, no," he mumbled. "I'll talk to you tomorrow. Be up by seven, and we'll go out for breakfast."

"All right." Daisy frowned and watched him climb the stairs with a puzzled expression.

When he'd disappeared upstairs, she reached over and turned over his cards.

To her surprise, they were aces and eights ... what Gideon had once called the dead man's hand. She shook her head and pulled her lips into a thin line.

She didn't put no stock in signs, or in luck, but Gideon believed in 'em powerful, and he'd be looking over his shoulder for the next few days, at least.

"Stupid cards," she muttered, and shuffled his hand back into the deck.

***

Daisy climbed up the stairs, closed the door of her hotel room behind her, yawned, and sat down on the bed. The hotel bed was real nice. It was stuffed with cotton wadding instead of corn shucks, and it was made up with a pretty quilt and cotton sheets. She kicked out of her shoes and cuddled up to the pillow.

But try as she might, she couldn't get to sleep. As soft as the bed was, it wasn't home, and the hotel room felt strange and uncomfortable.

It was too quiet, for one thing. She was used to dropping off to the soft night sounds of the mountains: to the purr of owls, or the hum of crickets, or the mournful wail of coyotes. She was used to the clean, cold night air, to the mist rising up from the creeks all around the cabin, to the fragrant hush of wind through the firs.

It was unnatural to go to sleep all boxed in, with the doors and even the windows closed up tight.

Daisy bounced out of bed and walked across the room to the window. It was dark outside; the only lights in the buildings were on the second floor, as the shopkeepers and their families settled in for the night.

Daisy opened both windows and let the night air flow in. She sat on the sill with one foot propped up and watched the street below for a while. The town rolled up after dark, and the only thing she saw was a silhouette or two in a window, and what looked like a dog trotting down the street.

After sixteen years on the mountain, even that felt strange to her.

But Gideon was dead set on living here. It was going to be a rocky road for her, that was for sure. Ever since they hit this town, she couldn't do nothing to suit him.

Daisy hugged herself and looked up at the ceiling.

Whenever she felt in need of comfort, she remembered how her mother had come to kiss her good night and hear her prayers before she dropped off to sleep.

Her mother's face was hazy now, a distant memory, but she still remembered how soft her voice was.

"Let me hear your night prayers, Daisy," her mother had breathed, and she'd put her hands together and prayed:

Now I lay me down to sleep
I pray Thee, Lord, my soul to keep
If I should die before I wake
I pray the Lord my soul to take. Amen.

Then her mother had leaned over to kiss her. "Good night, Daisy. Sweet dreams."

It had always made her feel so safe. Like everything was all right.

But she'd stopped doing it after she came to live with Gideon. Gideon hadn't been a praying man, and he'd stared at her when she asked if he was going to hear her night prayers.

"Ah—all right," he'd said and had listened patiently when she remembered to ask him, but when she forgot, he hadn't reminded her.

And bit by bit, she'd stopped praying.

Now, she'd almost forgotten how, but she sure enough needed some divine help if she was going to live in a big town like Wolf Table.

She glanced up at the ceiling, put her hands together, and murmured:

"Now I lay me down to sleep ..."

But somehow she couldn't get past the first line. She felt silly, praying a child's prayer. She needed something more grown up.

But the only person she knew who could help her with God was the Prophet, and he only came down to Wolf Table once or twice a year.

He lived away up on the mountain, higher even than her and Gideon, and he had an itchy foot. You couldn't bank on him being at his cabin. As like as not, he'd be out somewhere in the wilderness.

Gideon had called him a crazy man and told her to stay away from him, but Gideon hadn't seen what she'd seen.

Any anyway, if Gideon could believe in luck, then she could believe in miracles.

Daisy sighed and climbed back into the bed. She crossed her arms, looked up at the ceiling, and thought long thoughts for at least two hours before she finally dropped off.

Chapter
Thirteen

"Stand up straight, child."

Daisy sighed, squared her shoulders, and shifted her weight. Gideon had dragged her to a seamstress first thing and made her get fitted for a couple of dresses.

But she hated the blasted things. They were too long and too fussy, and just got in the way. How any girl could walk in them, much less run, was beyond her. And the bustle was just … she didn't have any words for how much she hated them silly things.

The seamstress looked up at her as if she'd read her thoughts. "How would you like a nice bustle on your dress, young lady?"

Daisy crossed her arms. "I wouldn't like it at all," she replied. "Them things look like somebody sneaked up behind and clapped a cabbage on your bottom."

The woman's mouth dropped open, and Gideon cleared his throat. "We'll hold off on those for now."

The woman climbed up from the floor, where she had been kneeling, and nodded at Gideon. "I have a selection of styles you can choose from, sir, and you can take your pick from the fabrics on that wall yonder."

Gideon nodded towards her. "Come over here and have a look, Daisy. You can choose any style and material you want."

His eyes returned to the seamstress. "We'll take two dresses at first, and see how that goes."

Daisy kicked at the floor, stuck her hands in her pockets, and slouched toward Gideon. He pointed her to a big desk with paper patterns tacked to the surface.

"How about that one?" Gideon prompted, and Daisy glanced at where his finger was pointing. A simpering young woman was twirling a parasol and showing off a fitted jacket over a big, pleated gown with flowing skirts.

"How'd I climb up to my deer stand in that thing?" Daisy objected and gestured towards it in appeal. "I'd end up hung!"

Gideon leaned towards her and whispered: "*Hush. We're not at home anymore, Daisy! You're a young lady, and I want you to start acting like one.*"

He cleared his throat and added: "How about this one? It's simpler."

Daisy glanced at it unhappily. "Looks like a torment to me."

Gideon sighed and turned to the woman. "We'll take numbers two and four," he told her, "and as for the fabric—she should have something cool for this weather. Cotton or linen. Which colours do you like, Dase?"

Daisy glanced at the bolts once. "Don't make no difference to me," she grumbled. "Gonna look like a fool in any one of 'em."

The woman made a huffing sound, and Gideon turned to her and smiled: "We've lived outside town for quite some time, and I'm afraid my daughter is something of a tomboy. We'll have the white linen with the little yellow roses, and the pale blue cotton with the little stripes."

"They'll be lovely on her," the woman replied and caught Daisy's eye. "You'll soon have boys buzzing around you like bees around honey, young lady."

Daisy opened her mouth, but Gideon gave her such a look that she closed it, but she'd been about to say that she expected to have to dodge rocks if she went sticking out in public wearing such ridiculous clothes.

"What about a hat?" the woman ventured. "The young lady will need some kind of hat, and a handbag."

"A hat *too*?" Daisy blurted, in a tone of horror.

"And boots," the woman added, with a glance at Daisy's leather moccasins.

"We'll take two pairs of boots in her size," Gideon replied, "one for every day, and one for dressing up."

The woman beamed at him, but to Gideon's embarrassment, Daisy was no longer there. The little bell over the door jangled, and when he looked out the window, Daisy was fast disappearing down the street. He pressed a few bills into the woman's hand and tipped his hat.

"We'll be back in a week or so," he told her and hurried out after his daughter.

"Daisy!"

Daisy glanced back over her shoulder and scowled. "Why d'you want to make my life hard, Gideon? I can't walk sewn up in no gunny sack, and I don't want to live crammed in so tight that I can lean out my bedroom window and shake hands with my neighbours!"

People were staring at them, and Gideon caught up to his daughter. He took her elbow and hustled her off the street and into an alley between two buildings.

"Daisy, you're going to have to settle down," he told her seriously. "You can't just blurt out the first thoughts that come into your head. Because most of the time, those thoughts aren't very polite. They hurt people's feelings."

"What, you mean you want me to lie?"

"Yes."

Daisy looked down and kicked the ground. "I hate this, Gideon," she grumbled. "I know you say it's for the best, but I hate it."

"Yes, I've noticed that. But I wager you'll come around, once you get used to it," he replied softly and brushed a twig of hair back from her brow. "Now come on. I'm going down to the stables and see if I can find some horses. One for you, and one for me."

Daisy's eyes snapped up to his. "You wouldn't pull my leg, would you, Gideon? A horse of my own?"

Gideon smiled and looked away. "A horse of your own. As long as you show me that you can be responsible with it."

Daisy shrieked and threw her arms around Gideon's neck, and he smiled and rolled his eyes up at the sky. "All right, Dase," he mumbled. "Though I'm sure I'm going to regret making you such a foolish promise."

Daisy grabbed his hand and pulled him back out into the street and towards the blacksmith's stables.

"Come on, Gideon! I know *just* the kind of horse I need," she added, her blue eyes afire.

"Strong, healthy, and broken in," Gideon told her. "A young lady needs a gentle animal because she will ride side saddle."

But his daughter's eyes were alight with a look that he knew well—and had learned to dread. She was so excited that she let go of his hand and went running down to the blacksmith's ahead of him. Gideon reached into his breeches pocket and pulled out a cigar. He'd managed to distract Daisy long enough to keep her from running away, but it was an open question how long that would last.

But for the moment, he decided to just be happy for small favours. He struck a match, lit the cigar, and followed her at a more sedate pace.

Chapter Fourteen

By the time Gideon reached the blacksmith's, he saw, to his alarm, that the big man had already been drawn away to the corral behind his shop. He glanced at the steaming pail of water, and the fire burning in the furnace, as he passed, and made his way out to the back. There was a big corral a few hundred feet back of the shop.

The blacksmith was holding the reins of a magnificent black stallion. "His name is Sampson," the blacksmith was saying. "He's like my furnace. He has fire in the belly, this one."

"Daisy," Gideon called uneasily and threw the cigar down. The corral was still about a hundred feet away, but he began to jog towards it.

"Can I try him out?" Daisy asked, and Gideon quickened his pace. "No!" he shouted but saw the big man nod, and the next thing he knew, Daisy had jumped onto the horse's back.

"Let him go!" she cried, and the blacksmith laughed and stepped back.

To Gideon's horror, the horse screamed, reared, and began bucking like a rodeo horse.

"Daisy!" he cried, "Jump, jump!"

The blacksmith turned towards him in amazement. "*Daisy?*" he echoed. "You mean that ain't a *boy*?"

"Didn't you hear me calling, you fool?" Gideon snapped, and the big man's face gathered darkness.

"What did you call me?" he growled and grabbed Gideon by his shirt.

But Gideon's eyes were riveted to the horse. It tossed its head and reared, and when that didn't throw Daisy off, it gathered itself, exploded over the corral fence, and roared past them and down the main street.

"Daisy!" he screamed, twisted out of the man's clutches, and went tearing after her as hard as he could run. "Somebody stop that horse!"

The black galloped down the street, scattering terrified pedestrians, and circled around and around as Daisy whooped and lifted one hand like a rodeo rider. Some of the boys watching from the sidewalks grinned and shouted: "Ride 'em, boy! That's the style!"

"Daisy!" Gideon screamed and snatched a rope off a hitching post. He tied it into a noose with frantic fingers and ran out into the street, but before he could lasso the brute, it screamed, tossed its head and bucked right onto the wooden sidewalk. The people standing there scattered in all directions, and with a convulsive kick, the stallion sent its powerful hooves right through the front window of Mrs O'Malley's café. Glass shattered everywhere, and the horse screamed and reared to throw Daisy off.

Gideon's mouth dropped open for a split-second; but then he recovered his wits and ran towards the horse, swinging the rope.

He threw the lasso, but the horse danced away just in time. Gideon watched helplessly as the stallion grunted, then leaped into the air and kicked, kicked again, and slowed.

"You're wearing him down!" one of the boys called, and Gideon cursed under his breath. That was all Daisy needed—encouragement!

"Jump, jump!" he shouted and sprang towards them, but to his consternation, the horse suddenly galloped off as if Daisy had spurred it.

He watched as Daisy grabbed the reins, pulled back and thrashed against the black, fighting it with her whole body. The horse screamed, tossed its head, and danced around and around, its black tail flying.

Gideon slowed to a walk, mouth open in amazement.

The horse grunted, kicked half-heartedly, and kicked again. But when Daisy leaned down to pat its flanks, it snorted, then allowed her to turn its head and ride it in slow triumph back to the blacksmith's, as every boy on the street cheered.

Gideon shook his head in dumbstruck amazement.

Every boy in town was running down the street beside her horse as she rode it back to the blacksmith's shop. The big man was standing outside, and Gideon saw him put his hands on his hips, throw his head back and laugh.

"Well, I'll be beat and hanged!" he roared, "A *girl's* done broke the meanest horse in my stable! Ride him, you little hellion!"

A slap of unpleasant surprise wiped a blank across her followers' faces, and Gideon's eyes narrowed. But to his relief, a tall blond boy broke out laughing. "I ain't never!" he hooted. "That's the toughest girl I ever saw! Ride 'em, Nellie!"

He slapped his friends on the back. "I saw her first!"

He laughed, and Gideon relaxed as he saw them smile reluctantly. "Come on!" he called, and they followed after him, chuckling.

"You better be careful, Jeremy," they warned him. "That one's a firecracker!"

Gideon hurried to the corral and arrived in time to see Daisy lean over and pat the black's neck. "He's a power!" she told the chuckling blacksmith. "Ain't never rode one like him!"

Gideon shouldered through the crowd outside the corral, and Daisy's eyes lit up at the sight of him. "I've made my choice, Gideon," she told him. "This one's mine!"

"You know better than to ask me for that monster!" Gideon told her severely. "You could've been killed! Get down off of that brute this minute. We're going back to the hotel!"

"Aw, Gideon!"

"Now!"

Daisy threw a leg over the horse's neck and slid down to the ground. The crowd of boys patted her head and shoulders as she passed, and the blond boy called:

"Hey—what's your name?"

Daisy looked back over her shoulder. "Daisy McCall."

The boy stuck his hand out. "I'm Jeremy McClary."

Daisy shook his hand loosely, and Gideon pulled her away. But the blond boy stared after her until she disappeared into the hotel on the other side of town.

The other boys noticed it. "What's wrong with you,

Jeremy?" they asked laughing. "You look like you done swallowed your tongue!"

Jeremy propped his elbows on top of the corral fence and rested his chin on his hands. "Boys, I'm going to marry that girl someday," he told them, and they looked at him, and then each other, and laughed.

"Good luck!"

Chapter Fifteen

Doc dragged his errant daughter back to the hotel. Mrs O'Malley and her husband were waiting for them in the lobby, and as soon as they entered, the man rose and cried:

"There they are!" He walked up and pointed an accusatory finger in Gideon's face. "Your daughter just destroyed our front window! It's going to take us a week to get all the broken glass swept up, and we're losing business as long as the window's busted out! What are you going to do about it?"

Gideon put up his hands. "I apologize for my daughter's impetuous behaviour," he drawled and yanked Daisy's arm. "You're sorry for breaking the O'Malleys' window, aren't you, Daisy?"

Daisy looked up sheepishly. "Yes, sir. I'm sorry the black busted out your window. I didn't mean him to do it."

The man's face reddened. "If you hadn't been riding him, none of this would've happened!" he retorted. "And we need more than an apology!"

"I will of course pay for your window to be replaced," Gideon replied. "Make out a detailed inventory of the damage and leave it at the hotel counter. I'll arrange for the damage to be repaired."

"What about the business we're losing?" the man

demanded.

"Add it to your estimate," Gideon replied wearily and dragged Daisy back upstairs.

He left her at her own room and told her: "I'm going out to look at houses. I want you stay in the hotel until I get back. We're drawing far too much attention in this town."

"Aw, I'll be bored to death," Daisy grumbled. "Let me come with you, Gideon!"

"You've caused enough trouble for one day," Gideon replied. "And if I find out that you left this hotel while I was gone, I'll—well, I'll think of something horrible."

"What about my lunch?" Daisy asked, and Gideon paused in the act of leaving.

"Tell the man at the counter to bring you a lunch from the café. Tell him he can add it to my tab."

***

He walked down the stairs and turned at the bottom to glare up at Daisy. She was still in the hall, but his frowning look made her sigh and drag herself inside her room.

***

Daisy walked to the open window and sat down on the sill with one foot propped in the frame. She watched Gideon walk down the street and disappear.

She flicked the window curtain with her fingers. Gideon was getting harder to live with by the hour. She had half a mind to go back up the mountain and hunt up the Prophet.

If she was lucky, she could lay out her problem, get the man's advice, and be back before Gideon returned.

The thought had no sooner crossed her mind than she gave the curtain a toss and skipped out of the room, the hotel, and the town.

Daisy breezed through the alley beside the hotel, out to the back yard, and up into the hills beyond. It was an hour's trip at least up the mountain to Gideon's cabin, but it was a cool, sunny day, and she was a strong walker.

***

She arrived at the cabin a little after noon and pushed the door open with her foot. There was salt-cured meat on the table, flatbread, and cheese. Daisy ate a couple of sandwiches, made a couple more, and stuck them in her pockets.

Then she grabbed the smooth, head-high walking stick that Gideon had made for her. It came in handy when you needed to pull yourself up a steep slope or if you were crossing a stream.

She walked outside, wiped her mouth, and looked up at the sky. By the position of the sun, she reckoned she had about four hours to find the Prophet, so she set off into the forest along a barely-visible trail that was the only road over that mountain.

She walked fast and took shortcuts across streams and over boulders where she could, and the oaks and aspens slowly gave way to the pines and firs of the higher slopes.

Daisy paused and pulled her arm across her brow. The sun was slanting through the trees and throwing bright spears of light into the shadowed forest. It was wilder up on the heights and more dangerous. Gideon had warned her a hundred times, but she hadn't paid him no mind.

The best hunting, the best views, and the best advice came from up here, and Gideon had always told her that if you wanted something good, you had to take a risk to get it.

Of course, he'd been talking about cards, like he always did; but she figured that if it was good advice, it should apply to everything.

At about three o'clock by the sun, Daisy parted the branches of a huge fir and peered through the green curtain. To her delight, the Prophet was at home. The log cabin was spouting a thin stream of smoke from a flue in the grass-covered roof, and she could hear his booming voice from where she was.

"Turn from your wickedness and your greed!" he was crying, "or every man among you will taste the righteous justice of the Lord—every mother's son!"

Daisy shrank back into her hiding place and swallowed. She had once come up here when she was about seven years old and had crouched inside this very fir tree. From the cover of its massive branches she had watched the old man walk out onto the rocky cliff just beyond his cabin door.

She had watched as he cried out and raised his hand to the sky in appeal, and a thread of lightning had branched down from a clear sky to touch his hand with a loud *pop*.

The flash and the thunder that shook the ground had made her eat dirt, but when she looked up again, the Prophet wasn't there anymore. She thought the lightning had knocked him over the cliff, but he was still there somewhere because soon the sound of his rough voice was echoing in the rocks.

"Amen! Amen! Amen! Worthy are you, Lord, of honour and glory and power!"

Then she looked up and a huge eagle was soaring on the wind, high above her. The hair had stood up on the back of her neck, and she turned tail and ran for home as fast as she could go.

Gideon had told her that the Prophet was a madman and didn't put any stock in what he said, but she'd never heard of anybody else in the world who was able to catch a lightning bolt like it was a raindrop.

Sometimes she wondered if the Prophet was even *human*. Her mother had told her stories of angels who appeared in human form to talk to men and then disappeared in a clap of thunder and a swirl of fire.

Either way, she figured the old man was worth talking to. She needed help, and she reckoned that since he was in touch with a higher power—since he might even *be* a higher power—the Prophet was the man to ask.

Still, it was only right to be cautious. You didn't just go strutting up to a man who could turn a lightning bolt. Daisy licked her lips, rubbed her palms on her pants legs, and stepped out from under the green curtain of the fir branches.

Chapter Sixteen

"Turn, turn from your pride and arrogance, and humble yourselves before the Lord!"

Daisy swallowed again and took a few tentative steps across the rocky yard outside the cabin. She put her hands to her mouth and called shakily:

"Hallo the house!"

The shouting stopped abruptly, and there was a long, pregnant silence in which Daisy could feel her heart beating. The door to the cabin opened, and an old man with long grey hair and bushy black eyebrows appeared in it. He was wearing buckskin breeches and a long white tunic over them, and he stood there without smiling, and without saying anything, for a long time.

"My name is Daisy McCall," Daisy cried. "I'm here because I'd like to talk to you. I need your help!"

The old man stared at her. "Your family died in an avalanche," he replied matter-of-factly.

Daisy frowned. "That's right," she replied. "Were you here when it happened?"

"I knew your father," he answered. "And your mother."

There was another long silence, and Daisy scuffed the ground with her foot. "Can I come in? I'd really like to talk to you."

The old man waved her on, and disappeared inside the cabin, and so Daisy followed.

***

The cabin was filled with smoke from the hearth because the old man was cooking stew in a cast iron pot over the fire. The inside of the house was so dark that it took Daisy's eyes a few moments to acclimate to the low light.

When they did, she saw that the inside of the cabin was cave like in its simplicity. Dried herbs of all kinds hung from the ceiling, and animal pelts lined the walls. There was a big table in the centre of the room, and everything else was pushed against the walls: chairs, a small bookcase, a tub for washing dishes, a cot.

"You were raised by that man who lives down the mountain," he went on gruffly. "The gambler."

Daisy frowned. "Gideon likes to play cards," she replied, "but I wouldn't call him a—"

"He's neglected your education."

At this, Daisy looked up and frowned. "Gideon's as good a man as any," she retorted, "and anybody says he ain't, better get ready to fight!"

The man's bright blue eyes snapped to hers.

"He's a gambler," he reiterated. "And he's being hunted. That's why he lives on this mountain. He's hiding from the men who want to kill him."

"Here now," Daisy replied in alarm, "You say that Gideon's in trouble?"

"His name isn't Gideon."

The old man walked to the hearth, scooped out a bowlful of stew, and handed it to her. She took it doubtfully and sniffed it before accepting a spoon.

The old man filled his own bowl, pulled two chairs off the wall, and threw a leg over one.

Daisy sat there in wary silence as the old man ate his stew. At length, he finished and threw her a shrewd look from his bright blue eyes.

"He's neglected your education. Your parents would have raised you up in the fear of the Lord. But the man you call Gideon doesn't know God, and so the little you remember of your parents' teaching has faded."

Daisy scowled at him. "How do you know my parents? I don't remember nothing about you."

But the old man ignored her question.

"You must seek your parents' God and come to know him as they did. That's what they both wanted for you—more than anything else."

"I didn't come up here to be told what I *have* to do," Daisy replied and put the uneaten bowl of stew on the table. "Or to ask you about God."

The old man nodded. "You came up here to ask me how to get your father to change his mind about moving into town. But you won't be successful. His mind is made up."

Daisy scowled at him. "How do *you* know?" she challenged him. "You're just making all this up, ain't you? I didn't come up here just to get my leg pulled!"

She jumped to her feet and would have stormed out, but the man's voice stopped her.

"His real name is Doc Dailey. A woman will greatly endanger him, and if he isn't careful, he'll be dead by this time next year."

Daisy whirled to confront him. "I don't believe you! You're just a lying, crazy old man, just like Gideon always said you was! And I'm sorry I came up here. I don't believe you ever knew my folks, and I know you ain't never met Gideon! You ought to be ashamed to scare me when I just come up here to ask for help!"

She threw the door open with a *bang* and ran across the rocky yard and into the thick stand of evergreens, but as she left, the Prophet's rough voice echoed in her ears.

"Woe to those who are wise in their own eyes, who pull away the shoulder, and who stop their ears! For the Lord resists the proud but gives grace to the humble!"

***

Daisy ran most of the way back to Gideon's cabin and arrived winded and worn out. By that time the sun had sunk into the west, and golden light was slanting low through the trees.

She'd only be able to make town before nightfall if she started down the mountain right then, but Daisy kicked off her moccasins and crawled up into her bunk. It had been her bed from the first night Gideon had brought her here, and it was the safest place she knew.

She pulled her pillow to her chest, and curled up around it. That old man had scared the living daylights out of her. But he was crazy; he had to be. There was no way he could know that Gideon was in danger, or—or when he'd die.

Daisy turned her face into her pillow. Just the thought of Gideon dying upset her terrible, and made a panicky feeling jump up in her chest.

But even if he was crazy, somehow the old man had known that her parents had died in an avalanche. And they'd been God-fearing people like he said.

And he'd never told her so, but it was also possible that Gideon had been a gambler once, him loving card games as much as he did.

Daisy pulled her mouth down. What if the old man wasn't crazy? What if he was right?

What if Gideon really was in danger? What if somebody was out to kill him?

The old man's last words to her rang in her ears like a mocking echo.

If he isn't careful, he'll be dead by this time next year.

He'll be dead by this time next year.

By this time next year.

"Oh Lord!" Daisy blurted out, "please tell me that old man isn't talking for you! Look out for Gideon, Lord! I've already lost my first parents," she added in a whisper. "I couldn't stand to lose him, too!"

Daisy turned her face back into the pillow and cried a little bit, but once she'd gotten the tears out of her system, she set her jaw and made up her mind.

If Gideon was sure enough in some kind of danger, like the old man had said, it was her duty, as his daughter, to protect him.

Up until then, she hadn't packed any iron when she

went into town, but that was about to change.

Daisy threw the pillow aside, climbed down the ladder, and pulled a revolver and a double-barreled shotgun from their places on the wall.

And as she loaded them, she was thinking: *Gideon kilt! Over my dead body.*

Chapter
Seventeen

Gideon knocked softly on Daisy's door.

"Dase?"

There was no answer from inside the room, and Doc knocked again. "Daisy, it's Gideon. Open the door!"

There was still no answer, and he frowned and pushed the door open. When he walked in, the room was empty, the bed was undisturbed, and the window was open.

The curtain fluttered in the evening breeze, and Gideon sighed and walked out.

If it had been any other child, he would've organized a search party and combed the town, but with Daisy, there was no need. His daughter had gone back up the mountain, and anything she might encounter with hostile intent, human or animal, would rue the day it challenged her.

Daisy probably would stay up on the mountain for a few days at least. He was prepared to humour her for a week or more because he knew it was going to be hard for her to adjust to a new way of life.

He was practically the only company she'd had for most of her young life. Wolf Table was a wide place in the road, a tiny town, but to a girl raised on the side of a mountain, it no doubt would seem crowded and confusing.

He reached into his pocket, pulled out a cigar, and lit it on the way back downstairs. He walked outside the hotel, leaned up against a post, and blew fragrant smoke into the evening air.

What little traffic there had been in town had thinned. The folk of Wolf Table had mostly finished work and turned for home, but the scent of frying meat lured Doc from the hotel entrance back down to Mrs Hartwell's.

He passed Mrs O'Malley's with a wry glance. After the twin debacles of the dead rat and the shattered front window, Gideon assumed that he would not be welcome at Mrs O'Malley's, even if he had the nerve to go there, and so he passed it by.

He noticed that the window had been covered with boards, and a message painted over them: *Café closed for repairs. We'll be open in a few days.*

He moved on to Mrs Hartwell's, further down the row, but if he had any trepidation, it was soon laid to rest. Mrs Hartwell smiled, welcomed him like a hero, and escorted him to a choice spot next to the window.

"We're so glad to see you here, Mr McCall!" she beamed. "Business has been booming for us ever since you came to town!"

Gideon noticed, with some embarrassment, that Mrs Hartwell had inherited all of Mrs O'Malley's usual customers. Her café was twice as full as it had been on his previous visit.

"I'm glad to be of service," he told her.

"We have fried trout and cornbread, or beef stew and cabbage tonight. You can have green beans or carrots with each one. Which do you want?"

"I'll have the trout and cornbread, with green beans and coffee."

"Coming up."

Gideon settled into his chair and tapped the ashes of his cigar into a tray. The street outside was getting dark, and the people inside the café were practically the only ones in town still stirring.

There was no night life in Wolf Table, or in any of the other little towns between Cheyenne and Denver, or at least, none to speak of.

Gideon took a contemplative pull on his cigar. Someone could make a killing if they opened up a gambling saloon in one of the little towns on the train line. It would draw all the locals for miles and bring business to the town when train passengers stopped there to play.

Yes, someone could make a killing. It just wasn't going to be *him*.

Mrs Hartwell arrived with a steaming cup of coffee, and Gideon thanked her and took a sip. It was bitter, pure acid, and he reflected that somebody could also make a killing if they opened a decent café in the town, and it was an open question whether a gambling saloon or a decent café would make more money. The people of Wolf Table were probably starving for good food just as much as for excitement.

As he sat there, a couple of middle-aged ladies rose and crossed the room to his table. He put his napkin on the table and stood up to greet them.

"Good evening, ladies. Would you care to have a seat at my table?"

A pink-cheeked matron giggled and shook her head. "Oh, we don't want to impose on you, Mr McCall! We heard that you and your daughter have come to live here, and we just came by to welcome you to Wolf Table, and to invite you to our church this Sunday. It's the last building on the road, the chapel. You've seen it, I'm sure."

"I have indeed, ladies. And thank you for your gracious invitation," Gideon drawled, but inside, he was trying to come up with some excuse that would spare him the necessity of sitting through an hour-long sermon.

'Are you a Christian man, Mr McCall?' the second lady enquired with a direct look from her guileless blue eyes, and Gideon temporarily drew a blank.

'Ah—I'm told I was baptized as an infant in St John's Cathedral in New Orleans,' he replied. 'But I have to take that on trust.'

The two ladies blinked at him, and then looked at each other, and the first one sputtered: 'Well, then, we hope you and your daughter will join us this Sunday, Mr McCall! Our pastor is a circuit rider, and he'll be in our town then. We won't see him for a month after, so be sure not to miss him!'

'I'll make every effort to be there, ladies.' Gideon smiled.

'We'll look for you, Mr McCall!'

'We hope you'll be able to attend.'

They returned to their table, and Gideon sat down again. His food arrived soon after, and he set to with as much enthusiasm as he could muster. After growing up on New Orleans cuisine, most everything else seemed bland and uninspired by comparison, and homesickness jabbed him like a knife.

He closed his eyes. What he wouldn't give to be in New Orleans at that moment, sitting at a card table with a glass of bourbon at his elbow and a Havana cigar in his hand!

And afterwards, to stroll into a restaurant at two in the morning and dine on beignets, scrambled eggs as light as air, and smoked, sugar-cured ham!

Judge Carter had driven him into a wilderness exile for ten years, but he had never stopped longing for his civilized, urbane life. And he'd begun to hope, in his heart of hearts, that Judge had moved on and forgotten him.

He was betting on that, anyway. He'd spent the afternoon looking at a couple of houses a mile or two out of town and planned to buy one before the week was out. It was past time for him to introduce Daisy to the world.

But he knew Judge well enough to stay sharp, and to watch his back.

He was going to have to play the role of Gideon McCall, mountain man and backwoods prospector until his dying day.

Because the bounty Judge had put on his head was still good, and probably would be hopefully pursued, right up to the day of his funeral.

Chapter Eighteen

The elderly minister adjusted his glasses and read out of his thick black Bible:

"And he said, Thy brother came with subtilty, and hath taken away thy blessing.

... And Esau hated Jacob because of the blessing wherewith his father blessed him: and Esau said in his heart, The days of mourning for my father are at hand; then will I slay my brother Jacob.

And these words of Esau her elder son were told to Rebekah: and she sent and called Jacob her younger son, and said unto him, Behold, thy brother Esau, as touching thee, doth comfort himself, purposing to kill thee.

Now therefore, my son, obey my voice; arise, flee thou to Laban my brother to Haran; And tarry with him a few days, until thy brother's fury turn away."

Gideon crossed his legs and assumed an expression of patient interest. On mature reflection, he had decided that firstly, it would be rude to turn down an invitation to church, and secondly, it would be wasteful. He knew almost no one in Wolf Table, and he was going to need acquaintances if he hoped to introduce Daisy to young people her own age.

The church was a good place to meet potential friends for Daisy, although he was paying a price for the privilege. The two ladies from the restaurant, Mrs Simmons and Mrs Taylor, had hailed him with joy when he arrived at the little chapel and would not let him sit by himself.

They had divided him between them; Mrs Simmons was sitting to his right, and Mrs Taylor to his left, and now and then they would glance at him, and he was compelled to nod, and look attentive.

Gideon scratched his moustache lightly. He had only a vague recollection of the story of Jacob and Esau. The gist of it seemed to be that Jacob had swindled his brother out of money and property, and had to skip town, because his brother wanted to kill him for it.

It was a story that had some distressing similarities to his own past, and was therefore not a comfortable story to hear.

The minister closed the Bible up and leaned over the rough wooden pulpit. "Have you ever been driven away from home?" he asked. "Have you ever fit with your family bad enough to have to leave? The Lord has a word for you.

"God is waiting for you in the wilderness. You may have lost the comforts of family and home. You may be lonely and poor. You may even be in danger. But the Lord will meet you in your lowest place, as he met Jacob. Listen!

"*And Jacob went out...and he lighted upon a certain place, and tarried there all night, because the sun was set; and he...lay down in that place to sleep.*

"*And he dreamed, and behold a ladder set up on the earth, and the top of it reached to heaven: and behold the angels of God ascending and descending on it.*

"And, behold, the Lord stood above it, and said, I am the Lord God of Abraham thy father, and the God of Isaac...And, behold, I am with thee.

"...And Jacob awaked out of his sleep, and he said, Surely the Lord is in this place; and I knew it not."

The old man looked up from his Bible. "The Lord was waiting for Jacob in the wilderness! Jacob thought he was friendless and alone, but the Lord was in that place. He just didn't know it!

"Have you ever overlooked the Lord? He's right there in your work. He's in your home. He's in your wilderness most of all.

"O Lord, give us eyes to see, like you give Jacob! Give us the eyes to see you, when we think we're alone!

"Give us the good sense to know that the whole earth is the house of God, and the gate of heaven, and that you're right there waiting—if only we open our eyes!"

***

To Gideon's weary resignation, the sermon, and the singing after, lasted almost two hours. After which followed a round of introductions, as his new acquaintances presented him to their friends.

Gideon smiled politely as he was introduced as "Gideon McCall, a prospector up on Smoke Mountain. He has a daughter too, isn't that right, Mr McCall?"

"Oh please," he replied smoothly, "call me Gideon. And yes, I do have a daughter. Her name is Daisy. She wasn't able to come with me this morning, as she has returned to our cabin for a few days. She'll be bringing back some things we have need of."

"Well, we'll certainly look forward to meeting Daisy,

won't we?" Mrs Simmons nodded. "How old is your daughter, Mr Mc—I mean, Gideon?" she corrected, with a giggle.

"Daisy is just sixteen," Gideon replied, "and I fear has suffered from a lack of maternal supervision. I have been practically her only companion for the last ten years. Her mother died in an avalanche on the mountain." He lowered his eyes and sighed heavily, and to his satisfaction, the ladies jumped to the conclusion he had hoped. His confession was met with a rush of sympathy.

"Oh, how awful!"

"We're so sorry for your loss, Gideon."

"It must have been very hard, to raise your daughter all alone."

He raised his brows and nodded sadly. "I did my best," he replied, "but of course even I could never replace the tender guidance and feminine wisdom that her mother would have given her. There are so many things that Daisy still doesn't know. I can only pray that she finds help from other quarters and can—flourish as a young woman in spite of her handicap."

"Oh, we'd be happy to teach your daughter anything she might like to know, wouldn't we, ladies?" Mrs Taylor cried, and the little bunch of bonnets bobbed in agreement. "You just bring her to church, Gideon, and we'll be glad to take her home after, and school her. Does she cook?"

Gideon shook his head. "No."

"Can she sew?"

"I'm afraid not."

"Can she sing?"

One end of Gideon's lip curled up, imagining their faces if he told them what kind of songs Daisy sang. She'd learned them from the miners and loggers they had occasionally met over the years: *Pistol Annie*; *Pee in Your Own Pot*; *Drive them Oxen*, and one of her favourites, a shocking ditty that was made up almost entirely of swear words.

"Not well, I fear."

The ladies were momentarily nonplussed, but rallied. "Well, never mind it! You just bring her down to us, and she'll soon learn, you'll see!"

"Ladies, you are very kind."

"Nonsense! We just want you and Daisy to feel welcome. Are you hungry, Gideon? We're going over to Mrs Hartwell's for lunch. Why don't you come with us?"

"Why, I'd be delighted," Gideon told them, and allowed himself to be led away.

Chapter Nineteen

Daisy arrived back in town a little after noon, with a bulging leather pack slung over her shoulder. She was carrying one of Gideon's shotguns in one hand and a pistol in the other. Most of the people who saw her got out of her way; her blonde brows were drawn low over her eyes, and both her expression and her angry walk suggested that she was thinking about shooting someone.

Daisy blew past the startled hotel clerk and took the stairs two at a time. The man leaned over the front desk to watch as she reached the second floor. She slammed the door behind her, and there was an ominous silence, broken only by a sound like a backpack hitting the bed, and another like a gun being loaded.

The hotel clerk mopped his face with a rag, then jumped as her door popped open again, and Daisy came trotting downstairs. She was holding a huge pistol in her hand and only paused long enough to ask: "Where's Gideon?"

The man stammered: "I—I think he went to church, but church is out now. They all usually go out to lunch after, so he's probably—"

But his grim-looking guest didn't wait for him to finish. She stalked out of the hotel and went striding down the street with such a look of purpose that the man decided that if she came back, he was going to hide in the back room.

***

Daisy strode down the street, scowling. The Prophet had said that a woman was going to endanger Gideon, and that if he wasn't careful, he'd be dead by this time next year.

She didn't know if the old man was crazy or not, but why should she take a chance with the only family she had?

She was going to make double-dog sure that no other woman had a chance to mess with Gideon for the next twelve months. After that, he was a free man—but not a day before.

One thing was for dang sure: nobody was going to punch Gideon's ticket while *she* was around.

She paused on the threshold of Mrs Hartwell's and scanned the lunch crowd for her father. Yes, there he was—sitting at a table surrounded by women and as unsuspecting as a little lamb.

Daisy narrowed her eyes. The Prophet hadn't said what kind of woman would endanger Gideon, or what age of woman.

It could be *any* of them.

She set her jaw and went walking up to Gideon's table. She raked his companions with a suspicious glance.

"Well, I'm back, Gideon," she told him. "You all right?"

Gideon looked up at her in surprise. "Perfectly fine," he replied. "I met these charming ladies at church today. Allow me to introduce Mrs Simmons and Mrs

Taylor, and their daughters Linda Simmons and Rachel Taylor. Ladies, this is my daughter Daisy."

The women's round eyes travelled from Daisy's chopped-off shock of hair, to her shirt and suspenders and breeches.

"How do you do," the girls said, in tiny voices. Their mothers were speechless.

Daisy turned a chair around, threw a leg over it, and slapped her pistol down on the table where everyone could see it.

"Howdy," she grunted, and nodded towards the gun. "Hope you don't mind me bringing my iron. Never go anywhere without it." She gave them all a keen look, just to show them she meant business and had the satisfaction of seeing the girls quail.

Gideon put a hand lightly on her shoulder. "Daisy, why don't you put the pistol away. I doubt you'll need it while we're eating." He motioned for Mrs Hartwell, who walked over with a smile.

"Daisy, would you like meatloaf or corned beef?"

"Ain't particular."

"She'll have the corned beef." Gideon reached for the pistol and set it down on the floor beside his chair. "Coffee or tea, Daisy?"

"Coffee," Daisy told him, still scanning the others. "Gotta keep my eyes open."

The girls on the opposite side of the table goggled at her, and one whimpered: "Ma, isn't it time we were going home?"

Her mother laughed tunelessly and sputtered, "We've

only just got here, Linda! And you have a chance to meet Daisy before anyone else. She's going to be your new schoolmate; isn't that right, Daisy?"

She turned to Daisy for confirmation, but Daisy replied: "They'll have to catch me first! I'd rather be shot than go to school. I can hunt and fish as well as Gideon, and that's all I need to live up on the mountain."

The old woman opened her mouth in speechless dismay, and Gideon replied, in a tone of rebuke: "That wasn't very polite, Daisy. I want you to apologize to these nice ladies."

Daisy replied bluntly: "Apologize for what—for saying what I mean? I hate the idea of sitting in one place all day and being asked questions."

Mrs Simmons sputtered out an uncomfortable laugh and replied: "I daresay she has that in common with many of her classmates!"

But Gideon frowned. "Daisy, apologize."

Daisy hunched a shoulder. "All right, I apologize," she said, in a disgusted tone. "But—"

"No *buts*," Gideon told her severely and leaned over to reinforce the rebuke.

Their food arrived soon after, so Daisy applied herself to her meal and said little else. But she kept a jealous eye on Gideon, and raised her spoon, ready to smack Rachel Tucker's hand when she saw the girl pass the salt to Gideon and smile.

"Hey—do that again, and I'll pop you!" Daisy warned her, with a thunderous frown, and the girl quailed before the look in her eye.

Chapter **Twenty**

"I've never been so embarrassed in all my life!"

Gideon turned around, hands on hips, and glared at his errant daughter, who was staring at him with an expression of perfect innocence in her big blue eyes. It was evening, and he'd been lecturing Daisy for most of the day.

He'd even followed her into her hotel room to make sure she didn't forget what he said.

"What possessed you to bring that pistol, and to lay it on the dining table like you were going to shoot someone?"

Daisy shrugged and bit an apple. "I didn't like them women."

"That much was clear to everyone! But I raised you to be more polite to other people. Or—at least, I *hope* I raised you to be more polite."

Gideon ran a distracted hand through his shaggy mane of hair. "You can say what you like to me, Daisy, but you can't just blurt out the first thing you think when you're with other people!"

"Aw, what do you care what them old heifers think?" Daisy grumbled. "The blazes with 'em. Let's go back home, Gideon." She kicked the baseboards in frustration. "This town makes me feel like I'm smothering!"

"We're not going back home, Daisy," Gideon replied in a softer tone. "In fact, I'm going to buy a house tomorrow. It's not far from town. I think you'll like it."

Daisy's blue eyes filled with dismay. "A house? What do you want with a house when you got a good cabin up the mountain? What's come over you?"

Gideon sank down into a chair by the door and looked at her hopelessly. "I'm to blame for this," he muttered. "I raised you like a boy, and I shouldn't be surprised if you act like one, now."

He sighed and tried again. "Daisy, those young ladies you met at the table today—"

"Never saw a more mealy-mouthed pair in my life!"

"—They were behaving like young ladies should behave. They were polite and demure—"

"What's demure?"

"Why, demure means modest and reserved. Quiet. Respectful."

"Huh! *Demure* means a mush-mouth ninny, then! You want me to just sit there and stare like a blockhead, for hours on end, when everybody else is talking? It'll be a cold day."

Gideon raised an eyebrow. "You can't always be the one talking, Daisy. And you might learn something if you listen to others."

"Like what?"

"Humility, for one thing," Gideon retorted, "and manners, for another!" He closed his eyes, seemed to regroup for a moment, and then continued: "I know this has been a big change for you, Dase, and I'm going to take things slow. But I need you to cooperate, just a little."

Daisy sat down on the bed and nodded. "All right. What do you want me to do?"

"I want you to come with me to see the house tomorrow. And I want you to try on the dresses we ordered. The seamstress says that they're ready to pick up."

Daisy's expression twisted in disgust. "Aw, you ain't gonna be happy 'til I'm trussed up like a Thanksgiving turkey! Don't I get no vote in all this?"

"Of course," Gideon told her softly. "I'm doing all of this for you, Dase. You don't know that you need it, yet. But you will one day."

"I don't need to be sewn up in no bag," Daisy replied darkly, "and that's all them dresses are—big fidgety bags that don't serve no purpose but to get in the way! Whoever dreamed 'em up should go to jail. They're made to hinder you from running or climbing or hunting, and they're a danger to you just standing still. They catch on everything, and I'll break my neck if I try to walk in one!"

"Thousands of girls wear them every day without any problems," Gideon told her, arms crossed. "You're an intelligent girl, Daisy. I have faith that you'll learn how to wear them."

Daisy's eyes took on a mutinous look, and Gideon decided not to press her further. "I'm retiring for the evening, Daisy," he told her and rose from his chair. "I want you to retire, as well. I'll come get you for breakfast, and we'll go"—he closed his eyes and sighed—"*back* to Mrs Hartwell's, and on to see the house."

"All right," Daisy grumbled. "If I gotta, I gotta."

"There's one more thing," Gideon told her and extended a hand. "I want the pistol and the shotgun."

"But Gideon!"

"Now."

Daisy sighed and handed over the guns, and Doc looked over his shoulder to deliver this parting shot:

"If by a miracle some forgiving lady agrees to sit with us, I don't want you scaring her off with a gun!"

"Aw, Gideon."

But the door snapped shut behind him with such an air of finality that Daisy flopped across the bed morosely.

***

It was already dark, and the curtain over the open window fluttered in the evening breeze. Its cool breath drew Daisy from across the room, and she sat in the window with one foot braced against the frame.

The street below was dark except for the golden light behind the windows of homes and shops. There were few sounds except that of crickets humming, and the occasional sound of a door closing. A distant woman's voice called:

"Peter! Susan! Come back home; it's time to get to bed!"

Daisy watched the street below as two small dark shapes raced past towards the sound of the woman's voice.

But while she was watching, she noticed another dark

shape on the street below. It moved silently from one shadow to another, down the row of shuttered businesses, and moved all the way over to the hotel, under her window.

Daisy waited, and sure enough, there came the faint sound of someone stepping up on the sidewalk railing, grabbing the gutter, and pulling himself up onto the roof just outside her window. Daisy pulled her foot down and leaned out the window to extend a hand.

Clay took it, and Daisy pulled him into the room with her. Her tall visitor leaned against the wall and caught his breath while she settled back into the window frame.

"What're you doing back in town, Clay?"

Clay looked up at her through his dark hair. "I'm going frog-gigging in the pond outside town. Wanna come with me? I'm gonna roast frog legs over a fire."

"That's the best offer I've had since I came to this blasted place," Daisy told him. "I'll go, but I have to be back by dawn 'cause Gideon wants to show me the house he's going to buy down here."

"So you and Gideon really are going to move?"

Daisy grimaced. "Looks that way. He wants me to start wearing dresses, too. Can you see me in one of them foofy dresses?"

Clay grinned and shook his head. "No, I sure can't."

"You're the only one who's got any sense," Daisy grumbled. "I don't know what set Gideon off, but he's crazy these days."

Clay gave her shoulder an encouraging slap. "Well, don't think about it tonight. Come on."

"You don't have to ask me twice!"

Clay climbed out the window, crept down the roof and dangled off the edge until he found the sidewalk rail with one foot. He rested the other foot on it, and then jumped down lightly.

Daisy followed, and Clay stood clear as she balanced on the rail and then hopped down beside him.

"Let's go."

"Have you got the gear?" Daisy asked.

"Enough for me and you," Clay told her. "There's a pond down the road a little ways, full of frogs. We should have real good luck."

Daisy followed him down the darkened road, and they met no one on the way. Wolf Table closed up after dark since most of its inhabitants believed that all decent people were in bed by nightfall.

As they walked down the road, there was a distant rumble of thunder, and the night sky far away glowed suddenly with lightning.

"I hope it don't rain on us," Daisy mumbled. "I don't mind getting wet, but it's hard to see what you're doing."

Clay looked up. "It's going over the mountain," he told her. "We'll be okay."

Daisy frowned at the sky. "The old man probably called it up," she grumbled.

"What old man?"

Daisy shrugged. "Oh, I went to see the Prophet the other day. I wanted to ask him a question."

Clay turned to her in the dark. "You hunted up that crazy critter?"

"Yep."

"I wouldn't if I were you, Dase," Clay replied. "He's a strange one."

"You can say that again," Daisy mumbled. "I went up to ask him how to talk Gideon out of moving. But all he did was say that I was out of luck 'cause Gideon wouldn't change his mind. And looks like that's turned out true.

"But then he told me more stuff that I *hadn't* asked about: that Gideon was running from men who were trying to kill him. He said that Gideon was a gambler, and that his real name is Doc Dailey."

"Do you believe him?"

Daisy sputtered. "No. Except—the old man did tell me that my parents were killed in an avalanche. And that they were godly people. Don't know how he knew that."

"Maybe he knew them. He's lived up on the mountain a long time."

"Maybe. But I don't ever remember seeing him around, back then."

"Do you think what he said about Gideon was true?"

"Don't know. But it worries me. He said that Gideon had better watch out for a woman, that she was going to trip him up. And—he said that if Gideon warn't careful, he'd be dead by this time next year."

Clay fell silent, and then ventured: "Aw, I wouldn't put too much stock in it, Dase. It don't really matter what

Gideon was before he came here. The important thing is, he's your father now. None of that other stuff matters."

"I know it. And I ain't worried about what Gideon was before I knew him. I figure that's his business. What worries me is what the Prophet said about him—being dead in a year if he don't look out."

"Did the old man tell you what he meant?"

"No. And I was too mad to ask him. I lit out of there like my hair was on fire."

"Hmm."

Daisy sputtered out a laugh. "I just about scared a bunch of old hens to death today when I saw 'em at the restaurant eating with Gideon. I put the pistol on the table and gave 'em all the dead eye. You shoulda seen their faces!"

Clay chuckled. "I wish I could've seen it! Bet that was a sight!"

Daisy sighed. "It just goes to show how jumpy I am these days. Feel like I'm sitting on an anthill."

"Have you told Gideon what the old man said?"

Daisy turned to him in the darkness. "Good grief, no! He's told me a dozen times to stay away from the Prophet, and if he finds out I went to see him, he'll be mad for a week. He thinks the old man is crazy."

"He's right, Dase. You shouldn't let that old man worry you." He stopped, took her arm, and pointed to the right side of the road.

"There's the pond. Take my hand and follow me. The bank is slick, and you'll fall if you're not careful."

***

The two of them made their way down the treacherous bank. The ground and the reeds were slick with new rain, and more than once Daisy slipped and almost fell, if Clay hadn't hugged her to his side. She clapped her arms around him and almost brought him down as they laughed and stumbled, but they finally reached the muddy shore.

Daisy let go of him and shook her head. "That was close!" she sputtered. "Almost ended up with a face full of mud! Give me the light, and I'll hold it for you."

Clay handed her a dark lantern, and she opened it. A beam of light jumped out, and Daisy trained it on Clay's hands as he pulled two long spears with pronged ends out of their hiding place in the grass.

"I'll hold the light for you, and when you're done, you can hold it for me," Daisy offered, and Clay nodded, kicked out of his moccasins, and waded into the pond, spear at the ready.

Soon he had half-filled a burlap sack with frogs and was just on the point of handing the spear off to Daisy when a thunderous blast made them both drop everything and scramble madly up the bank.

A second blast followed, and Daisy half-fell. Clay threw an arm around her shoulders, and together they half-ran, half-limped to the road, and then ducked behind the cover of a big oak on the far side.

In the occasional dim flash of lightning, they could see a large shadow emerge onto the road. A man yelled out, pointed his shotgun towards the town, and emptied another round of rock salt from the barrel.

"You little devils!" he roared, "If'n you trespass on my

land again, it'll be the real thing next time!"

He turned back down the embankment and disappeared, muttering savage curses, and they watched his retreat with relief. After the man had gone, Clay looked down at Daisy.

"You all right, Dase?"

"Aw, he winged me," Daisy complained. "I got rock salt all up my left leg!"

"I'll help you," Clay told her. "Put your arm around my shoulder, and I'll put mine around your waist. I'll get you back to the hotel."

They made their way back to town as fast as they could, but Daisy had to limp along painfully. The salt pellets had been sharp, and the scrapes they'd created on her leg stung like fire.

"Aw, blast it, I won't be able to run for a week," Daisy grumbled. "The old rascal—what harm would it do him if we took a few frogs out of that pond?"

Clay scowled. "He's a fool. He signed a paper, and now he thinks he owns that land, and even the wild animals that cross it. But no one owns the land. One day, the earth will teach him."

"I hope the earth uses rock salt," Daisy muttered resentfully and hobbled back to the hotel, leaning on Clay's shoulder.

***

When they returned to the hotel, a little after midnight, they found the front door locked and the lower windows shuttered.

Clay murmured: "Think they'd open the front door if

we knocked and yelled?"

Daisy turned outraged eyes on him. "I can't let Gideon know I've been out tonight!" she told him. "No telling what he'll do! He might even make me stay in that old hotel room for a day or two more. I couldn't stand it!"

Clay looked up at the open window on the second floor. "It's a long way up there. Think you can make it, Dase?"

Daisy leaned on her good leg and squinted up at the window. "I dunno. I can't put weight on this leg or it'll give way."

Clay bit his lip. "I'll help you get up on the railing, and then I'll lift you so you can grab the gutter and pull yourself up."

"All right."

Clay leaned down and helped lift Daisy up until she was standing on top of the sidewalk railing. He held her steady as she swayed back and forth on one foot.

"Can you grab the gutter?"

"I got it."

"I'm going to lift you on three. One ... two ... three!"

But at that moment, a commanding voice cried: "Put your hands up, or I'll shoot!"

Clay, still wrestling to hold Daisy up, cried: "I can't put my hands up!"

The cold kiss of a shotgun barrel against his back made him push Daisy up with a mighty heave and then throw his hands up into the air.

Daisy yelled and scrabbled for a handhold on the roof,

and her legs kicked in the air over their heads. The hotel manager yelled in outrage:

"Come down from there, young man, or I'll blow you to the moon, along with your partner! Try to break into my hotel, will you?"

"I'm falling!" Daisy shrieked, and scrabbled at the tiles, but she tumbled off the roof despite it. She knocked Clay right onto the hotel manager and then fell on both of them herself. The shotgun was knocked sky west and blasted shot to the moon, and the man wallowed on the ground, groaning, with both Daisy and Clay sprawled on top of him.

"Get off me!" he screamed, and Clay scrambled up and bolted off into the darkness. "Hey!" the man shouted, "Somebody grab him before he gets away!"

He pushed Daisy off him and struggled to his feet.

Daisy pulled herself off the ground, wincing in pain, and the lights came on in the hotel. Daisy saw Gideon's window go up and bit her lip as he stuck his shaggy head out and cried:

"What's going on down there?"

"You should ask your daughter!" the hotel manager cried furiously. "I caught her and some boy climbing across the roof!"

"Daisy! Come inside this instant!" Gideon cried, and Daisy began to hobble off, but the hotel manager cried:

"You're going to be liable, Mr McCall, if they did damage to this house!"

"I know it," Gideon replied, and closed the window.

Chapter
Twenty-One

"How on *earth* did you get so skinned up?"

Gideon grimaced as Daisy lifted her pants leg to reveal a half-dozen scrape marks across her calf.

"I got shot with rock salt," Daisy replied.

"Shot! By who?"

"Oh, some old blockhead at the pond just out of town," Daisy replied darkly. "Clay came by and wanted to go frog gigging, and so we—"

"Clay! Where is he?"

"Oh, he lit out when the hotel manager's shotgun went off," Daisy replied. "Clay knew it'd rouse the whole town. It wouldn't-a done me any good if he'd stayed, and he knew it."

Gideon stared at his daughter as if he feared for her sanity. "What possessed the two of you to climb in through a second storey window? You could both have been killed!"

"It was the same way we went out," Daisy shrugged, "and it would've been fine coming back, except my left leg was gimpy and made me slow."

"You mean neither one of you thought to *knock on the front door?*" Gideon demanded, and then shook his head. "Never mind—it makes no difference now! By breakfast the story will be all over town!"

He pulled his hands over his face and stared at Daisy over them.

"Daisy—the pond you went to—was it the first one out of town, on the right side of the road?"

Daisy's face lit up. "That's right! How'd you know?"

Gideon closed his eyes and shook his head. He didn't answer for a long moment, and then replied, in a grim voice: "The man who ran you off is Abraham Petersen, and the house he lives in is the one I'm trying to buy."

Daisy's mouth fell open. "*Ohhhhh.*"

Gideon glared at her. "If I thought you did this on purpose—"

"Oh no, Gideon, my hand on it! I didn't know it was the same place, I swear!"

Gideon stared at her grimly. "I told you this afternoon that I wanted you to stay here. If you had obeyed me, this would never have happened!"

He shook his head and turned for the door. "There are still some hours left before dawn, so I want you to wash those scrapes with soapy water and dab a little alcohol on them." He handed Daisy a little silver flask, and she opened it and sniffed suspiciously.

"It's going to sting, but it will keep the wounds from getting infected. Once you've done that, I want you to go to bed and stay there until I call for you at breakfast!"

"I will, Gideon."

Gideon paused in the doorway to deliver the awful

parting shot: "And tomorrow, you are going to put on one of the dresses I ordered for you, and you are going to wear it when we go out to see the house. Hopefully, Mr Petersen won't guess that he's seeing you for the second time today!"

He slammed the door behind him, and Daisy raised her brows and whistled in awe. That was the maddest she'd ever seen Gideon.

Of course, she hadn't done what he said, and he had a right to be chapped about it, but still.

The way he was carrying on, you'd think she'd set the house on fire.

Daisy went to the washstand and began to wash the scrapes on her leg. The water alone made them burn like fire, and when she dabbed a bit of Gideon's liquor on a cloth, and swiped it over her leg, it burned so bad it made her eyes water. She stomped on the floor and gritted her teeth but refused to yell out.

She had the strong feeling that she'd drawn way too much attention to herself for one day.

Daisy shed her clothes and crawled into bed wearing her undershirt and baggy shorts. Soon the new sheets and soft pillow soothed her fast asleep: but in spite of all the other things that had happened, it was the Prophet's words that still echoed in her dreams:

His real name is Doc Dailey. A woman will greatly endanger him; and if he isn't careful, he'll be dead by this time next year.

***

The next morning Daisy woke to the beams of the rising sun. The sun had just crested the mountains, and its rays reached all the way from the craggy heights to caress her cheek with their golden fingers.

She sighed and stretched and frowned. Her left leg was telling her that it was badly skinned up, and she threw off the covers to inspect it. She had a half-dozen red scuff marks on her leg, and she was so sore that she was certain to be walking with a limp that day.

She stood up gingerly and winced as she made her way to the washstand to splash cold water over her face and wash up a bit. She still had flecks of mud on her hair and face and arms, and she did her best to erase all the guilty signs of her previous night's work.

She didn't want to hex Gideon when he went to buy the house.

Daisy whistled a little bit to herself as she scrubbed her face and neck. If their new house had a pond out back, it might not be quite as bad a change as she'd thought. Once Gideon had the place, she and Clay could go frog gigging all they wanted, and no one else would be able to squawk about it.

They could even go swimming in the pond when the weather was warm, or ice fishing when it froze over in the winter.

A knock at the door made her turn her head. "Come in."

Gideon opened the door and poked his head in. "I have your dress here from the seamstress," he told her. "I want you to call me when you've put it on, so I can see how it fits you."

He placed a tissue-wrapped package on the bed and walked out of the room again. Daisy put her washcloth down and went over to look at it.

She unfolded the tissue paper and pulled out a beautiful pale blue linen gown. She tossed it out full-length over the bed and examined it. It was a pretty thing, all right: she could tell the seamstress knew what she was doing. The stitches were tiny and perfect, and each tiny button and bit of trim were sewed on just so.

Daisy rubbed her chin and stared at it. She didn't have a clue how to put it on except to throw it over her head and wriggle into it like a nightshirt.

So she grabbed the huge hem, threw it over her head, and tried in vain to wriggle up past the waist. It was just too small to get her head through.

She wriggled out of it, threw it down on the bed again, and studied it for a minute. It looked like the top part could be detached from the bottom, and so she turned the jacket up to peer inside. Sure enough, there were some kind of doodads that kept 'em together.

She unsnapped the jacket from the skirt and tried again, and to her relief, this time she was able to get into them. But even so, there were no fewer than 20 tiny buttons on the front of the jacket, and it was going to take a long time to get the fidgety little things fastened.

But she grunted and cussed her way through every one. Gideon was mad enough, without her setting him off all over again.

Daisy finally got everything put together and took a look at herself in the mirror over the washstand. She could only really see her face and neck, but she looked all right, as far as she could tell, and so she walked out to show Gideon.

Gideon was waiting for her downstairs, and he looked

relieved to see her. "There you are! Come on, Daisy. We're going to have to hurry and get breakfast if we're going to meet Mr Petersen at ten o'clock."

He extended his hand to her, and Daisy skipped down the stairs, but the relieved look was suddenly wiped off his face. He looked at her funny as if she had a bug in her hair.

"Oh ... Dase ... um. Just—just wait here for a minute. I have to get something before we can go."

Daisy frowned. "But you just said—"

"Never mind what I said. You wait right here, and don't go anywhere until I come back."

Daisy sighed and flopped down into a chair to wait for Gideon. He was behaving like a crazy man, and the Prophet's words came back to worry her. Maybe the Prophet had been warning her that Gideon was in danger of getting soft in the head.

Daisy sat in the chair, twiddled her thumbs, and looked around and smiled at the other patrons who passed her by, but she began to notice that they were staring. She looked down at herself, thinking she might've got some flecks of dried mud on the dress, but it was clean.

Before long, Gideon came back. His face was as red as a ripe apple, and he gave her a big white shawl.

He leaned over and whispered into her ear. "I want you to put this around your shoulders. Don't take it off, not even to eat!"

She scowled at him. "What is it now?" she complained. "Ain't I done enough yet?"

"Just do as I say!" Gideon hissed. "I forgot to buy you

something very important!"

Daisy frowned. "What?"

"A corset!"

Chapter
Twenty-Two

"Well, good morning, Mr McCall! And is this young lady your daughter?"

Daisy frowned and shuffled her feet under her skirt, but Gideon grabbed her elbow and presented her to Abraham Petersen. He was a tall older man, with a shock of white hair and a bristling moustache.

"Yes, this is my daughter Daisy. Daisy, say hello to Mr Petersen."

Daisy squinted up at the older man and nodded mutely. Gideon had clapped a big bonnet on her head to cover her short hair, and she felt like a fool.

"Hello."

"How do you do, young lady!" Mr Petersen frowned a bit as he looked at her face. "Your face looks familiar. Have I seen you before?"

Both she and Gideon looked up sharply and cried: "Oh, no!"

"It must've been someone else then," Mr Petersen smiled. "Well, come on in and take a look at the house. I've kept it up as well as I could since the missus died, but now that I'm an old bachelor, I figure I'd do better living in town. This place is getting too big for me, but it'd be just right for a man with a family."

He opened the door and let them come in. The

Petersen farmhouse was a single-story white clapboard with a porch, a porch swing, and a big oak in the front yard. The interior was clean and spacious, with wooden floors that creaked underfoot, a big stone fireplace in the front room, and a nice parlour off to one side with a big foot pedal organ.

Mr Petersen looked at it wistfully. "That organ was Mrs Petersen's pride and joy," he murmured. "But I can't stand the blasted thing. I'll throw it in if you buy the house."

Daisy gave it a curious look as they passed, but Mr Petersen led them further in. "The house has three bedrooms in the back, a nice big kitchen with a wood burning stove and a pump, a dining room, and an attic bedroom for guests."

He led them out onto the back porch. "The back yard's pretty big, and there's a stout outhouse off through the trees there. A two-seater, with a nice tin roof." He gestured towards the pond. "The pond is stocked with plenty of fish, and I have about ten acres beyond that's good rich bottom land. You can plant it in most anything if you've a mind to farm."

"What would you want for it, Mr Petersen?" Gideon asked.

The older man rubbed his chin. "I'd want about four thousand for the place."

"Four thousand," Gideon echoed.

"I know it's a lot of money, but I'll have to live on it, now that I ain't farming anymore," the older man replied.

Daisy rolled her eyes to Gideon's face and saw him nod. "I understand perfectly, Mr Petersen," he replied softly. "And I will meet your price."

The older man looked startled. "You will?"

"Yes. I have been blessed with some small success in my—er—efforts." He reached into the pocket of his leather breeches and pulled out a wad of bills that made the older man's eyes bug out.

"You said four thousand?"

The man nodded wordlessly, and Gideon counted the money out in his hand. "One thousand, two thousand, three, and—four."

"It's a pleasure doing business with you, sir!"

"And with you," Gideon assured him. "If you'll come down to the lawyer's in town and transfer the deed, we'll call it a deal."

"I'll do it. Just let me get my hat!"

The old man walked off to find his hat, and Daisy leaned over and whispered: "I never knew you had that much money, Gideon!"

"I don't advertise it," Gideon drawled. "You remember that, Daisy—never tell other people how much money you have."

"It's never been a problem with us before," Daisy reminded him. "Never had much need for money before we came to town and had to slick up like—"

"I'm ready when you are, Mr McCall," Mr Peterson beamed, and Gideon turned to Daisy.

"Is it all right if my daughter stays here while we conduct our business?"

"Oh, perfectly fine!" the older man smiled. "It's your

home now!"

"We'll be gone for a while, Daisy," Gideon told her. "You stay here until we come back."

"All right," Daisy sighed, and watched as the two men strode off towards town, arm in arm.

Once they were gone, she strolled through the house, room by room. It was a nice place, compared to the cabin, and would probably be a lot easier to live in, but she still didn't like it.

Daisy took off the bonnet and threw it down on the dining room table. She would've gladly thrown off the dress, too, but she didn't have anything else to wear, and she was sure that Gideon would be mad if they came back to find her skinny dipping in the pond.

Daisy walked out to the back porch, sat down in a rocker, and propped her feet up on the porch railing. The pond was the best part of the whole place, in her opinion.

But it wouldn't make up for all the things they'd be missing: the deep stillness of the night sky on the mountain, and the cold, clean air; the icy streams and the lush hunting, and the freedom. The freedom, most of all.

Daisy closed her eyes. That was what it hurt the most to lose. The freedom to go hunting all night, or spend the day in a tree, or to explore a cave in the rocks, or a dozen other things. Gideon had never interfered with her unless he thought she was going to break her neck.

There had been a few times he'd stopped her, on that account, but she could count them on the fingers of one hand.

She didn't like living in town for another reason, too: it was going to be harder to protect Gideon when he was living only a mile or so from the railroad depot. Anybody could find him who wanted to.

The little house Gideon had just bought was sitting on a road going into town and was bordered by another road in the back, just behind the pond.

If the Prophet was right, and there were men hunting Gideon, he was a sitting duck in this place. Daisy picked a stick up off the porch and threw it over the lawn in disgust.

She was just going to have to do the best she could.

Gideon was in a strange mood, and there was just no talking to him.

Chapter
Twenty-Three

"It's your play, Miss Dubois."

Kate Dubois smiled faintly. "I raise five thousand." She took five chips from the top of her pile and threw them into the colourful jumble in the centre of the table.

A portly man to her left shook his head. "Too rich for my blood. I fold."

"Mr Donnely?"

A grizzled cowboy adjusted the cigar in the corner of his mouth to mumble: "I'll see your five and raise ten."

"Mr Fouchard?"

The slight, elegant Frenchman uttered a soft profanity and threw his cards down. "Fold."

All eyes at the table reverted to her. "Miss Dubois?"

She met the cowboy's eyes. "I call."

The cowboy unfurled his cards on the green baize table—an unmatching five, six, seven, eight and nine.

"I have a straight."

Everyone turned to Kate. She put her cards on the table: four aces and a nine of hearts.

"Four of a kind."

The cowboy cursed ruefully and then extended a brown hand. "Heck of a player, ma'am. Congratulations."

"Thank you, Mr Donnely," Kate replied primly, and scooped the chips up.

She'd been having a real run of luck since she'd come to Denver. A female poker player wasn't exactly a novelty, but she was often the only woman at the table, and her opponents were losing to her so consistently that Kate had begun to believe that she was throwing them off their game.

Not that she *meant* to, of course.

She sorted her chips into the rack, and then carried it to the cashier, who counted out ten thousand dollars in nice crisp bills. "Congratulations, ma'am." He grinned—and winked.

Kate smiled back. The cashier was the owner's son, a blond, good-looking boy she estimated to be a good ten years younger than she was herself, but it was fun to imagine that he was trying to flirt with her.

She was a bit past thirty, and lately, she was beginning to feel it.

She closed up the little carpet bag and marched out of the gambling hall and onto the streets of Denver. It was early evening, and there were several large establishments still open, but not as many as the town was once famous for. Denver wasn't nearly as wild as she had feared when she first arrived; the merchant class had all but taken over, and the gaming saloons that had survived were more genteel than their frontier predecessors.

And that suited her right down to the ground.

She passed a couple on the sidewalk, and the man caught her eye and beamed at her, prompting the woman to take his elbow and jerk his attention back where it belonged. He coughed and looked down, and Kate swallowed a smile.

She understood quite well that the more respectable citizens of Denver saw her as an adventuress. Their logic was that only a disreputable woman would frequent a gambling hall—a place of avarice, drunkenness, and in some cases, prostitution.

She had carefully avoided the establishments that offered female companionship, but it was a fine distinction in the eyes of many, and her scruples had not saved her reputation.

Female gamblers were generally looked at askance by more conventional women, and some of the women in town had made it clear that they wished her gone.

Their opposition made her standing in town somewhat tenuous, and it complicated her social life in many ways.

But the men she met in the gambling halls were perfect gentlemen. They might be brawlers once they walked out into the street, but they had always shown her admirable courtesy at the gaming table.

It was the respectable, proper women who were badly behaved towards her: most of them perfect strangers to her, too. But since she never stayed in any one place for very long, she was generally able to maintain her good humour.

Kate returned to her hotel—the most luxurious in all of Denver—and walked up to her rooms to retire for the evening. She had the suite on the top floor, which consisted of a bedroom, a sitting room, and an indoor bathroom complete with a porcelain tub straight from New York. After sitting at a poker table all day, Kate was ready for a hot soak, a dinner delivered to her room, and a good book.

She unpinned her hat and set it down on a mahogany table in the sitting room but was soon interrupted by a soft tapping on the door.

"Who is it?"

A male voice coughed. "It's Calvin Burke, Miss Dubois. We played poker last night at the El Dorado."

Kate smiled and walked to the door. When she opened it, a handsome blond man stood there, hat in hand.

"I was hoping that you'd let me take you out to dinner tonight," he said, with a smile.

She had only just opened her mouth to reply when another man appeared just behind him. She caught a glimpse of his face over Mr Burke's shoulder and recognized the dark, rather elegant fellow as another of her former poker opponents from two nights ago.

"Good evening, Miss Dubois," he said and bowed with a smile and a flourish. "I hope I haven't caught you at a bad time."

The blond man turned, frowning. "As a matter of fact, you have," he informed the newcomer. "I was just about to ask Ms Dubois out for the evening, and three's a crowd."

The dark man eyed him coldly. "Is that so? I'm going to need to hear Miss Dubois say it," he replied.

Kate raised her hands. "Gentlemen—"

The blond man turned to face the newcomer and

punched his chest with a brown forefinger. "I'm telling you to shove off, and if you're smart, you'll listen."

"Is that a threat?"

"Whatever you want it to be, slick!"

Kate raised her voice in alarm. "Gentlemen, please! I'm really too tired tonight to go out anywhere, and I—"

But the blond man suddenly put his fist into the dark man's teeth, and he went flying backwards against the opposite wall. When he recovered, he answered with a lightning-fast right to the blond man's jaw, and soon the two men were rolling on the floor, fists flying.

"Oh, stop it!" Kate cried and noticed with dismay that the doors to neighbouring rooms were popping open as the other lodgers took in the disturbance.

"What's going on?"

"Somebody call the manager!"

"This is what they get when they let that disgraceful woman rent out rooms in a nice hotel!" one woman snorted. "She's a magnet for rascally men!"

Kate shot the woman a pained glance but held her tongue, and soon the manager and his young son came running up to break up the fight.

"Gentlemen, this is a respectable establishment!" the manager hissed and pushed between them. "I'm going to have to ask you to leave immediately, or I'll call the sheriff!"

The two rumpled antagonists glared at one another, and then glanced at Kate, who was watching them sympathetically from her doorway. They grumbled, but trudged off peaceably, and the manager turned to

Kate and asked:

"Are you all right, ma'am?"

"Perfectly." Kate smiled. "Thank you. I don't really know either one of those gentlemen, and it was becoming awkward."

The manager smiled uncomfortably. "If I can help with anything else, just let me know, ma'am."

"I will, and thank you."

Kate turned back to her own rooms and closed the door behind her, but not before hearing the woman down the way snort and cry: "It's women like her who give this town a bad name!"

***

Kate sighed and drifted to the picture window that overlooked the street. She watched as both of her would-be suitors exited the hotel and walked off in opposite directions.

They hadn't known it, but both her hopeful visitors had been doomed to disappointment that night. She wouldn't have gone out with either of them.

It wasn't because they weren't handsome and charming. It wasn't because she had anything particular against them. It was because they each fell short in one critical respect.

They weren't Doc Dailey.

Kate put a hand to a fine golden chain around her neck and pulled out a beautiful diamond ring. It flashed and glowed in the lamplight as she turned it this way and that.

It was the engagement ring that Doc had once given her, and from the night she had first gotten it, she'd never taken it off. More than once, when the cards had turned against her, she'd been tempted to throw it into the pot, but she never had. That ring was her good luck charm and had brought her good fortune and pleasant memories for ten years.

It was all of Doc that she had left.

Kate sighed. It was absurd to carry a torch for Doc after all these years. It was just her bad luck that she had to love the man who'd gotten away.

Kate smiled and wondered where Doc was and what he was doing. He was probably married by now, with a houseful of children, a receding hairline, and the beginning of a paunch.

But she always saw him as he had been that last night on the train: tall, blond, broad-shouldered and muscular, impeccably groomed, elegantly dressed, and so in love with her.

She'd rushed out into the Kansas City depot without any money that night, with only the clothes on her back. But she always landed on her feet, and soon she'd wangled a seat on a train speeding towards Denver. That was where she and Doc had been bound.

But when she got to Denver, to her despair, there was no sign of Doc. No one had even seen anyone who looked like him. She had stayed in town for months, hoping to get some word of him, but there was none.

It was like he'd fallen off the face of the earth.

In her darker moments, she feared that Judge Carter had killed Doc, or more likely, had him killed. She didn't doubt for a moment that Judge had tried. Judge was proud and short-tempered, and he had more than enough money to keep things hot for Doc.

But Doc was one of the wiliest men she had ever known, and something in her heart still clung to the hope that he'd survived.

That she'd see him once more, even if it was too late for the two of them.

Kate turned away from the window, tucked the ring back into the neck of her gown, and smiled at her own foolishness. Maybe that silly hope was the real reason she moved from city to city and played round after endless round of poker when she'd long since won enough money to retire.

She was hoping to walk into a gambling hall one day and see Doc Dailey lift his bright blue eyes to hers.

Chapter
Twenty-Four

A soft knock on the door of her bedroom woke Kate the next morning. A high, brisk voice called out in French: "*Déjeuner*, Kate."

Kate opened one eye. She had arranged for her little companion, Emil, to open the door and leave a breakfast tray in her room each morning, because after a late night of poker, she often got back to her suite at two or three.

She was usually dead to the world at dawn, and for many hours afterwards, but on that morning she stretched and sighed and shrugged into her dressing gown, and then walked out to inspect the elegant tray.

It was silver, with a little rose in a vase, and the covered plate was heaped with tempting things: scrambled eggs with cheese, salt cured bacon, buttered biscuits, ham, gravy, and sliced fresh tomatoes.

Kate walked to the big window overlooking the street, placed the tray on a little table, and sat down to enjoy her meal while watching the passing scene below.

Emil came back into the room and set a folded newspaper beside her on the table. "The Denver paper was the only one they had," he announced.

Kate glanced at him. Emil was about six years old, a dusky, handsome, and fiercely intelligent Creole child.

She and Emil spoke French when they were together, but Emil could also speak passable English.

The child had come to her a year earlier when she won a rice plantation from a New Orleans planter who might or might not have been Emil's father. The man had informed her that Emil came with the farm, and that she had 'won' him.

She had replied, with some heat, that an honourable man would never dream of giving away a child, but to her amazement, the man had abruptly walked out of the room and abandoned Emil on the spot.

And so Kate had acquired a companion on her travels.

She glanced at the boy. He had pulled a chair up to the table and was busy making himself a plate off the food on the tray. He was a handsome child, with a head of dark, tousled curls and light green eyes. She loved to dress him up like a little New Orleans dandy, in fine linen shirts and little brocade vests, fine broadcloth trousers and little leather boots. She had pierced one of his ears and given him a little gold ring to wear in it, like Jean Lafitte himself, and it had delighted him.

"I am a pirate!" he had cried and gone slashing through their hotel rooms with an imaginary cutlass.

She had originally intended to take Emil to an orphanage, but one day had melted into another, and then another, and she had found that idea less and less appealing the longer Emil stayed with her.

She told him they were *bons amis*, and that was what he called her.

But the longer Emil stayed, the fonder she became of him, and now she was playing with the idea of adopting Emil outright.

Not that any formal legal procedure would likely be necessary.

She had taught him how to play poker and faro, and how to cut cards, and to her amusement, he was so good at it that he was already competent to deal at any gambling hall in town.

Kate turned back to the view of the street and sipped hot coffee from a delicate china cup. It was Sunday morning, and the sidewalks below were filling up with people on their way to church. The faint sound of church bells penetrated the walls of the hotel, and their pleasant chimes added a cozy zest to her meal.

"See, Emil?" Kate gestured to the people walking on the sidewalks below. "All of the people are going to church."

Emil looked up at her with his light green eyes. "What's church?"

Kate's china cup paused on the way to her lips, and she suffered a brief jab of guilt. Her own family had not been devout, nor had they gone to church, but she had the vague sense that she wasn't doing right by Emil unless she taught him some kind of moral code.

So far, the nearest she'd come to a moral code, was to tell Emil that nobody liked a poor loser at cards.

She patted her lips delicately with her napkin. "Church is a place where people go to learn about God, *petit*."

"How?"

She blinked at him. "Why—a minister tells them Bible stories, and—encourages them to—be good."

Emil made a face. "What's the Bible?"

Kate shifted her weight uncomfortably. "It's a book about God."

"Does it have pirates?"

She laughed softly. "No."

"Then it is certainly boring." Emil turned his attention back to his food, and Kate watched him eat fondly.

She was going to have to make a decision about Emil soon. It wasn't fair to the boy to keep him with her if she wasn't going to adopt him. He would soon be old enough to go to school, and it would be selfish and wrong of her to keep him out, and to drag him from town to town.

But if she adopted Emil, she was going to have to change a lot of things in her life; and that was why she still hesitated.

It was fun to dress Emil up like a doll, and to spoil him, but a child was a lot of responsibility, and she'd never been the motherly type. She kept ungodly hours and frequented places that sometimes attracted dishonest or even dangerous people.

She kept a pearl-handled ladies' pistol up her sleeve at all times and its matching mate tucked into her skirt pocket. She had seldom been held up or offered unpleasantness on her travels, but on those rare occasions, it had been a special comfort to be able to get in the last word. She had once shot the hat off a man's head when he accosted her one evening and had delivered herself from the hand of another by ramming the full length of her formidable hat pin into a particularly tender spot.

There was no denying that her life was risky, and she was constantly on the move. It was an exciting and rewarding life so far, but it was no life for a little boy.

Emil's childish voice interrupted her thoughts. "You look sad, Kate. Did you lose money last night?"

"No, *petit*."

"What then?"

"Oh, I was just thinking. But one should never think over breakfast. It takes away all pleasure in the meal."

Emil nodded and picked up a strawberry with his fingers, and Kate sighed and tucked a napkin into his collar. "A gentleman never eats with his hands at the table," she told him. "You cut the berry with your knife and fork, and eat it like everything else.

"And you must always use a napkin, like a gentleman, or you'll stain your beautiful vest!"

"I am certainly a gentleman."

"A gambler must *always* be a gentleman," she agreed and smiled to see Emil straighten up instantly and tuck the napkin deeper into his shirt.

Chapter
Twenty-Five

"I think I will go downstairs."

Kate glanced at Emil's determined face indulgently. He had told her that he wanted to watch the people passing by outside, but she suspected that Emil's real mission was to watch the hotel patrons playing pool and maybe beg a turn with a cue.

"Oh, all right. But don't leave the hotel, and don't be gone long."

She smiled to see his face brighten and watched him straighten his jacket and walk out of the room. Emil loved games of all kinds and was never happier than when he was watching or playing.

Kate poured herself a second cup of coffee. The church bells were still tolling melodiously outside, and it reminded her of Sundays in New Orleans, during her childhood. Sunday mornings there had been filled with the soft sound of church bells.

The soft, deep tones had always sounded civilized and urbane to her. She associated them with the sight of pretty ladies and elegant gentlemen walking to church in their finest clothes and little children running along behind them in frills and velvet.

Kate took a delicate bite of ham and a sip of coffee. The memory of those families walking to church in New Orleans, long ago, made her a little homesick.

Her parents had died years before, and she had been an only child, but she still had family in New Orleans.

She'd been away a long time.

She buttered a slice of toast and smeared it with jam. The thing that had always kept her from going back was the knowledge that Judge Carter was still there. He owned almost every gambling hall of any consequence in the city, as well as the *Natchez Queen*, and even though she'd deduced by now that Judge hadn't put a price on her head, she still didn't want to return to his territory. She had a morbid fear that if she went back to New Orleans, Judge would find out somehow, and she never wanted to see him again.

There was no denying that she missed her home now and then. Even the crisp air and beautiful mountains around Denver were a poor substitute for the ancient, moss-covered oaks, cobbled streets, and sleepy elegance of New Orleans.

But the west had its points too. Gambling out here was still free, as Doc had once told her, not controlled by any one man, and even though upstanding citizens still looked at her askance, by and large, the west was more tolerant of women like herself, who didn't play by the usual rules.

Kate lifted a napkin off the silver tray and found a folded newspaper underneath. She shook out the paper, took a contemplative sip of coffee, and read the day's headlines.

It was mostly local business doings, though the front page was occasionally punctuated by the account of a shooting or a robbery. Kate wiped a crumb off her dressing gown.

Kate was in the act of turning the page when an

article caught her eye. Her mouth fell slightly open as she read:

GAMING MAGNATE VISITS DENVER.

DENVER—Southern gaming magnate, Mr Judge Carter, will visit Denver in early July to celebrate the opening of his new gaming emporium, The Lucky Seven. Mr Carter is the owner of a large group of gaming establishments in New Orleans and elsewhere, including a riverboat, the *Natchez Queen*.

"I'm excited to open my first gaming house west of the Mississippi," Mr Carter said. "The Lucky Seven will offer a new gambling experience in Denver, with faro, roulette, poker, and other popular games of chance in an elegant setting suitable for both male and female patrons. It will also offer guests an unrivalled dining experience, with a team of French chefs imported from New Orleans."

Kate felt the paper slip from her hands. She stared at the table for a moment in stunned surprise.

She suddenly felt unsafe, though on reflection, it was an absurd fear. Judge had no way of knowing that she was in Denver, and even if he did, it had been ten years.

Surely he had let go of his anger by now and moved on with his life.

Still, the thought of being in the same city as Judge Carter was *No*. Especially when she thought of Emil.

Kate folded up the newspaper decisively. It was time to move on. It was time to go to San Francisco and to hope that she'd found a place beyond Judge Carter's reach at last.

Kate rose, swept back into her bedroom, and opened the doors of the huge chifferobe. She was throwing her gowns onto the bed when another soft knock came at the door.

"Yes?"

The manager's soft voice murmured on the other side of the door. "There's a gentleman in the lobby asking for you, Miss Dubois."

Kate stared at the door, and a cold shudder worked its way up from her heels to the crown of her head.

"Did he give a name?"

"No, ma'am. He just said he's an old friend."

Kate frowned and bit her lip. "Tell him I'll be right down."

"Yes, ma'am."

Kate frowned and began dressing, and as soon as she had buttoned herself up into a red silk gown, she opened the top drawer in the bedside table and tucked the two pearl-handled pistols into her sleeve and dress pocket.

Then she lifted a small hat from the top of the dresser, placed it carefully on her head, and secured it with a murderous hat pin more than six inches long. She sighed, turned her head this way and that before the mirror, and went down to face whatever awaited her.

But the laughing eyes that were raised to hers at the bottom of the stairs didn't belong to Judge Carter, as she had feared; they belonged to Broadway Bobby, a career gambler who had often played faro on the *Natchez Queen*. He was a wiry man of indeterminate age, with close-cropped white hair, bright blue eyes, and a face as wrinkled and brown as a dried apple.

"Kate!" he laughed, threw his arms out, and Kate smiled and went into them without hesitation. "I knew it was you! I saw you coming out of the Occidental last night, but I was a touch the worse for wine." He shook his head. "What are you doing here in Denver? I thought you and Doc had long since settled down somewhere."

Kate looked down at her hands and then up at her friend's smiling face. "Doc and I parted ways," she murmured.

"Oh ... I'm sorry to hear it," Bobby commiserated. "But I'm glad to see you! Are you dealing anywhere?"

"Oh, no. I'm just playing now."

"It looks like Lady Luck's been good to you," he observed.

Kate smiled. "I can't complain."

Bobby put a hand on her arm. "Did you see the newspaper this morning? Judge Carter's opening a new saloon in town. He's coming out here. May be here already. Thought you'd like to know." He gave her a sage wink. "A word to the wise!"

"Yes, I saw it." Kate licked her lips and glanced towards the hotel entrance.

Bobby leaned in and whispered: "Don't trust him, Kate. I heard that he set a bounty hunter onto Doc after you left the *Queen*."

Kate frowned, and Bobby glanced at her sympathetically. "But if you and Doc went your ways—well, I guess that wouldn't have nothing to do with you."

Kate caught an unhealthy glint in her old friend's eye and mustered her best smile. "No, it really wouldn't."

Bobby's eyes searched her face. "Well, then—I hope we'll see each other again, while you're in town." He smiled uncertainly. "Old times, and all that."

"It's always good to see a familiar face," Kate assured him. "Good luck in Denver, Bobby."

"And to you, Kate."

Kate maintained an air of perfect calm, but she was conscious of Bobby's keen eyes boring into her back as she left. Now that Bobby knew where she was, she could almost see him hurrying off to find Judge Carter in the hope that Judge would pay him for the information.

Or even, in the hope that he could collect the bounty Judge had offered on Doc's head.

The thought sent Kate searching for Emil. She paused in the door of the hotel's pool room and was astonished to see Emil with a cue stick in his hand. She waited until he had made his shot—a surprisingly good one, for a boy his age.

She called out to him in French. "*Nous partons maintenant*, Emil."

He frowned. "*Maintenant?*"

"*Oui.*"

The little dandy set his cue stick down carefully across the table, bowed to his smiling adult competitors, and took Kate's hand.

She led him upstairs as quickly as she dared, and told him, "Go and pack your things. We're leaving town."

Emil's big eyes found hers, and she smiled reassurance. "I'm bored silly here. Aren't you?"

Emil shrugged a shoulder. "Not yet."

"How would you like San Francisco, *petit*? It's much bigger than Denver, and on the ocean, too. Lots more people, lots more games."

"Could I play pool there?"

She opened the door to her suite and swept him before her. "Oh, of a certainty."

Once they were inside, she locked the door behind her and gave Emil a little nudge towards his bedroom. "Go on now, hurry. We're leaving this afternoon."

And once the little boy had disappeared, Kate returned to her own room and began tossing her gowns into a trunk.

Chapter
Twenty-Six

"Cheyenne and points north, link to the Transcontinental east west line, Platform Three!"

Kate led Emil across the huge marble floor of Denver's Union Station. People were moving back and forth across its vast expanse like currents in the ocean: businessmen in suits and hats, labourers in baggy jackets and pants, women in elaborate gowns and hats, cowboys in jeans and boots, Indians in shawls and moccasins, and every other style of clothing imaginable.

Kate held her head up and moved through them like a clipper on the waves. She was elegantly dressed in a charcoal grey travelling gown, a massive hat, and a discreet veil. She was trying to blend in with the crowd.

But Emil made that a challenge. Every matron who passed smiled at the dapper little man, and Emil, knowing he was a handsome fellow, nodded and smiled as flirtatiously as if he had been older, and they younger.

Kate glanced down at him in amused exasperation. She was going to have trouble with Emil because he was destined to break hearts. He was already cracking them, even as a six-year-old.

"Stop flirting," she whispered, and he glanced up at her with a look of such perfect innocence that he almost fooled her.

"You're *such* a little showboat."

When they arrived at the correct platform at last, Kate handed their tickets to the porter with a gloved hand. The man smiled and stepped aside to admit them to the first class car. Kate helped Emil climb up the steep steps and then whisked him to their private compartment.

They would change trains in Cheyenne, and then ride the Transcontinental all the way to San Francisco—and safety.

Kate settled into her seat, glanced nervously out the window, and pulled the shade down. After a while, a porter came by, and she bought a paper bag full of peppermints for Emil and a ladies' magazine for herself, and before long the train whistle sounded.

The porter took his leave, the train began to move, and Kate relaxed. Soon they would be in San Francisco, and she was even toying with the idea of buying a house and settling down there with Emil. She could afford to do it, and it would put her unfortunate acquaintance with Judge Carter forever behind her.

An hour passed by, and Kate was so deep in the latest fashions from Paris that she didn't notice at first when the train slowed, and then stopped. Emil raised the window shade and looked out curiously.

"Why are we stopping?"

Kate glanced out the window, and to her bemusement, the scene was not that of the Cheyenne train station, but of a stand of fir trees, and forest beyond.

It looked like the wilderness.

A loud voice in the corridor outside called: "Ladies and gentlemen, there has been a landslide across the track ahead. We apologize for the inconvenience, but we're going to have to turn back for Denver since it will take days for us to clear the track."

Kate rose and opened the compartment door. She caught the porter as he walked past. "Please, sir—is there a town nearby where I can stay while the track is being cleared? I don't wish to return to Denver. I'm willing to wait here until repairs are made."

The man scratched his head. "The nearest town is Wolf Table, ma'am," he replied, with a glance at her elegant clothing, "but it's pretty rough around the edges. They have a hotel, but I doubt it's what you're used to."

"Oh, I don't mind," she replied quickly. "May we stop there?"

"Certainly, ma'am," he replied. "I'll tell you when we get there."

"Thank you."

She sighed and looked down at Emil. "It looks like we're going to be living rough for a few days," she told him, and closed the door.

"What! You mean among the *sauvages?*"

She frowned incredulously. "No, of course not! What gave you the idea that we'd be living with Indians?"

"This is where they live, *n'est-ce pas*? In the woods?"

"I suppose, but we're going to a town."

"Thank God!"

Kate sat down again and almost laughed at Emil's expression. He looked as if he thought they were about to be scalped.

"It will be all right, you'll see," she told him.

***

To her surprise, the train began moving backward within a few minutes, and she sat watching in uneasy admiration as the scenery began to slide past in reverse. It took them about fifteen minutes to return to the Wolf Table station, and the porter came and knocked on her door.

"Ma'am, this is your stop," he told her.

Kate gathered up Emil, and her things, and the porter brought her trunks out and set them down on the small train platform. He tipped his hat to her and pointed to the hotel.

"There's your lodging, ma'am. We should have the slide cleared in a few days. A week at most. When you come back, just tell the porter what happened, and you won't be charged again."

"Thank you," she replied faintly, and turned to assess their new surroundings. The Wolf Table Hotel was a simple clapboard house with a sign hanging over the front door. It was primitive, just like the rest of the town, but it was a safer place to wait than Denver, and so they had to endure the inconvenience.

Still, the raw look of the place was daunting. The only street was a dusty wagon track through town, and there were no more than two dozen buildings from one end of it to the other.

Then there was the problem of their trunks. There was no one manning the little depot, and her trunks were far too heavy for her to carry.

She took Emil's hand, led him down the steps, and then crossed the street to the hotel. There was a young man standing on the sidewalk not far away, and she met his eye hopefully.

"Excuse me, but would you be willing to help me with my trunks? We've just arrived, and they're too heavy for me. I'd be glad to pay you."

The boy was tall and dark and was clearly an Indian, and Emil's eyes bugged out of his head as the boy nodded.

"I'd be happy to. And you don't have to pay me."

He crossed the street and retrieved her trunks, one by one, and carried them into the lobby of the hotel. Kate noticed that the manager gave the boy a murderous look but managed to deflect his attention before he could act on it.

"I'd like to rent some rooms for myself and my boy," she told him.

The man's scowl disappeared. "Of course! We have a vacancy. How many nights?"

"I'm not sure yet," Kate replied, stripping off her gloves. "I suppose I should reserve the rooms for a week."

The boy turned to go, but Kate stopped him. "It was very kind of you to help me," she told him. "Let me do something for you in return."

A proud look glinted in his dark eyes. "It's all right, ma'am," he told her. "Thank you is enough. I hope you enjoy your stay."

Kate watched as the young man walked out and then down the street. "What a nice boy!" she murmured.

The manager cleared his throat. "I'll carry your trunks upstairs, ma'am," he told her. "You're welcome to wait in the sitting room yonder until your rooms are ready."

"Thank you."

Kate extended her arm toward Emil, and the little boy sighed and allowed himself to be shepherded to the open parlour just to the left of the stairs.

But he made a face at her, and a flash of disgust lit his vivid eyes.

"This place is like the end of the world!" he told her in French, but she only laughed and replied:

"We'll find some way to amuse ourselves, I promise," and smiled when the little boy looked skeptical and replied:

"Bah!"

Chapter
Twenty-Seven

Gideon emerged from the little office downtown and shook hands with Mr Petersen. "It's been a pleasure," Gideon told him, and the old man smiled.

"That's a load off my mind," Petersen confessed. "You got the keys to the house. I'm staying with my brother for now, and I'll be back on Saturday to get what's left of my stuff. I hope you enjoy the place as much as I have."

"I'm sure I will," Gideon replied, and Mr Peterson put up a hand in parting and walked down the road.

Gideon tucked the deed into his pocket and turned towards the hotel. Once he'd paid his bill with the manager and packed their things, he and Dase could settle into the new house.

He crossed the street and entered the hotel. He found the manager behind the front desk, and the man frowned, straightened up, and cleared his throat.

"Checking out, Mr McCall?"

"Yes. I'm ready to settle my bill."

"Well now, let's see." The man put on a pair of glasses and consulted a written list. "You have the cost to replace the café window that got kicked out when your daughter rode that wild horse through town."

Gideon straightened and gave the man a frowning

look, but he went on:

"And then you have the two rooms, for five days, and the cost of the repairs I had to have made to the roof when your daughter and that Indian decided to break in."

Gideon stared at him. "My daughter's name is Daisy," he replied coldly, "and her friend's name is Clay."

The man didn't look up. "*Mmm-hmm.*

"Altogether, that comes to ... thirty-five dollars, and sixty-two cents."

Gideon raised an eyebrow but counted out the bills without hesitation. The manager stared in shock as the rough mountain man produced what most men would consider a month's wages without so much as blinking.

"Thank you," he murmured in surprise, and opened his register to count out change.

Gideon stuffed his cash back into his pants and looked away from the manager. In the silence that followed, he became aware of a pair of voices, speaking in a soft patois he hadn't heard for years but that he recognized instantly.

"He's as hairy as a bear!" a young voice piped in French. "Look at that beard! And they're both dressed like Indians. See how their shirts flap loose in the breeze!"

"*Shhh,*" a soft voice replied. "Mind your manners. It isn't polite to talk about other people."

"The big one looks like he sleeps in the woods!" the little voice observed. "He must be homeless. Give him a dollar, so he can get some food!"

"Emil!"

Gideon frowned and turned his head. There was a young woman and a little boy sitting in the little parlour. The boy's bright eyes met his with a look of frank speculation.

The woman had half-turned towards the child; but the sound of her voice made Gideon's eyes widen in dawning recognition. He tilted his head slightly, and his heartbeat quickened.

She turned back, and he could see her face clearly at last. Gideon inhaled sharply and had to turn his eyes away.

He couldn't let Kate see that he was *overcome.*

"Here's your change." The manager held out a few dollars, and Gideon took the money mechanically. He stared at the floor for a few more moments than was seemly, and the manager added: "Is there something else I can do for you?"

Gideon looked up. "Who—who is that young lady in the parlour?" he asked softly.

The manager shrugged. "She's a guest here, just arrived today. She signed in as"—he adjusted his spectacles—"Miss Kate Dubois."

A half-laugh escaped Gideon's lips, and he shook his head. "Thank you."

The man frowned at him. "You're welcome," he replied slowly. "Please have your things out by five this evening. It's hotel policy."

"Yes, yes," Gideon replied and looked at Kate again. She was reading a magazine, and the little boy had discovered a wooden puzzle on a table and was fidgeting with it.

He stared at Kate, his greedy eyes drinking in every detail: The tilt of her elegant black hat, and the jaunty sweep of its little grey ostrich feather; her downturned eyes; the shining auburn tendril that had escaped her updo and curled prettily down her cheek, and the soft curve of her throat.

She looked just the same to him as the girl who'd said *yes* on the train to Denver ten years ago.

She was dressed in a tailored gown, a charcoal grey pinstripe that was almost severe in its simplicity but that hugged her elegant figure without being one stitch too tight. There was a lacy white ruffle at her throat and two more that cascaded over her wrists, and the delicate toes of her expensive leather boots just peeped out from underneath her frilled skirts.

Gideon's eyes moved to her left hand, and to his joy, Kate's ring finger was bare, but the little boy bore silent witness to the fact that ten years had passed since their last meeting.

It was inevitable that a woman of Kate's beauty would find love again. But what he wondered at that moment, was why she'd signed into the hotel alone, except for the boy, and under her own name.

The manager cleared his throat again, and Gideon moved away from the desk, but he couldn't ignore Kate, couldn't walk past without reaching out to her in some way.

He walked up to her slowly and waited. She noticed his shoes, and then looked up at him with a puzzled smile.

"Hello, ma'am," he croaked. "I'm Gideon McCall. I

notice you're new here. I—I just wanted to say, welcome to Wolf Table."

He stared into her face painfully, wondering if she'd recognize him under the bristling beard, if she'd know his voice, his eyes.

But Kate smiled politely and nodded just a touch.

"Thank you, sir. That's very kind," she replied smoothly. "The train track to Cheyenne was blocked by a landslide, and I and my little boy are staying here until it can be opened again."

Gideon looked down and nodded. "I see. Well—I hope you both have a pleasant stay, ma'am."

Kate smiled again, and nodded, and he backed away, feeling like a fool. But his heart was beating like a steam piston all the way up the stairs, and when he opened the door to his room, he caught Kate looking at him over her shoulder.

Chapter
Twenty-Eight

Gideon opened the front door and entered his new home like a sleepwalker. Daisy called to him from the back porch.

"Is that you, Gideon?"

"Yes."

He threw their things from the hotel down onto the floor and drifted out to the back porch. Daisy was cleaning fish on the back steps with a small knife.

"There's plenty for both of us," she told him brightly. "I'm gonna like this pond. Clay will, too. Did you see Clay in town?"

Gideon stared at her dully. "No."

"Well, when he comes back I'm going to invite him down. It won't be as much fun to gig frogs from here, as from another place we might get run out of, but I guess you trade the excitement for the convenience."

Gideon sat down in a chair and stared at his hands. Daisy glanced up at him and observed: "What's the matter, Gideon? You look like you been clopped upside the head with a rock."

"I was."

Daisy looked at him again and then grinned and returned to her task. "Aw, I should've known you was funnin.' What happened?"

Gideon turned his eyes to her face. "I met a woman I haven't seen in ten years. Kate Dubois."

Daisy looked up sharply. "Kate? You mean the woman you holler out about sometimes in your sleep?"

A faint flush moved up Gideon's face. "Yes."

Daisy frowned. "Look here, Gideon—you ain't gonna go goofy over some old gal at your time of life, are you?"

Gideon looked at her. "My time of life?" he echoed incredulously.

Daisy shrugged. "Well, ain't no use beatin' around the bush about it. You're past thirty now, ain't you, Gideon? Your best huntin' days is behind you. Ain't no shame in admittin' it."

Gideon sputtered out a laugh. "I think I have a few good years left."

"Why, a man your age is just limpin' along, that's all. Can't hunt all night no more, can't climb worth a flip, and grunts when he runs.

"And how old is *she*?" Daisy went on and shook the knife at him. "Probly way past her sparkin' days! And I'll bet she's lost a tooth or two in the back of her mouth."

Gideon put his hands on his hips. "It might surprise you to know that thirty-five is not old!"

Daisy looked at him pityingly. "That's what folks say when they want to make you feel better," she told him and gathered up the cleaned fish. "But don't worry, Gideon. I'll go and cook these. You better rest after walking in from town."

Gideon glanced at her indignantly but forbore to argue. He was still in shock and in no condition to debate.

He stared out at the pond and pulled his hand across his mouth. It still felt like someone had punched him in the stomach. Kate, alive and well—and here in Wolf Table, of all places!

She clearly hadn't recognized him, and he wondered if he should've told her who he was.

Maybe he should still tell her.

She was only planning to stay in town for a few days. He only had this one opportunity.

Daisy glanced up at him from the fire. "How many fish do you want, Gideon?"

"Four," he replied, and watched sadly as Daisy coaxed fire out of a little pile of sticks and twigs.

No, he couldn't reveal himself to Kate. He knew she wouldn't betray his secret, but it might get out even if she didn't mean it to, and he had Daisy to think of, not just himself.

He was already taking a risk, just to move into town.

Judge Carter had set bounty hunters onto him, and he couldn't expose his daughter to that danger, no matter how badly he wanted to talk to Kate.

***

He was brought slowly back to reality by the smell of roasted fish. He looked down to see a plate full of grilled trout floating in the air in front of him.

"There you go," Daisy's voice was saying. "Hot off the

fire!"

Doc sighed, wiped his eyes, and nodded.

"Thank you, Daisy."

Chapter
Twenty-Nine

Daisy stretched out in a little hammock on the back porch of the house and crossed her arms behind her head. It was about an hour after sundown, and the air was filled with the sweet smell of mown grass, flowers, and just a tinge of leftover smoke from her fire.

Fireflies had begun to rise from the grass, and Daisy watched as their little yellow lanterns bobbed and winked in the air.

The new place was pretty, all right, and she was surprised by how quick she was settlin' down to it. It was a real relief to find at least one good thing in Gideon's crazy plan.

But Gideon was going downhill fast, and it worried her. He'd been addled all day long. She couldn't get no sense out of him no matter what they talked about.

He was thinkin' about that woman, that Kate-what's-her-name. And it was plain to her now, which woman she had to protect Gideon from.

The Prophet had been right.

The thought sent a shudder up Daisy's back. The Prophet had been right about everything so far, and it looked like he was going to be proved right on the rest of what he said, as well.

And that meant only one thing: she was going to have to run that woman off before she ruined Gideon, just like the Prophet had warned.

Daisy bit her lip. The Prophet had said that Gideon wasn't even his real name. That he was a gambler, name of Doc Dailey.

Daisy spoke the name softly. *Doc Dailey* felt strange on her tongue, but in the end, it didn't matter to her what her pa called himself—Gideon or Doc or Jack Sprat.

The important thing was to keep him *alive*.

She glanced through the porch window. A light still burned in the living room, and she got a glimpse of Gideon pacing back and forth inside. She shook her head. The next thing you knew, Gideon was going to be talking to himself.

Daisy sighed and looked up at the sky. Her duty was clear, and so she made up her mind to do it.

***

The next morning, dawn found the back porch of the little house empty, and the hammock swinging. Daisy had forsaken it, and was already walking down the road toward Wolf Table.

Daisy arrived in the little town just about breakfast time. The residents had just begun to stir, and the smell of frying bacon hung over the main street as Daisy walked boldly into the hotel.

She found the front counter empty. Daisy looked this way and that and leaned over it to peek at the ledger. There was only one name in it, in Rooms Two and Three.

Daisy pushed back and took the stairs two at a time. She hurried to Room Two and rapped on the door.

"Breakfast!" she called softly, and when the door opened, she pressed in.

A little boy stood on the other side, and she pushed him back unceremoniously.

"Hey!" he objected. "Who are you?"

But Daisy had already found the door that connected the two rooms and blew through it.

She found Kate Dubois still rolled in her blankets, and she strode over to the bed and threw the covers off onto the floor.

Daisy pulled her pistol out of her breeches and pointed it at the woman's head. "Get up!" she commanded.

The woman opened one eye and then opened it wide. She put her hands into the air and slowly sat upright, trembling in her nightgown.

"Who are you?" she gasped.

"Never you mind," Daisy answered; and then half-turned towards the boy standing in the doorway. "And you, short stuff—get over here where I can see you!"

The boy walked in slowly, his solemn eyes watching her.

"Don't bring him into this!" the woman replied quickly. "If you want money, I'll give you money. Just leave my little boy alone."

"I don't want your money," Daisy told her gruffly. "I want you *gone*. I want you to get up and get dressed and get the blazes out of this town!"

"All right," the woman answered evenly. "But the line

to Cheyenne is blocked, and we have to wait until the railroad can open it again."

Daisy frowned. "Oh. Well, then—I want you to ride out!"

The woman's wary eyes watched her. "We don't have any horses," she replied, "and I don't have enough money to buy one."

"You can rent one, down to the stables," Daisy told her. "Get up and get moving!"

The woman sat up, hands in the air. "I don't know you, young man," she added carefully, as she put her feet into her slippers. "Why do you want me to go?"

Fire flashed from Daisy's blue eyes. "Because you're a danger to my pa!" she cried. "He's beside himself, just having laid eyes on you! You're bad luck to him, lady—worse than you know! Don't ask me questions. Just get up, and get on out of here!"

"Who is your father?" the woman frowned. "How would he even know me? I'm a stranger here."

"You knew him once," Daisy murmured, and to her irritation, tears sprang to her eyes. "And if you ever loved him, you need to get out of here before you ruin him!"

"Loved him?" the woman echoed, with a frown. "What do you—" Kate suddenly raised her eyes sharply to Daisy's. "What is your father's name?" she breathed.

Daisy saw hope burning in the woman's eyes and cursed under her breath.

"His name is Gideon McCall," she replied stubbornly.

"The man who spoke to me yesterday?" Kate

murmured. "But he was—" Her voice trailed off, and she suddenly clapped a hand to her mouth and sobbed out something in another language.

The woman raised swimming eyes to Daisy's face. "Your father—he was once called *Doc Dailey*—wasn't he?"

"No!" Daisy shouted. "He's Gideon McCall, and he's going to go on being Gideon! Now get up, and get out of here!"

But the thunderous sound of someone rushing up the stairs outside made Daisy close her eyes in defeat and lower the pistol.

It was Gideon's voice—*Doc's* voice—shouting:

"Daisy, stop it—put the gun down!"

The little boy's eyes bugged. "Can he see through the door? How does he know?"

"He's my pa," Daisy groaned and went to open the door.

"*Was* my pa."

Daisy opened the doorway to find Doc filling it. His blue eyes were blazing, and he glared at her, but his eyes quickly moved past her to the woman standing there in her nightgown. She put a hand over her mouth and dissolved into tears.

"Doc!" she cried, "Doc!"

He took two steps into the room, and the woman threw her arms around his neck, and he buried his face in her hair, and they both wept.

"What's going on?" the little boy demanded. "You're all

mad!"

Tears sprang to Daisy's eyes because the Prophet's terrible words were coming true right in front of her. Doc was rocking the woman back and forth in his arms and crooning to her in some strange language she'd never heard, and it was plain as print that he wasn't Gideon, and never had been.

Her whole life had been built on a lie.

"I'm going home," she mumbled, and set the gun down on a table. Nobody tried to stop her, and by the time she got to the bottom of the stairs, she broke out into a run.

Chapter **Thirty**

Doc looked down into Kate's face and laughed shakily. "Kate! I thought you were dead!"

Kate closed her eyes as Doc found her mouth and gave her a desperate kiss. When she opened her eyes, Doc was looking down at her, and his eyelashes were wet.

"Why did you leave me that night on the train?"

She caressed his face. "I didn't leave you," she murmured. "I was chased away! A man came to my compartment that night on the train and put a gun to my head. He told me he knew who we were, and that if I didn't get the money and bring it back to him, he'd kill us both. So I did what he said!

"But when I got back to my own compartment, I kicked him and ran off the train at the Kansas City Station. He followed me, but he mistakenly attacked some other woman on the platform, and he was captured. But the train left before I could get back on.

"I came to Denver as soon as I could. I searched for you," she said earnestly, "but no one had even seen you!" Kate closed her eyes because tears threatened to overwhelm her, but Doc kissed her again and took her in his arms.

"I was in Denver for less than a day," he murmured into her neck. "That monster who attacked you was a bounty hunter. He found me too, and I had to kill him. But he lasted long enough to tell me you were dead, and I believed him. Thank God he lied!"

They embraced each other in silence, and rocked back and forth, until the little boy retired to his own room in disgust. They stood there, whispering and holding one another, for a long time.

***

Kate caressed his face with her hand, and tears filled her eyes again. "I still can't believe it," she marvelled. "It's really you!"

Doc kissed her again, and when their lips parted, she rested her head on his chest. "What will we do now?" she wondered aloud, and looked up at him.

"Pick up where we left off," Doc told her. "Unless there's some reason why we can't. Are you married?"

Kate shook her head. "Are you?"

"No."

She smiled and snuggled in deeper, and Doc laughed and tightened his hold on her. "I'll have to buy you a ring," he mused aloud, but Kate smiled and tugged on the chain around her neck. The huge diamond he'd once given her flashed and glittered in the light.

"You kept it!" Doc marvelled and took the magnificent diamond ring in his fingers.

"I've worn it around my neck from the day we parted," she told him and watched as Doc loosed it from its chain. He raised the ring and smiled crookedly.

"Marry me, Kate?"

Kate laughed indulgently. *"Oui, je t'épouserai,"* she whispered and gave him her hand. Doc slipped the flashing ring back on her finger. He leaned in for another kiss, but Kate put a hand up between them and laughed:

"No, not even one more kiss until you shave off that scratchy beard!" She looked up at him and smiled. "I want to see the man I adored in New Orleans. I want to kiss my lover—not a hairy bear."

Doc laughed outright. *"Hairy bear?"*

"Yes. It's what Emil named you when he first saw you downstairs. And he wasn't far from the truth." She twined her white arms around his neck and looked up at him in appeal.

Doc's smile faded. "I can't tell you how sorry I am for what Daisy did to you and your little boy," he murmured. "The two of you must've been terrified! But she was bluffing. The gun she used wasn't even loaded.

"Is your little boy all right?"

Kate nodded. "I think so. What possessed your daughter to do such a thing?"

Doc sighed. "Daisy's lived in the wilderness all her life. I just brought her to town a few weeks ago, and it's been rough for both of us. It's not like her to be insecure, but lately she's been behaving—differently. I think she's afraid that I might get married. She's been a little defensive."

"She seemed almost desperate," Kate murmured. "Where did she go?"

"She went back up to the cabin. I think I'm going to let

her stay there for a few days. Then I'll go up and talk to her when she's had a chance to cool down. I'll have to punish her for this, but I want to do it when we're both calmer."

Kate smiled up at him. "Very well. I've waited ten years, so I can be patient when you go up the mountain.

"But in the meantime—go to the barber, Doc—*s'il vous plait?*"

Doc kissed her hand gallantly and stood up. "I bow to your wish, my lady."

Kate looked up at him and smiled. "I'll be waiting."

Doc sighed and tried to linger, but Kate laughed, pointed at the door, and pushed him away. He walked out of the hotel room, and after he was gone, the door to Emil's room opened and the little boy stuck his head in.

"What's going on?" he demanded. "Who was that fellow?"

Kate waved him over to the bed. "Come over here beside me, *petit.*"

The little boy walked over to her bedside, and Kate put an arm around his shoulder. "Emil, that was Doc. He and I were—very good friends, many years ago in New Orleans. We were going to get married, but some bad things happened, and we got separated for a long time. We met again this morning, for the first time in ten years!"

Emil's light green eyes frowned at her. "Are you going to marry him, then?"

"Yes, *ma chérie.*"

Emil scowled. "Are you mad? He looks like he sleeps on the ground! I refuse to let you marry a beggar!"

Kate laughed delightedly and hugged him close. "He's not a beggar, Emil. But even if he was, I would love him. You cannot control love, you see. Once you love someone, you're quite helpless."

"Bah!"

Kate caressed his dark curls and smiled into his eyes. "You're going to like him very much, Emil. He was once as handsome as you. Quite the dashing young man."

"What happened to him? It must have been something terrible!"

Kate's smile faded. "Yes. Yes, it was." Her smile crept out again. "But it's over now, Emil. I sent him to the barber, and when he comes back, you won't recognize him, I assure you."

The little boy looked into her face with a serious expression. "If you have chosen, there is nothing to be said. If he makes you happy, I'll endure him. But only if he shaves."

Kate laughed and hugged him close. "You make your *bonne amie* so happy." She sobered and straightened his little silk dressing jacket. "When I marry Doc, you'll naturally come to live with us, *petit*. Would you like that?"

Emil nodded solemnly. "I would like to go on living with you," he told her. "Will it be here, in this town?"

"I'm afraid so, *cherie*."

The little boy sighed gustily and nodded. "Well, one must resign oneself."

Chapter
Thirty-One

Doc walked into the town's only barber shop and caught the proprietor's eye. The bald, aproned man straightened up and smiled.

"Good morning! How can I help you, sir?"

Doc gestured towards his beard. "I'd like to take this thing off."

The barber tilted his head and considered. "I'm not one to turn down business, but are you sure? It's a beauty. Must've taken a long time to grow it out that length."

Doc settled down into the barber's chair. "Ten years."

The barber looked down at him. "You're sure?"

"Positive." Doc closed his eyes and settled in as the barber flung a towel over his chest. "And I'd like my hair and moustache cut and trimmed very precisely. Do you have a style menu?"

"Yes sir."

The man produced a loosely bound book with gentlemen's hairstyles. Doc perused them critically. "Are these the latest styles?"

"Maybe not the very latest," the man confessed. "I got this mailed to me last year from New York."

Doc's bushy moustache twitched, but he replied: "Very well. I'd like the Number Three, the Park Avenue."

"Yes, sir." The barber took a pair of shears and began cutting. "I don't think I've seen you around here. Are you new in town?"

"Fairly. I've been here a week or two."

"Where you from?"

"Up on the mountain. I lived in a cabin above Pine Ridge."

The man whistled. "That's wild country, all right. I don't know how you made it work."

Doc folded his hands across his chest and looked up at the ceiling contemplatively. "I don't either."

"Got any family?"

"One daughter. I've just become engaged and will be marrying soon."

"Well, congratulations," the man said with a smile. "I see now why you'd want this off. Most women these days don't like a long beard on a man. Are you getting married in town?"

"We haven't discussed it."

"The church isn't big, but it's pretty, with those old oak trees all around. There's also Lake Aspen if you'd prefer something outside." He snipped off a hunk of beard and it fell into a growing mound of blond hair on the floor.

"Is there a shop in town where I can buy formal attire?"

"Sunday clothes, you mean?"

"Yes."

"We have a mercantile that sells men's clothes, but they're mostly flannel and denim. We have a seamstress who can make up something to order. She carries some fine linen and twill material."

Doc stifled a sigh and made a mental note to go on a shopping trip to Denver. "Thank you."

The barber put the shears onto a table and reached for a finer pair. He worked them in the air a few times before approaching Doc's bristling moustache.

"You know, you're right. This is taking years off your face," the barber observed, and Doc rolled wry eyes to his.

"You don't say."

"*Mmm.* I took you for fifty when you first came in. But you're in your thirties, aren't you?"

"That's right."

"That beard made you look like a completely different person!" The barber finished with the shears and soaped up a barber's brush. He began lathering up Doc's face, and Doc closed his eyes.

***

Doc stayed at the barber's for almost two hours, but when he emerged at last, his blond hair was short, sleek, and elegant, and his moustache was smaller by half and trimmed precisely. His jaw was as smooth as a baby's bottom and pleasantly fragrant of bay rum.

He paused on the sidewalk before resigning himself to

the mercantile. He didn't especially want to dress like a cowboy, but he had to have something to wear on the trip to Denver.

His only consolation was that whatever he ended up with would look better than the baggy shirt and buckskin breeches he had been wearing.

The shop owner looked at him twice when he walked through the door. "Good morning, sir," he said uncertainly. "How can I help you?"

"I'm looking for a suit of clothes," Doc replied, glancing at the dry goods side of the store without much hope.

Recognition dawned over the man's face. "Why—you're the newcomer, the man with the beard!" he exclaimed.

Doc smiled wanly. "I got a shave."

"I wouldn't have known you! Well, come over here, and I'll show you what we have. Most of what we carry is for every day since that's what folks mostly need," he explained. "But I do have a few fancy duds over in the corner."

Doc followed him to a dusty corner in the dry goods shelves, and the shop owner pulled out a collarless white linen shirt, and a pair of black trousers. To Doc's surprise, there was also a silk vest in an unusual blue-grey shade.

Doc picked up the vest and rubbed the silk between his fingers. "Is there someplace I can try these on?"

The man looked doubtful. "I have a broom closet in the back."

"Do you carry any dress shoes?"

The shop owner rubbed his chin. "Got some black boots."

"I'd like to try them all on." Doc paused and glanced at the broom closet in distaste. "Is there a mirror in the broom closet?"

"I can bring you one."

Doc stifled a sigh, draped the garments over his arm, and walked to the rear of the store as reluctantly as if he was marching to the gallows.

Chapter
Thirty-Two

Kate fastened a dangling gold earring to her ear and turned at the sound of a soft knock at her hotel room door. She dotted a tiny bit of Parisian cologne on her wrists, and over her blue satin gown, and smoothed her shining ringlets back from her shoulders.

"Come in."

The door opened, and for the first time in ten years, the Doc Dailey she remembered walked back into her life. Kate put a hand to her mouth and tears pooled in her eyes. Doc looked almost the same to her. His blond hair was as severely styled as always, his moustache was precise, and his clothes—well, *those* would have to do until he could get better ones. He was dressed like a frontier shopkeeper, in a plain white shirt, a blue vest that looked homemade, and a pair of baggy slacks and dull black boots.

But for the first time, Doc looked like himself, and she threw open her arms. He walked into them gladly, and they communed with one another delightfully until Emil could stand it no longer and stamped his foot on the floor in the open doorway.

He was dressed in a little high-collared jacket, a vest of red velvet, tailored breeches, and shining boots. He was wearing a little top hat and looked ready for an evening on a riverboat.

Kate looked down at him from her place in Doc's arms

and smiled. "Come, Emil, and say hello to Doc."

The little boy straightened, walked up, and bowed stiffly. "Your servant, sir," he said in French and swept his little hat off his head and tucked it under his arm.

"And yours," Doc replied correctly and in the same language. His lip twitched slightly, but he maintained an air of admirable gravity. He released Kate and knelt down to look into Emil's eyes.

"I'm very glad to make your acquaintance, sir," he told the boy in a confidential tone; "I am told that you're a formidable poker player. We shall have a game this evening if it pleases you."

Emil looked up at him. "For what stakes, sir? I am accustomed to playing for expensive things."

Doc's eyebrows shot up, and he looked back at Kate's laughing face. "Oh—shall we say then, a brand new suit of clothes in Denver, from the finest gentleman's couturier, and a meal at The Silver Swan, and a complete and faithful replica of Andrew Jackson's army with a hundred tin soldiers and two cannons, and a box full of sweets?"

Emil bowed again. "Your terms are agreeable to me, sir," he replied. "I will indulge you at your convenience."

"I shall look forward to it," Doc told him and reached into his pocket. "And in the meantime, here is a token of my sportsmanship." He presented the little boy with a five dollar bill. "You may spend it freely in town this afternoon if you like, and I'll do my best to win it back this evening."

"Mèrci, monsieur. We shall call it an opening wager,"

Emil told him and pocketed the bill. Emil bowed again and turned to Kate.

"Can I go downstairs and amuse myself?"

"Yes; but only if you don't go too far," Kate replied.

"No fear of that," Emil replied and put on his hat. "There's nothing beyond the end of the street."

They both watched him go, and Doc turned to Kate in bemusement.

"He's quite the little man. Can he really play poker?"

Kate gazed after the boy. "He knows almost nothing else. I won him in a poker game," she said with a sigh.

"*Won* him?"

Kate's smile faded. "Emil was with an older man, and the man just abandoned him at my table when he lost the game. Emil has been with me ever since. He's been at the tables all his life. I taught him to play poker and faro. He can deal as well as an adult now."

"I see," Doc murmured.

Kate looked up at him. "Do you mind, Doc?"

Doc took her in his arms and smiled down into her eyes. "No. I'm sure we'll get along well, Emil and I. The real question is, do you mind about Daisy?"

Kate pursed her lips, looked down, and then up at Doc. "Is she your—your *natural* daughter?"

Doc raised his brows. "You mean, did I find love up on that howling mountain in the middle of nowhere? I'm afraid the answer is no."

Kate sputtered and laughed. "You know what I mean."

"You're jealous!"

"Not of Daisy," Kate assured him. "Of the idea that you could love any woman but me."

"Good news then," Doc murmured and took her chin in his hand. "I never have." He leaned forward, kissed her, and then kissed her again.

She looked down and smoothed her hands across his chest. "You spoke of going to Denver. But perhaps we shouldn't. Do you remember Broadway Bobby, Doc? The little man on the *Natchez Queen* with the New York accent?"

"I remember that he was a cheat," Doc growled.

"I met him a few days ago in Denver. He told me that Judge is coming out here, may be here already. He's opening a new gambling hall in Denver, and he's in town for the ceremony."

She looked up at him. "That was what drove me here. I was on my way to catch the Transcontinental to San Francisco. To get as far away from Judge as I could."

Doc's expression darkened. "He throws a long shadow, doesn't he?" he murmured and looked down at her hands. "I'm tired of hiding from that man, Kate."

"We've found each other again," Kate urged. "And as long as I'm with you, Doc, I don't care where we live, or how. The only important thing is that we're together, you and I, and our children. We've got them to think of, too."

At that, Doc nodded. "You're right, of course. Revenge is an ... expensive luxury." He tightened his mouth and shook his head.

Kate watched him uneasily. "Let's go shopping in

Cheyenne instead, Doc," she urged, but Doc's bright blue eyes held a gleam she remembered.

"I promised the boy we'd go to Denver, Kate," he said evenly. "And so Denver it will be."

"We can't go right away, in any case," Kate persisted. "We couldn't go without your daughter. Where is she, Doc?"

"I'll have to go get her," he replied. "She's up in that cabin on the mountain, sulking. You may have to be extra patient with her, Kate. I apologize."

"You needn't, Doc," Kate assured him and smiled. "Nothing could vex me now.

"And nothing in this world could make me unhappy!"

Doc smiled at her again and took her into his arms.

Chapter **Thirty-Three**

Daisy stopped to catch her breath, turned around, and looked down the mountain. Wolf Table was just a dark smudge on the edge of sight, and that suited her down to the ground.

"I'm done with you," she mumbled and wasn't sure if she meant the town or Doc, but it didn't much matter.

It would work out the same, either way.

Daisy walked the rest of the way to the cabin and when she reached it at last, she closed its wooden door behind her. She climbed the little ladder to the loft and curled up in her bed. Her whole chest ached, but she didn't cry. There was no point in it.

Doc had a right to live his life the way he wanted to, and so did she.

Doc was free to marry that woman and bring her back to that house he just bought, and be happy.

She didn't have no claim on him; he wasn't really her pa. It had been real nice of him to raise her up, seein' as how she wasn't his, but she was grown now, and she could let him go.

If the Prophet's words came true, she'd grieve for Doc, but she couldn't stop him from doing what he wanted. Didn't have no right to, no way.

Daisy turned her face to the wall and sighed deeply. She felt a terrible heaviness in her chest and had never been sadder in her life.

But she could be glad about one thing: she was back home on the mountain at last, and that much at least felt *good*.

***

Daisy fell asleep and slept heavily all that night. The next morning, it took the sound of a loud voice calling to rouse her.

"Hallo the house!"

Daisy sat up in bed and rubbed her eyes. It sounded like Clay, and she clambered down the ladder and went to open the door.

"Hallo the house!"

Daisy peered out and ran a hand through her short hair. "Hello!" she called, and sure enough, Clay appeared a few hundred yards from the cabin.

"You back now, Dase?" he called, as he approached.

"For good this time," Daisy told him and flopped down onto a log lying outside the door.

"Where's Gideon?"

Daisy looked down at the ground and shrugged. "In town. And he ain't Gideon." Daisy rubbed her nose and looked away. "Turns out the Prophet was right. His name is Doc Dailey."

Clay frowned and came to sit down on the log beside her. "How do you know?"

Daisy sniffed. "Aw, some old gal came to town, and she and Gid—*Doc* were sweet on each other once, or something.

"I tried to get out ahead of it. I went to the woman's hotel room and tried to run her off, but it didn't work. Doc figured out where I'd gone and followed me, and—well, he's gone back to his old life now, and that's fair enough, I guess. He gave me ten years, and that's more than I had any right to expect."

Clay nodded without saying anything, but he put an arm around Daisy's shoulder, and she suddenly turned her face into his chest and broke down in tears.

Clay put his chin on her hair, closed his eyes and let her cry herself out. After a while, he looked down at her with a frowning expression.

"You'd be miserable down there anyway, Dase," he told her. "You've been free too long. You live like my people live, out under the sky. Once you do, you can never be happy living any other way.

"It's like living in a cage."

Daisy nodded. "You're right. I know you're right." She wiped her nose. "And I'm going to be fine, once I get used to—the way things are now."

"Did Doc tell you that he wanted to part ways?" Clay asked gently.

Daisy shrugged. "Didn't have to. You could see it, plain as day. He found his lady friend, and they don't need to be saddled with an old scruffy thing like me, that's half bobcat."

Clay sputtered and shook his head. "You're half bobcat all right, Dase." He smiled. "But maybe you should let Doc tell you what he wants, and what he don't. Maybe you ran off too quick."

"No, I ain't going back," Daisy replied softly. "You're right; I belong here." She sat up straight and clapped her hands clean. "Maybe we'll visit back and forth a little, but Doc has gone his way, and I'll go mine."

She stood up, took a deep breath, and put her hands on her hips. "You know, I ain't been deer hunting in more'n a month. What say we go out tomorrow and get a nice buck or two?"

Clay smiled at her. "Suits me."

"That should set us up." Daisy nodded. "Plenty of meat to last us for a long time. And I got potatoes growing in a little patch out back of the cabin, and some watercress, and some onions. There's still a sack of corn meal in the cabin, and a little lard for cooking."

"You're going to be okay," Clay told her, and Daisy shot him a look of gratitude; but if she wasn't really sure of that, she sure wasn't going to let on.

Chapter
Thirty-Four

Clay stood as still as a shadow in the mottled green forest. He leaned against a tall pine, holding his rifle, as a magnificent buck picked its cautious way down the hill on the opposite side of the creek. The buck took one careful step, its ears twitching, then another, on its way down the steep bank.

Daisy stood motionless a few trees over, her rifle in her hands. She carefully inched the rifle up to her shoulder, slowly, slowly, and Clay lifted his own gun.

The wind flowed up through the ravine suddenly, sighing through the firs and lifting the branches of the trees like a rising tide. The buck's nostrils flared, its eyes widened, and it suddenly bounded up the hill. The two rifles cracked simultaneously, but the buck gained the crest of the hill in two mighty leaps and disappeared.

"Blast!" Daisy exclaimed, lowering her gun, "I was sure we had him! He was a big one, too."

Clay set his rifle on the ground and leaned against it. "Well, we've had a good day. We got plenty of rabbits and some grouse. Come on, we'll go back to your cabin and cook 'em up."

Daisy threw him the game bag, and Clay slung it over his back and led the way back down the barely-visible footpath that wound through the trees. They were high up on the mountain, not far from the tree line, and it was another hour's trek down to Doc's cabin.

The trail followed the creek as it wound down the mountain and slowly gained strength. The water gradually widened from a swift, shallow stream to a strong current rushing noisily over the rocks.

About halfway down to the cabin, the stream tumbled over a rockface in a waterfall of about five feet and widened out into a pool. Daisy called to Clay and turned aside to the stream.

"What're you doing?"

Daisy propped her gun against a tree and sat down on the grass. "I'm going to take off these shoes and dunk my feet. They're hot as an oven. We've been walking all morning, and a little cold water's going to feel good." She looked back over her shoulder and patted the mossy rock beside her. "Come on."

Clay glanced up at the sun as it pierced the canopy and fell in vivid shafts on the forest floor. "It's past noon. This is why we never make good time. You're always stopping to do something."

"We've done our hunting, ain't we? What's the harm in taking a break?" Daisy set her moccasins on the mossy rock and gingerly lowered her feet into the icy water.

"*Woo!* That's cold!" she yelped and yanked her feet back before gingerly dipping them back in again. "But that water sure feels good."

"Come on, Dase."

Daisy looked up at her companion. "What's the matter? You're as itchy as if you done sat on an anthill."

"I'll feel better when we're out of the high country," Clay replied. "This is bear territory."

"Good! Maybe we'll bag one while we're up here."

Clay looked away impatiently. "You've never hunted bear, Dase. It's dangerous."

"Well, you're the one always telling me about how many bears the Pawnee brought down with their bows," Daisy objected. "If you can bring down a bear with a bow, it should be a snap to bring one down with a rifle."

"I'm not going to argue with you," Clay told her with a dark look. "Come on."

"All right, all right." Daisy pulled her feet out of the water and stuck them back into her shoes. Clay offered her a hand and pulled her up, and they returned to the trail.

But he scanned all around the footpath as they walked and seemed ill at ease until they finally reached the safety of the cabin in the mid-afternoon.

Daisy pushed inside and flopped down at the wooden table. "Happy now, Grandma?" she taunted him.

Clay gave her a short look and tossed the game bag onto the table. "Yes, very happy," he retorted. "Do you want to know why? I saw fresh bear tracks in the woods. Huge ones, Dase."

"Why, you"—Daisy sputtered and threw her shoe at him. "Why didn't you show me then?"

"I was afraid you'd want to follow them," Clay told her. "It was Old Crunchy, Dase. There's only one bear on this mountain with paws that big."

Daisy looked up, and he continued: "The tracks came way down the trail. Further than I've ever seen before. It worries me. We need to keep our eyes peeled for him, Dase. And don't leave anything outside the cabin that could draw him."

"Why, I thought you was a hunter," Daisy replied scornfully. "Why don't we just go out, get the dang bear, and stop worrying about him? Didn't your people bring down all sorts of monstrous bears with just their bows and arrows?"

Clay shook his dark head. "All those stories I told you about my people bringing down bears with their bows—that happened once. Maybe twice. But it was a miracle both times. The best chance you have to bring down a bear is to blast it as many times as you can with a double-barreled shotgun.

"It's suicide to stir them up, Dase. You can't outrun a bear. It runs twice as fast as a man, even uphill. You can't escape it by climbing a tree. A bear can out climb you—even a Grizzly. And you can't hide because a bear can smell a man a mile away. The best you can do is pray it doesn't want to eat you because the bear always sees you before you see it."

Daisy frowned and stuck her hands on her hips. "Why the fool did you tell me all that big pack about hunting bears, then?"

Clay looked away and took a deep breath. "I was trying to—I was kind of trying to impress you, Dase."

Daisy stared at him. "Impress me? Why? You know me, I know you. Ain't no need for puttin' on no show. What's got into you?"

Clay shook his head and opened the cabin door. "I'm turning in. I'll see you later."

"We ain't even got this game cleaned," Daisy objected. "Ain't you going to stay and have dinner?"

"No. I'll see you later."

"Ain't you even going to take your half back home?"

But Clay didn't answer. Daisy rose, went to the cabin door, and watched in puzzlement as her friend kicked at a tree root, picked up his rifle, and disappeared into the trees.

"Everybody's bat crazy these days," Daisy muttered and closed the door. "Must be the moon."

***

Daisy spent her evening cleaning the rabbits and the grouse, and then pan-fried them on the little wood-burning stove pushed up against the cabin wall. Daisy picked the hot meat out of the pan, yelped, and licked her fingers before enjoying a tasty morsel.

"Clay, you're sure missing some good eats," she told him and shook her head.

She sat down, relished a hot meal, and then went outside. She built a fire to burn the bones and offal, and left it there to char.

By that time a long day of tramping over the mountainside was beginning to catch up to her, and she yawned and stretched, threw the bar across the cabin door and climbed up into the loft.

Chapter Thirty-Five

By two o'clock in the morning, the moon began to slip down from its zenith in the night sky. Its white light slanted through the window from the tops of the pines on the westward side of the cabin.

Daisy murmured in her sleep, turned towards the wall, and settled in. The only sound outside was the soft hum of crickets and the occasional full-throated *whoo* of a distant owl.

But another soft sound added to the forest ambience: a subtle scuffling sound just outside the door. A swiping noise, the subtle rustle of sticks falling, the sound of something small being knocked over.

Daisy rubbed her eyes, sighed, and turned over, facing towards the door.

The scuffling sound continued in the stillness and gradually intruded on her consciousness. She opened a bleary eye and frowned as it went on: a heavy shuffling, a soft grunt, the sound of something small and metallic falling onto the ground with a faint ring.

Then a sudden pandemonium exploded like a bomb just outside the window. There was a loud crash and the sound of frantic chickens clucking and flapping. It sounded like some big animal had knocked over the henhouse.

Daisy's eyes opened wide, and she sat bolt upright, heart pounding. She grabbed the sides of the ladder and came sliding down in one swoop.

One of Doc's shotguns was propped against the wall, and Daisy loaded it feverishly. Then she crept to the side window and peered out.

There was a huge, silvery shape in the moonlight, snuffling through the ashes of her fire. Electricity raced down Daisy's spine and tingled in her fingers and toes. It was Old Crunchy, there was no doubt, and he bit the head off one of her chickens as she watched.

She stared at him in disbelief. Even on all fours, he was half as tall as a man. The only living thing she'd ever seen as huge was a bull buffalo.

Daisy swallowed and clutched the gun. Clay had been right. She'd have no hope against that monster, maybe not even with a shotgun. If it charged her, she'd have one chance to get off a blast, and if it didn't hit the Grizzly in just the right spot, it probably wouldn't do more than make him mad.

She watched in awe as Old Crunchy suddenly stood up on his hind legs. He reared up above the cabin, practically blotting out the moon. He looked ten feet tall in the dim light, and the deep sound of him snuffing the air reminded Daisy of a blacksmith's bellows.

The bear suddenly came down on all fours, and the weight of his massive body shocked the ground with a *thump* that Daisy felt inside the cabin.

To her intense relief, the bear abruptly disappeared, but with a speed she could hardly believe, even though she'd seen it with her own eyes.

One instant he was there; the next he just—wasn't.

Daisy's mouth dropped open slightly. It was a good fifty feet from the cabin door, across the clearing to the cover of the trees, but Old Crunchy had done it in a split second. It boggled her mind that the big Grizzly could move that fast, but he had.

After she was sure the bear had gone, Daisy slid down the cabin wall and put a trembling hand to her mouth. She didn't know what she would've done if that monster had tried to break in. It would only have taken one swipe of the bear's massive paw to smash the cabin door all to splinters, and her only other way out would've been through the little window.

She'd gotten off lucky.

But she had to admit that the mess was her own fault. Clay had reminded her not to keep anything outside that would draw a bear, and she'd been careful to burn up the remains of their game but had forgotten about the chickens.

She knew she should go out and check on the henhouse; she knew she should search for any birds left alive, but there was no way she was stepping foot outside that cabin until the sun was in the sky.

Daisy set the shotgun carefully on the floor and pulled her hands over her face. For the first time in her life, she didn't feel safe in the cabin. Old Crunchy could come back at any time. There was no sure-fire defence against that monster, and no escape.

A vivid shudder worked up her back. She'd never forget the night Clay had first told her how Old Crunchy got his nickname. They'd been sitting over a campfire in the woods after a day of hunting. Clay had leaned toward her, and the firelight threw the planes of his face into stark relief.

"There was an old prospector worked a claim in the high country on the other side of this mountain," Clay had told her ominously. "Hadn't nobody heard from him in over a month, and when they went to check on him, they found his dead body outside his cabin. He'd been torn up something horrible, and one of his legs had been tore right off him, just below the knee."

She had shivered and glanced into the darkness surrounding them, and Clay went on: "And when they went searching around his cabin, they saw that monster Grizzly sitting in a clearing not a stone's throw off. They said his big fangs were solid red, and he was crunching a leg bone of some kind between his teeth—*crrrunch crrrunch crrrunch!*"

"All right, you told me. Let's move on," she'd complained, but Clay had grinned and added:

"There was only a few neighbours lived anywhere near the old man, and they didn't know him that well, so they decided he wasn't a close enough friend to get kilt over and went back to their own houses instead of goin' out to hunt that Grizzly.

"So Old Crunchy just kept gettin' bigger and bigger and bigger every year until now he's a high as a house, and got a mouth like a barn door, and fangs as long as your arm!"

And after having seen the bear herself, Daisy had to admit that Old Crunchy lived up to his legend. That thought was unsettling enough to keep her sitting against the cabin door, wide awake and staring until the eastern sky went pink with dawn. And though daylight offered her no special protection against Old Crunchy, she finally felt comforted enough to drag herself back up the ladder and collapse in her bed.

She fell asleep instantly and slept half the day away, and when she woke in the afternoon, some of the horror of the previous night had worn off.

***

Daisy climbed down the ladder, lifted the little burlap curtain, and peeked out the window. The henhouse was gone, and in its place was a litter of sticks scattered out all over the yard. Feathers were everywhere, and more than one dead bird was splayed out on the ground, but she saw no live ones.

Daisy pulled her mouth to one side. She couldn't blame those chickens for skinning out. If she was a chicken, and her henhouse had been attacked by a Grizzly, she'd still be running.

Daisy sighed, dipped her hands in a little wash bowl and splashed her face with water. She was going to have to clean all that mess up, and good, too, if she wanted to head off another nighttime raid.

She was going to have to get used to not having any eggs for breakfast too, it looked like because there was no point in setting it all back up again, just to bring that bear back down on her.

Daisy sighed, went to the front door, and opened it a crack. She scanned the yard and the trees beyond but saw nothing but ashes and feathers littering the ground.

Still, she reached for the shotgun before stepping outside and held it at the ready as she walked over the yard and around the side of the cabin.

The henhouse litter was an awful mess, and Daisy grumbled under her breath as she surveyed the damage. She'd have to get rid of the dead birds, burn up the splintered wood, and rake dirt over the ashes of her fire until not even the memory of grilled meat was left.

She raised her eyes to the trees and noticed that the bear had torn some of them with its claws. She tilted her head in disbelief as she counted off the distance—the marks were twelve feet above the ground. The bear's claws had hooked deep into the trunks and carved ragged gashes in the wood.

She gave the trees another wary glance as she walked around the back of the cabin and up the other side. The bear's massive paw prints were stamped deep into the grass and soft dirt around the cabin, and Daisy shuddered, thinking of how close the bear had come to her. The Grizzly had been just on the other side of the cabin wall as she slept, and if it hadn't knocked over the henhouse, she might never have known it was there at all.

Daisy arrived at the cabin door again and surveyed the yard and the trees. The golden beams of daybreak were flowing through the treetops, and dew glittered on the grass. It was going to be a pretty morning, and it was still cool.

Best to get started while it was still comfortable out.

Daisy glanced at the trees again. The morning breeze ruffled their leaves, and a pleasant scent of fir tinged the air.

She propped the shotgun up against the cabin wall, to be ready at a moment's notice, and she began to rake dirt over the campfire ashes. They had been scattered so widely that she was obliged to tear up most of the yard to cover them, and by the time she was finished, she was thirsty.

Daisy leaned the rake up against the cabin wall, picked up the shotgun in her right hand, and a bucket in her left, and went down to the creek to get water.

Daisy threaded her way carefully down the little bank to where an icy creek chattered over the rocks. She dipped the bucket in, looked warily all around her, and hurried back up the incline and back inside the cabin again.

Daisy put the gun on the table, lifted the bucket, and poured the icy water into a big clay jar. She took a big gulp before emptying the last of it and walked back outside to do her other chores.

There were four dead birds on the ground, and she was going to have to sack them all up and—

Daisy looked up, and a wave of horror swept over her as the huge Grizzly suddenly appeared in front of her. It smashed through the underbrush with an ear-shattering roar and reared up to the sky. In the same instant, she swung the shotgun up.

The next thing she knew, she was flying through the air and then rolling over the grass on the other side of the yard. The shotgun clattered onto the ground beside her in pieces.

Her head was swimming, but she looked up. The bear stood on its hind legs and towered over her like a tree, its massive jaws gaping. *Oh Lord*, was the only thing she had time to think; and then the bear came down.

Chapter
Thirty-Six

"My name's Suzy. What's your name?"

Emil turned to face the little pigtailed girl who had sidled up to him outside Hiram Heller's mercantile. He swept off his hat and bowed gallantly.

"I am delighted to make your acquaintance, *mademoiselle*," he told her. "My name is Emil Dubois, and I am entirely at your service."

The little girl blinked at him and smiled shyly. "I like your clothes," she told him, "but why are you so dressed up? Are you going to a wedding?"

"Not yet," he told her. "But I will soon."

"Oh, I see." She nodded. "It must be a real fancy wedding for you to slick up so fine. I've never seen a boy who looked so good in clothes!"

Emil raised his brows and shrugged. "These are from my hometown, New Orleans," he informed her and pulled out the end of his vest just enough so the little girl could feel the velvet material.

"*Ohhh.* That's beautiful."

"Do you live here, Suzy?"

"Oh yes. My pa is the doctor in town."

"What is there to do in this place? Do you have any

gaming halls, or pool rooms, or faro parlours?"

The little girl frowned. "What's faro?"

Emil stared at her, but his reply was interrupted by the arrival of another little girl, a freckled miss with blonde ringlets. She dimpled at him and then turned to his companion.

"Mornin', Suzy. Who's your friend?"

Suzy gave the little newcomer a frowning glance. "This here is Emil De ..." She gave Emil a frustrated glance, and he continued:

"My name is Emil Dubois. *Enchanté.*" He reached out and took the girl's palm lightly in his and lifted her hand to his lips.

The little blonde girl wiggled all over and laughed delightedly. "My name's Charlotte. Mighty pleased to meet you, Emil!"

Suzy put her hands on her hips and demanded:

"Why didn't you kiss *my* hand, Emil?"

Emil turned to her and extended his hand, and Suzy's frown cleared. She put her hand in his, and he lifted it to his lips.

"Isn't he just the beatenest thing?" Suzy giggled. "How long you been here, Emil?"

"Only a few days."

"Gonna be staying here?"

"I fear so."

Emil looked downcast momentarily and then reached inside his vest for a pack of cards. He took them out and shuffled them quickly as the girls looked on in awe.

"I will show you a magic trick." Emil shuffled the cards quickly and pulled out the ace of spades; shuffled them again and pulled it out again to their surprise; shuffled them a third time and pulled the ace again, to their laughter and clapping.

"You see? Magic."

Suzy looked down at the ground and twisted back and forth shyly. "Reckon you ain't got a girlfriend, have you, Emil?"

"I regret, no."

"I'd be glad to go out with you if you were to ask me," Charlotte volunteered, and Suzy scowled and cried:

"Why you selfish little heifer, I saw him first!"

Charlotte put her hands on her hips and retorted: "Didn't see *your* name on his forehead, Suzanne Williams!"

The two girls began to push each other, and things might have gone ill had Emil not cried: "Ladies! There is no need for unpleasantness. I have two arms."

He thrust out his elbows, and each girl looped her hand inside one of them.

Emil turned from one to the other and smiled, and as they passed, they attracted the attention of a group of frowning little boys who had congregated on the corner.

"Hey Suzy," one of them cried, "who's that fancy friend of yours?"

"His name is Emil, and he's from New Orleans," Suzy told him with a nod. "Brand new here, and my beau now—ain't that right, Emil?"

The little boy scowled at Emil. "Don't see nothing so wonderful about him," he scoffed.

"He's a man of the world," Suzy told him haughtily. "Not like some country boys round here who ain't never been out of town."

"He's my beau *too*," Charlotte was quick to remind them. "We're gonna share him!"

The little boy looked Emil up and down. "Why's your beau so duded up? Last time I saw someone dressed up like ol' Emil here, he was lyin' in a coffin," the boy scoffed, and his friends sputtered.

Emil straightened in outrage. "Here now!" he cried sharply, "I take exception! Do you apologize?"

The boy frowned at him. "Do I *what*?"

"Do you apologize?"

The little boy's expression hardened, and he stuck his jaw out. "Not a bit! You're dressed like a undertaker, and you talk funny, too!"

"Very well!" Emil replied and pulled a pair of gloves from his pocket. He walked up to the frowning boy and slapped him across the jaw with the little glove.

"I demand satisfaction!"

The other boy sputtered and stepped back. "Why'd you wipe my face, you fool? Was there a fly on my chin?"

Emil's green eyes flashed. "I would not be at all

surprised to learn you had insects!" he snapped, and the girls sniggered behind their hands. "I will meet you at dawn tomorrow, in this same place!"

"What's wrong with now?" the boy replied instantly. "I'll fight you right here! Put up your fists!"

Emil's lip curled. "I do not fight with my fists! I challenge you to a duel! Swords or pistols, sir?"

The little boy's eyes goggled. "Pistols? I ain't got no pistols!"

"Swords then!" Emil replied.

"I ain't got no swords either. Put up your fists!"

"Bah! I will choose," Emil declared and stalked out to the end of the wooden sidewalk. He pulled two narrow wooden balusters out of the sidewalk railing and produced a small knife from his pants pocket. He sharpened the ends of the wooden sticks as they watched, and when he was satisfied, he threw one to his antagonist.

"There!" Emil declared. "They are exactly the same! *En garde!*" He tucked his left hand behind his back and advanced on the boy with the pointed stick in his right.

"Be careful, Emil!" Charlotte cried and put her hands to her mouth, but Suzy jogged her friend in the ribs and asked:

"Ain't this *exciting?*"

***

The sound of children shouting in the street below made Kate's brows twitch together. She moved to the window of her hotel room and parted the curtains.

To her horror, she saw Emil and another boy fighting each other with sticks as a crowd of children circled them and shrieked encouragement.

"*Oh!*"

She gathered her skirts and hurried out of the room. She glided down the stairs and swept out into the street.

She took a moment to place Emil, and was about to sally forth to put a stop to the fight, but Doc's hand on her arm made her look up with a frown.

"Don't, Kate," he told her. "Let him fight his own battles."

"Neither of them should be fighting!" Kate replied indignantly. "They could get hurt!"

"Emil's going to have to fight those boys sooner or later. Do you see those two little girls on the sidewalk?"

Kate's eyes moved unwillingly to where Emil's new friends were cheering him on.

"He's already got two little girls on his string. That means a fight with the other boys," Doc told her softly.

"How do you know?" she demanded.

"I had the same problem all through my childhood," he drawled.

"I won't teach Emil that violence is the way to solve his problems!" Kate objected, but Doc smiled and put his arm around her waist.

"A little boy has to be raised differently than a little girl," Doc murmured in her ear. "Let them sort it out,

Kate."

He nodded towards the street, and Kate turned her eyes to where Emil and the boy were slapping the sticks against each other furiously. The little boy suddenly raised his stick and tried to beat Emil over the head with it, but Emil blocked the blows with his own stick, and then, with a lightning-fast flick of his wrist, swept the stick out of his opponent's hand and sent it spinning onto the ground.

Emil dived forward and touched his opponent's chest with his stick.

"*Touché!*" he cried. "Do you yield, sir?"

His opponent's answer was to take to his heels, and Emil pressed the stick to his nose and marched back to the sidewalk in triumph.

Doc laughed softly, and Kate pulled away from him to rush to her son, but when she reached him, she found he was not alone. He was basking in the adoration of his two female friends.

"I never saw anything like that in my whole life!" Suzy exclaimed. "You sure taught old Bobby Jordan a thing or two!"

"Oh, Emil, you were so brave!" Charlotte told him and put a hand on his arm. "I was so afraid for you!"

"A man of honour does not think about danger," Emil told her, and Kate put her hands on her hips.

"Emil, come with me," she told him, and extended her hand.

But instead, Emil turned to his female friends. "This is my mother Madame Katherine Dubois," he told them. "And these," he told her, "are my new *copines*, *mademoiselles* Suzy and Charlotte."

Kate raised an eyebrow and crossed her arms. "Hello," she said smiling. "It's very nice to meet you. But I'm afraid Emil must go now."

To her relief, Emil turned to his admirers, swept off his hat, bowed deeply, and murmured: "*Au revoir.*"

"Bye, Emil," they echoed and watched with round eyes as Kate took his hand and led him back inside the hotel.

Chapter
Thirty-Seven

The three of them had lunch in the café, and Kate was conscious that they had inspired a great deal of curiosity in the other diners. It was unusual that a mountain recluse and a sophisticate from New Orleans would keep company with each other.

Kate took a sip of tea and looked away as the other women assessed her gown of ivory-coloured brocade, the dark red lace at her throat and sleeves, and the ruby drop earrings that flashed and trembled with her every move.

They glanced at Emil, in his little high-collared jacket and velvet vest, and then at the newly-shaved Doc, wearing his linen shirt and homemade vest and breeches.

She usually didn't interrupt others, but when Doc began, "I want you to come to my house," Kate cleared her throat and interjected: "*En français, s'il vous plaît.*" She tilted her head slightly to the left, and Doc glanced over just in time to see a pair of older women turn back to their meals.

"I'd like you to come over to see the house I just bought," he went on in French. "I hope you'll stay with me until the wedding. It will be far more comfortable for you and Emil at my house than in that cramped little hotel."

Kate glanced over at the other tables. "Before we're

married? You've chosen a small town, Doc. Imagine the gossip it would invite!"

"What are you talking about?" Emil demanded in French, and Kate switched instantly to Creole.

"We have the children to think of, as well," she went on. "If we live here, they must eventually choose their friends and lovers in this place. For their sakes, we must observe the conventions."

"You're right," Doc conceded, with a contrite look. "I wasn't thinking. Forgive me."

Kate smiled up into his eyes. "For *anything*."

Doc reached out across the table, and Kate took his hand. But Emil pursed his lips and shook his head.

"This food is vile," he observed in French. "Must we always eat here?"

"Emil!"

"This coffee is undrinkable, even with milk and sugar. And this meat"—he poked it with his fork— "is as tough as an old shoe, and there is no sign of any dessert. When I think of the cakes and pies we had in Denver, I could cry."

Doc sputtered and lifted his own cup to his lips, but Kate gave her son an admonishing look.

"Emil, it is very rude to criticize your food at the table. Even if what you say is"—she glanced around her— "perfectly *true*, a gentleman never hurts other people's feelings."

"Very well, but my stomach has been hurt, and I think for good," Emil retorted and put his napkin down. "If we are to stay here, this problem must be solved."

"It is not for you to tell your parents what must be done," Kate replied firmly. "Now settle down, and eat your meal."

Emil sighed heavily and poked the meat again with his fork. They went on eating and talking softly, but a moment later, a commotion in the doorway of the café made them look up. Doc sat up straight and frowned because Clay was standing there, searching the room with his eyes. When he saw Doc, he hurried to their table.

"You've got to come with me," he gasped and bent over to catch his breath. "Something's happened to Daisy. I left her at the cabin the night before last, and I went to check on her this morning. She's gone, but there's bear marks all over the place, and her shotgun was thirty feet from the cabin door, emptied out and broke in two. It's Old Crunchy, Doc. Has to be!"

Doc sprang to his feet, and Kate put a hand on his arm. "What can I do, Doc?"

"Stay here with Emil," he told her.

"Where are you going?"

Doc turned to her. "I'm going up to the cabin to search for Daisy. I'll be back."

"Doc!"

But he and the Indian boy were already outside, jogging across the road, and they soon disappeared. Kate watched them go and then turned to Emil in confusion and dismay.

"Finish up your plate. We're going back to the hotel."

"Has that insane girl been eaten by a bear?"

"Hush, Emil!"

"You know, I ask myself, why do we stay in a place where it is possible to be shot before breakfast and eaten by bears?"

"Be quiet!"

***

Doc burst into the blacksmith's shop and told the startled owner, "We need two horses right now!"

The man looked up at him. "Out back," he replied frowning. "It's a dollar a—"

Two five dollar bills fluttered over the counter, and the two men were gone. The blacksmith glanced after them in confusion and followed slowly, wiping his hands.

But by the time he reached the corral, they'd already slapped bit and halter on the strongest of his horses, and were riding bareback out of the corral with shotguns and rifles slung over their shoulders. He watched as they turned the horses into the road, and then across it, out past the clapboard buildings and up towards the mountain.

"Hey!" he shouted after them, "they're not for mountain climbing!"

But the men had already urged the horses, and he watched helplessly as they galloped across the meadows back of the main street, and up into the cover of the trees.

Doc spurred his horse up the narrow trail that threaded through the trees. It was an hour's walk up to the cabin, but they could cut that time in half if they drove the horses.

His blood ran cold in his veins as he turned Clay's words over in his mind. Daisy was gone, and the shotgun was broken.

Broken.

He kicked the horse, and it surged up the rocky incline. He couldn't allow himself to imagine what might have happened. He had to keep focused, couldn't let his mind wander.

But it wandered anyway. He saw Daisy as she'd looked when he pulled her from the rubble of the avalanche. Her blonde hair had been caked with dirt, her eyes had been closed, and her breathing had been weak. She'd almost died that night because he hadn't known what to do.

She had laid there on the cot like a broken doll, and all he could do was watch by her bedside and hope that she'd make it.

That same sense of helplessness gripped him as he urged the horse through the trees. He should never have let Daisy stay up in that cabin by herself, should never have left her alone that long.

If he'd started earlier, if he'd taken some thought beforehand and not thrown Daisy into town life like throwing her into a pond, maybe she would've adjusted better. He'd been lazy and careless; he'd raised her like a boy because boy skills were what they needed.

What he'd needed.

He hadn't thought of Daisy and what she needed, not

really. All of this was his fault.

He pulled a hand over his mouth and blinked back tears. The thought of Daisy dying alone and terrified, up on the bare mountainside, while he was enjoying himself in town, made him almost desperate.

And if he found out that Daisy was dead, he was going to kill that God-cursed monster if he had to fight it with his bare hands.

He kicked the horse again.

***

They reached the cabin by mid-afternoon, and Doc threw himself down from his mount and burst into the cabin.

"Daisy?" he called raggedly.

"*Dase*?"

He found the cabin empty and turned to the yard. Just as Clay had said, the signs of the bear were everywhere. The paw prints stamped into the ground were as big as pie plates.

Clay knelt down in the grass. "The Grizzly came up from the creek," he said quietly, "and Daisy's footprints meet the bear's over by the chicken coop. There's no shell casings on the ground there, so she didn't shoot him. There aren't any more prints of hers going away."

He wiped a hand over his eyes and stood up again. "The bear's prints go across the yard fast, over to where the gun is." They walked across the yard, and Clay picked up the shotgun. The stock had been torn right off the barrel, and the trigger dangled in the air as Clay picked up the pieces.

"The bear stood up on its hind legs, and—"

"Stop!" Doc cried suddenly. "Stop it! I don't want to know."

Clay looked up at him and then looked down at his feet. They were silent a long time, and the wind ruffled the fir trees. Doc looked up at the sky, blinked, and nodded.

"Can you track the bear?"

Clay nodded grimly. "It's hard to miss him. He went back down to the creek, up the slope on the opposite side, and up into the high country."

Doc turned to look at him. "You don't have to come with me. But I'm going to go get that monster. I'm going to kill it if it's the last thing I do in this world!"

Clay's dark eyes met his. "I'll come with you."

Doc nodded. "I'm going to search around here for a while first, just in case Daisy's—somewhere near."

***

They searched the yard, and all around the cabin for a radius of a mile in all directions, but the broken shotgun and her footprints were the only clues that Daisy had been there. There was no other sign of human life anywhere to be seen. The ponderous bear's marks and prints dominated the landscape and left an unmistakable trail up the mountain.

They stopped for a while after, and Doc went inside the cabin to get a drink of water and to be alone. When he came out, Clay was seated cross-legged in the grass near the broken shotgun. Doc watched as Daisy's young friend slowly shaved off all his hair with a knife. When he'd finished, Clay lifted white feathers towards the sky, and chanted solemnly from deep in his chest, and for a long time.

Chapter
Thirty-Eight

The next morning, they rose with the sun and took off on foot across the creek, and up into the forest. The Grizzly's massive paw prints were stamped all over the soft mud of the creek bottom, and the signs of his passage were plain up the hill beyond. Torn branches, bent bushes, and now and then, scored tree trunks marked his sprawling trail over the mountain.

Clay kept a sharp watch, glancing all around as they made their way up under the tree cover, but Doc kept his eyes on the trail. He lusted for that monster's blood, and he was going to have it. Two rifles, two shotguns, and four bags full of shells would avenge Daisy's death, and he prayed, give him some sense of peace.

It was just beginning to dawn on him that they might never find her body, or worse, that they would find it in that monster's den. He couldn't allow himself to imagine that, and so he kept his eyes doggedly on the trail, clutching the rifle in his hands.

The trail climbed higher all that morning, winding up the mountainside, crossing and re-crossing creeks, and at one point, stopping in a patch of long grass. They paused to look at where the Grizzly had stopped to wallow on the ground; the grass was crushed down as if a covered wagon had fallen on its side.

They stopped to rest briefly, to take a drink from a stream, but were soon on their way again. The forests of the lower foothills were slowly giving way to high, open meadows, and beyond them, the forests of the high country, thick with firs and mountain pines.

Clay nodded towards a tree a few dozen feet ahead. The air was working alive with bees, and a ravaged honeycomb lay shattered and oozing on the ground.

"We're not far behind now," Clay murmured. "They're still stirred up. Look sharp."

"Let's split up," Doc told him, and Clay moved off a few hundred feet to the right as they passed the beehive on either side.

They moved silently through the trees, looking warily from left to right, moving slowly. The sun was climbing to noon, shining down through the thinning trees. They were approaching the crown of the mountain, and the ground was increasingly rocky. The oaks and aspens of the foothills had given way to towering pines and firs, but even they were becoming sparse. They were in bear country, and not far from the tree line.

Doc stopped for an instant to wipe his brow with his forearm. They'd been hunting all day, and while Clay was used to that, he wasn't anymore. He suddenly remembered Daisy telling him that he was over the hill, and sputtered, and then put his hand to his eyes and wept.

He swayed against his rifle. He'd lost the only companion he'd had in the years he'd spent in these mountains, his quirky, funny, tomboy daughter. No one but Kate understood him better or loved him more.

Now she was gone—lost forever—and it felt like half of his heart was gone, too. No matter how happy he and

Kate were together in the years to come, he'd lost his only daughter, and he'd never be right again.

"Oh, Daisy!" he moaned, "my Dase!"

Doc lifted his eyes and caught sight of Clay's shaved head glimmering through the trees off to the right. The boy wasn't one to wear his heart on his sleeve, but he was mourning openly now.

Maybe Daisy would've fallen in love with him, and maybe not. But they would never know, now.

Doc lifted frustrated eyes to the sky. It was obscene, a violation of the natural order, that an animal should rise up and kill a human. That it should kill a defenseless girl, who could do it no harm! It was strange and wrong; it was never meant to be.

But the monstrous, unthinkable thing had happened.

Doc wiped his eyes and took a new grip on his rifle. They were close now, and he had to stay focused. He had to kill the monster, wipe it off the face of the earth.

A sudden movement to his right made him turn his head. Clay had raised his arm and was pointing over to his left.

Doc turned quickly and stiffened. His eyes narrowed and his mouth twisted in deep hate. There it was, the hulking brute that had stolen his daughter's life and wrecked his own. It was a huge, honey-coloured mountain of hide and hair, watching them with small, close-set eyes from across an open space of about a hundred feet. The bear's ears went up, and it rose upright on its haunches.

Doc raised his eyes in disbelief as Old Crunchy reared

up—more than a thousand pounds of rippling muscle and sinew. His paws were monstrous and tipped with knifelike claws four inches long.

The thought of Daisy bleeding on the other end of those claws made Doc jerk his rifle to his shoulder. "Die, monster!" he screamed hoarsely and unleashed round after thunderous rifle round into the bear's chest.

He walked steadily forward, still firing, as the bear slammed back down on all fours and charged him. The grizzly opened its massive jaws and rushed at him like a freight train.

He heard Clay screaming "Shoot his eyes!" heard the boy's rifle firing blast after blast; then the bear was on him.

Doc emptied his last round right into the bear's face, and when the bear opened its jaws, he swung the empty rifle and smashed it across that massive head like a railroad hammer.

He could hear Clay's voice crying, fainter and fainter in the background. He was still yelling, and there was a sound like a shotgun going off, but even that faded, in the end.

Chapter Thirty-Nine

"Gideon! Gideon!"

Daisy woke to the sound of her own cries. She was semi-conscious, confused, and in pain.

A voice mumbled in the background on the other side of that jumping wall of pain. It rose and fell, and the meaning of its words danced just beyond her understanding.

"You shall lie down, and none shall make you afraid, and I will rid evil beasts out of the land."

Daisy turned her head restlessly. Strange visions flashed through her brain, mingling with the fire in her body. She didn't know if they were memories or dreams, but they splashed across her mind more vividly than anything she'd seen in the waking world.

The grizzly had towered above her, and she'd scrambled away just in time to dodge its crushing paws as they slammed down. The bear opened its maw and screamed at her, and the shock of the blast passed through her body and into the ground like the thunder from a passing train.

She'd curled up into a ball on the grass, with her arms folded over her head. She expected to be torn limb from limb, and when that didn't happen, she moved her arm just enough to look up through her hair.

There was a blinding flash like lightning, and when she looked again the bear was standing upright, and a strange man was wrestling with it. His hair was as long as a woman's and dazzling white. It flashed in the air around his head and rippled with blue fire. The grizzly and the man swayed back and forth as the fire branched down the man's back and raced into his arms. The man clamped his glowing hands over the bear's paws and shoved it away from her.

The grizzly roared, staggered back, and fought the air. Daisy watched in disbelief as the white-haired man threw himself against the bear's chest and pushed it away again. The blue fire pulsed through the man's body, gathered itself into a knot, and suddenly forked like lightning through his arms and hands and into the bear's chest. The grizzly screamed, twisted away, and went galloping into the cover of the trees.

Daisy watched in terror as the man with the floating hair turned around to look at her, but her mind was playing tricks on her. He was huge one moment, with burning hair and fiery eyes, and the next, he was a shrivelled old man with grey hair and bristling brows.

His appearance changed back again, and threads of fire ran up his arms as he lifted them to the sky, clasped them together over his head and cried: "I have done it!"

A white bolt from the sky answered. It struck the man, and his whole body burst into flame.

She'd goggled at his burning body in horror, then her eyes had rolled up in her head. She passed out; and even after she came to, what followed was a strange hallucination in which dreaming and waking swirled together in one long, confusing jumble.

***

Daisy groaned and grimaced in pain. Somebody was moving her.

An arm behind her head lifted her up into a half-sitting position, and something trickled down her throat. It was very bitter. Daisy coughed, and the arm lowered her back down again.

The voice went on muttering, and this time she was able to catch a word or two before they floated away on the soft stream of sound.

"Do not fear, for I am with you; do not be dismayed, for I am your God. I will strengthen you and help you; I will uphold you with my righteous right hand."

With that, hands settled gently on her head, and warmth radiated slowly down from the crown of her head, through her neck and chest, and thighs, down her legs, to the soles of her feet. The warmth eased her sore muscles, and her pain gradually faded. An overwhelming weariness closed over her like warm water, and Daisy sighed and slipped down beneath its soothing wave into a deep sleep.

***

When Daisy woke, she gradually became aware that she was lying on a cot in a tiny cabin. Blankets covered her, and a pillow supported her head.

She wrinkled her nose. There was a faint scent of smoke in the air, even though it was high summer, and the fireplace was cold. The cabin was dark and small and empty except for her, but there were signs that whoever lived there wasn't going to be away for long. There was a half-eaten loaf of bread on the table, a piece of cheese, and a cup of steaming coffee.

Daisy tried to sit up, winced, and fell back again. Her ribs felt cracked, at the very least. Her whole midsection was sore, and pain jabbed her every time she drew a breath.

Her eyes moved uneasily around the little cabin, from the little fireplace to the plain wooden table to the dried herbs hanging from the ceiling, and her heart jolted against her ribs. She recognized the place now. She was in the Prophet's cabin, and after the weird things she'd seen, she wasn't sure she was any safer with that strange old codger than she'd been with the bear.

That fiery man couldn't have been real, but the sight of him had given her the scare of her life, and she was still shook up bad. If she could, she would've skunk out of that cabin like a scalded cat and kept on running until she was back in town and hid up under a bed someplace, but she was busted up, and couldn't walk, much less run.

She pushed her hair back from her face. She still felt groggy and sick, but it was a miracle she was alive. She was thankful for that.

But she would've been more thankful someplace else.

Daisy shuddered, remembering that unearthly face, with its fiery eyes and floating hair, and the old ghost of her childhood—the fear that the Prophet might be a lot more than he looked—reappeared and laid a cold hand on her shoulder.

Everything he'd told her had come true so far, and when she was a kid she'd once seen him stop a lightning bolt with his bare hand. The fear that she'd witnessed yet another heavenly apparition spurred Daisy to fling off the blanket and throw her feet onto the floor, but the effort made her yell with pain, and she fell back on the cot, gasping.

She closed her eyes and pulled her hands through her hair. There was no escaping the Prophet's lair, at least not for the moment.

She was stove up, and there was nothing she could do about it.

***

When an hour and more passed, and the Prophet didn't return, Daisy became restless. She was starting to get hungry, and while her fear of the old man kept her from reaching for his dinner, she couldn't help it if she wanted to.

Her eyes roamed over the rest of the little cabin. There was very little in it; just a few sticks of furniture, a few pots and pans for the fire, some hunting guns, and a few furs to throw over the cot when it got cold.

But after a while, Daisy noticed a little shelf above the cot, halfway up the wall. It had only one thing on it—a big black book.

Daisy frowned and reached for it. The book looked strangely familiar.

The front cover read: *The Holy Bible*, in fancy gold script with a lot of swirls, and Daisy caught her breath in amazement because she remembered this book. It had belonged to her parents and had been her mother's special treasure.

Daisy frowned as she opened it, and resentment and confusion flared in her. How had that old man gotten his hands on her mother's Bible when she herself didn't have one scrap to remember her parents by?

Daisy opened the book and pressed her hands over the front pages reverently. Those pages were full of the names of family members written in her mother's neat hand. Their family name was Jansson, and her mother had told her that their grandparents on both sides had come from Sweden. Their names had been recorded in blue ink, these people she'd never known: Karl and Inga Jansson, and Leif and Ola Engstrom, and their children.

Her mother used to hold her on her lap at night and tell her about them, and then her mother read to her out of this book.

She hadn't thought about it for years. Gideon—Doc—wasn't at all a religious man, and the memory of this book, and the stories her mother had read to her out of it, had faded.

Daisy swiped her nose with the back of her hand. She was already pretty shook up, and to see this book now brought back powerful memories. Much of her early life had faded, but she remembered her mother's bright blonde hair, and blue eyes, and pink cheeks; and her soft voice and hands.

She turned the pages and smiled at the once-familiar pictures of strangely dressed men with turbans and flowing robes, and barefoot women with veils over their faces and bracelets on their arms.

She flipped from one picture to another. There was an angry-looking old man holding a pair of stone tablets over his head; a barefoot boy sitting down on the ground, surrounded by sheep; a beautiful queen bowing before the king, and an old man standing in a pit full of lions.

She turned to the pictures in the back of the book.

The first picture called up a smile because it had been one of her favourites. It was of a smiling young man surrounded by children. The caption read: *Let the little children come to me.*

"Well, you must be feeling better."

Daisy jumped and slammed the book shut. The old man had snuck up on her and was standing in the doorway. She stared at him warily and said nothing.

She followed him with her eyes as he walked in, slung a pack from off his shoulder, and threw it down on the table. "I guess you're hungry by now. I've got some smoked meat, and bread, and cheese. Enough for a sandwich if you want one."

When she didn't answer, he added: "I've got water and coffee if you're thirsty."

He glanced over at her and nodded. "See you found my book."

To her own amazement, Daisy replied angrily: "This ain't your book. It belonged to my mother. How come you got it? How'd you get hold of it?"

The old man shrugged and lifted a piece of bread to his mouth. "I found it lying on the mountain," he told her.

Daisy scowled at him. "Found it? You would've had to dig it out from under ten feet of dirt, mister," she replied, "and there ain't a grain of sand, nor a mark one, on it!"

The man's bright blue eyes flashed at her from under his bushy eyebrows, and a thrill of fear snaked down Daisy's back. She closed her mouth and watched him in silence as he assembled a sandwich on the rough wooden table.

"I'm going out again, so I won't be here to fix your dinner for a while," he told her. "You better go ahead and eat."

He put the sandwich and a dried apple on a plate, and filled a cup with water, and set them both on the floor beside her. Then he lifted the pack and slung it over his shoulder again.

"I'll be back later."

To Daisy's deep relief, he walked out on those words, and the cabin door slammed shut behind him. Daisy closed her eyes and tried to slow her heart down because it was jerking in her chest.

But the old man was gone, and she was going to call it good enough.

She reached for the plate and put the sandwich in her mouth. It wasn't bad, and she was hungry, so she gobbled it and the apple up and washed them down with the water.

She felt much better afterwards. The food put heart into her. Her fear faded a bit, and she started to feel more like her old self.

Because she'd already decided that she wasn't going to wait for the Prophet to come back. She was going to hightail it and do her best to never meet that old man again.

And she was taking her mother's Bible with her.

Daisy tried to sit up, and this time the pain was more manageable. She took her mother's Bible, crammed it down inside her shirt, and tucked her shirt into her breeches. Then she threw the blanket off and leaned over to grab a walking stick propped by the door. She took one of the thinner blankets, folded it into a thick pad, stuck it under her arm, and pinned it there with the stick.

When she tried to stand, the heavy Bible flopped down to her stomach and threatened to pop her shirt open. But she pressed her left arm under it as she braced the stick with her left hand and swung it with her right.

It only took her a few tries to learn how to walk with the stick, and fifteen minutes later she was limping her way down from the high crag the cabin perched on. Soon she disappeared into the forest, and a bright-eyed hawk, sitting on the limb of a huge fir tree, was the only one to see her go.

It jumped into the air, spread its big wings, and soared silently overhead as Daisy stumped doggedly down the forest trail below.

Chapter **Forty**

"Doc?"

Clay threw his shotgun down and scrambled to where Doc lay splayed out on the ground. The dead grizzly lay not ten feet beyond, its massive head bloody with rifle and shotgun blasts.

Clay put his hand on the older man's chest. There was no heart beat that he could feel.

Clay grimaced. "*Doc?*" He shook Doc's shoulder, but he was afraid to touch his head. It was tilted back at a strange angle, chin to the sky.

He had watched in horror as the grizzly charged Doc. It was over in a heartbeat, and even though they'd both pumped the bear full of leads, Old Crunchy hadn't fallen until he'd swiped Doc forty feet back and five into the air. The older man had landed hard on the rocky ground and rolled for a long way, but even so, the bear was on him instantly.

He'd blasted the bear on the run with double-aught buck, and only then had it slumped to the ground. The monster hadn't gotten a chance to savage Doc, and that was a mercy, but it might not matter, after all.

Doc's neck looked like it was broken.

Clay leaned back on his heels and looked up at the sky. His eyes were dazzled with tears, and he shook his head in silent misery.

He wiped his face with his hand, and as he did, he caught a slight motion out of the corner of his eye. He turned, and to his surprise, an old man was standing under the trees about fifty feet away.

"Hey!" Clay jumped up and waved his arm. "Help me! This man's been mauled by a bear!"

But the old man just stood there looking at him, and Clay frowned and yelled again. "Can you help me? I think his neck may be broken!"

A faint noise made him turn back quickly, and to his joy and amazement, Doc opened his eyes and groaned.

Clay scrambled over on his hands and knees. "Doc? Can you hear me? Don't move!"

The older man writhed in pain. "Clay, is that you?" he whispered.

"Yes. Be careful not to move. You've probably got broken bones. I'll ask the old man if he can help us."

But when he turned to look, the old man was gone. Clay stood up and shaded his eyes, but there was no sign of him. Clay scowled, wondering what kind of man could turn his back on a life and death crisis, but he didn't get long to fume.

Doc was mumbling, "We got him, didn't we?"

Clay turned towards him and knelt down again. "Yeah, we got him."

He scanned Doc's body. His hands were clenching weakly, and that was a good sign, but his legs were still. He bit his lip, wondering how he was ever going to get Doc down off that mountain. He could go back for the horses and build a drag sled, but it would be dark before he could get back, and he didn't want to leave Doc alone and lying so close to a carcass, after nightfall. There were wolves and pumas and many other bears in that wilderness.

Clay rubbed his jaw. Maybe he could build a sled and pull Doc down the mountain himself. It wouldn't be easy, but at least it would be downhill most of the way. Once they reached the cabin, he could put Doc into his bed and go for the doctor.

Daisy would've wanted Doc to survive, more than anything, and so Clay was determined to give it his best.

He turned to Doc. "Doc, I'm going to build a sled and pull you down to the cabin. I want you to lie quiet while I do. Don't try to move, okay?"

Doc closed his eyes and nodded.

Clay gave him a worried glance and hurried off to the trees. He had a hunting knife, and he used it to break and saw limbs for the sled. He didn't bother to shape them and left the branches trailing. He didn't have time for more than the crudest sort of frame.

They had to get down off the mountain before nightfall.

It took him thirty minutes, but he managed to make a long frame for Doc to lie on that would keep him flat and above the ground. He'd left the limbs long at the head of the frame, so he could push it along. He'd lashed many bushy pine branches underneath to serve as crude runners and shock absorbers.

The rig was very simple, but it would have to do, and

he prayed that it would be enough.

Clay pushed the sled up beside Doc and looked down at him in doubt. It was risky to move him, but he had no choice.

Clay knelt beside Doc and took the older man in his arms. Doc was a tall, broad-shouldered man, and he was very heavy, but Clay gritted his teeth and lifted him just long enough to drop him onto the sled.

The motion made the older man cry out in pain, and Clay looked down at Doc in dismay as he slumped on the rough wooden sled. A fringe of blond hair covered his eyes, and his head lolled over on his chest. He was so still that Clay grabbed his wrist to check for a pulse.

To his relief, it was still there, but Doc had passed out.

Clay retrieved the guns and the bag of shells and slung them over his shoulder. Then he grabbed the limbs of the sled, took a deep breath, and began pushing it downhill. It was a brutal, jolting ride over rocky terrain, and Clay couldn't help thinking that maybe things had worked out lucky after all. Maybe Doc was better off unconscious.

It was going to be a real bumpy ride down the mountain.

***

By sundown, Clay had dragged the sled two-thirds of the way down to the cabin. It had been slow going and hot work, and he was exhausted.

He stopped to pull his forearm across his brow and to catch his breath. His muscles were screaming, and he was winded from the violent bouncing of the sled down the steep slopes. Doc probably weighed close to two hundred pounds, and it was hard to keep control of the sled on sharp descents. More than once he'd almost lost control of it.

He looked down at Doc. If Doc had come to at any point on the ride, he'd probably passed right back out again, and Clay bit his lip when he thought about what the bouncing ride was doing to his passenger.

But he didn't have the time to worry about it for long. The sun was going down, and he had to get back to the cabin while he still had the light.

Clay pushed on, and to his relief, they'd left the worst and hardest terrain behind. The ground was becoming softer and more level as he pushed the sled down into the forests just above the cabin. He figured he had about twenty more minutes of twilight and made a hard push to close the distance in time.

The sled suddenly snagged on a rock, and Clay cursed savagely and yanked the sled free. As he wrestled with it, a sound came floating down from the slopes above them that froze his blood and made him straighten in dismay.

It was the sound of hunting wolves, howling and baying to one another on the mountain above.

Clay scanned the rocky slopes behind them and licked his lips. There was no chance he could outrun a pack of wolves with the sled, and he refused to put Doc at their mercy.

Clay threw the shotgun off his shoulder and loaded it feverishly. He looked back and around them, but there was as yet no sign of pursuit.

He glanced ahead, and there was a flat rock shelf above a small creek that would protect his back and give him the high ground. The rock face behind was too high and too sheer for a wolf to jump down, and the shelf was well above the creek, and flat and broad enough for Doc to lie on.

The only question was whether he could get Doc up there in time.

A shuddering howl floated down on the wind, and Clay threw the shotgun strap over his head and pushed the sled as hard and fast as he could. It jounced savagely, but Clay didn't stop even when a loud groan demonstrated that Doc was coming back around.

He reached the foot of the rock face and gauged the distance with his eyes. The shelf was twelve feet up the cliff, and not easy to climb. He'd have to carry Doc on his back all the way up the wall—two hundred pounds of dead weight.

An approaching chorus of yips and slavering growls settled the matter for him. Clay shot a worried glance behind them, and to his horror, the first wolf burst from the cover of the dusky trees and paused at the edge of the clearing.

Clay knelt beside the sled. "Sit up, Doc," he urged and reached around his shoulder. "I'm going to hurt you, but I can't help it. We have to get up that cliff. We're being hunted."

Doc frowned and glanced over Clay's shoulder. The sight of three wolves, watching them with glowing yellow eyes, made his own widen.

"Do what you have to," he whispered, and Clay took a deep breath and slung him over his shoulder.

Doc's head rolled back in agony, and his scream echoed in the trees as Clay staggered under his weight and clawed his way up the rocks.

Clay climbed slowly up the cliff, hand over hand, his face contorted in pain, and they both swayed dangerously as the wolves burst from the trees and exploded across the creek towards them.

Doc watched grimly as a bristling black wolf splashed through the creek and gathered itself to leap onto Clay's back and pull them both down to their death. His face twisted, but he snatched a pistol out of his shirt, lifted it, and fired so quickly that, had anyone witnessed it, it would have seemed that he was throwing the gun away.

The wolf was shot down mid-leap and jackknifed into the water and thrashed horribly. The others flared off into the trees temporarily, and Clay struggled heavily to pull them higher up the cliff.

Chapter
Forty-One

Kate took Emil's hand and led him down the street from the café to the hotel. The little boy tipped his hat gallantly to every female they happened to pass, regardless of age, and Kate noticed, with some alarm, that Emil was fast becoming the darling of Wolf Table. Even elderly women who raised their eyebrows at her elegant clothes, and young wives who pulled their husbands sharply sideways when she passed, beamed with transparent delight when Emil bowed and smiled:

"*Bonjour, belles femmes*! It is a lovely morning, is it not?"

It was a welcome distraction from her worry about Doc. She hated the idea of Doc going into the wilderness to hunt wild animals, and she hated to think what it would do to him if Daisy was really hurt, or even …

She closed her eyes and refused to let herself imagine it: but she wouldn't have a moment's peace until Doc returned with his errant daughter in tow.

That was the only outcome she would allow herself to contemplate.

To her surprise, as they strolled down the street, the train rolled around the bend, belching steam and sounding a long, loud whistle blast as it barrelled towards town.

"Well! The railroad has opened the line at last," she murmured, and Emil looked up at her.

"*Bon*! Now we can go to Cheyenne to have dinner," he suggested. "Perhaps the cooks *there* will show us mercy."

Kate looked around in embarrassment and leaned down to hiss: "What did I tell you about that?"

She pulled him onto the wooden sidewalk in front of the hotel, and they paused outside the door to watch as the train pulled into the tiny depot, belching steam. To Kate's surprise, a group of men stepped out onto the platform. The first was a reporter, who took a picture of the group with a bang and a flash.

The men were all dressed very elegantly, and one in particular seemed to be the centre of attention. Kate's mouth fell open slightly, and she instantly swept Emil into the lobby.

"What's going on?" Emil objected as she hustled him up the stairs. "Has that evil breakfast overpowered you?"

Kate opened the door and pushed him inside. "Quickly!" she commanded, and slammed the door shut and locked it.

"What's the matter?" Emil demanded.

Kate moved to the window and lifted the corner of the curtain. Through the sliver of window, she watched as Judge Carter and several other men laughed and posed for the camera.

"*Le maudire*! What the devil is he doing here?" she murmured.

Emil climbed up on a chair beside her and peeked out

the window. "Who are those men, and why do you stare at them?"

Kate nodded towards them. "You see the stocky one, with the red hair?"

"Certainly."

"His name is Judge Carter," she told him, in a low voice. "Doc and I knew him once. He is a very bad man."

Emil lifted his chin and regarded the group of men with a kindling eye. "I shall challenge him to a duel," he declared.

Kate laughed and hugged him. "You would certainly triumph," she assured him. "But I do not require that you defend my honour today. We will wait here and play cards until they go away."

Emil jumped down from the chair and set a small table out in the middle of the room. "Shall I deal, or shall you?" he asked.

"You may deal today," Kate murmured and glanced out the window again. She watched in rising alarm as the men walked down from the platform and crossed the street, coming straight for their hotel. She recalled that she had signed into the hotel under her real name; and while she didn't believe that Judge Carter would look at the ledger or spend the night in such a dowdy place, his nearness made her very uneasy.

She could clearly hear his gravelly voice downstairs, and Emil lifted his head and piped: "Is that him?"

"Hush," Kate murmured and listened intently. She hadn't heard Judge's voice for years, but it was every bit as unsettling as it had been. It was the voice of a brute, a violent man hiding behind a civilized veneer.

Judge Carter had hired an assassin to murder Doc and had almost been successful. Judge deserved to be hung on the courthouse square, but instead he was riding to Denver in triumph to open the latest in his empire of gaming halls.

Kate set her mouth in frustration and anger. Life was unfair. She had often observed it, but not until then had she felt the sting of that truth.

The sound of her little son's voice called her back to the present.

"I'm ready," Emil told her, and Kate let the curtain fall and joined him with a smile.

But she wasn't at ease until the train whistle sounded again. She put her cards down and moved to the window, and she was only comforted when she saw Judge climb back onto the train and ride away.

Even so, she couldn't be still, wondering why Judge had come to Wolf Table; and after she and Emil had finished their card game, she drifted downstairs and engaged the manager with a smile.

"I heard voices," she told him. "Will there be new guests here in the hotel?"

The man's voice sounded excited. "I still can't believe it," he told her. "I shook hands with that nabob, Judge Carter, the man who owns the Lucky Seven down in Denver! They're having their grand opening this week, and he's touring the towns all up and down the Denver line. He had his picture taken right here in my hotel! He gave me this advertisement with his own hands!"

"How thrilling," Kate murmured. "May I see it?"

The manager handed her an advertisement. There was an engraving of a tall, elegant building, and underneath it, ten lines of copy. The advertisement was emblazoned in bold red letters:

GAMING MAGNATE JUDGE CARTER OPENS THE LUCKY SEVEN.

BIGGEST AND BEST CASINO EVER TO OPEN IN THE MILE HIGH CITY.

FOUR FLOORS OF FARO, POKER, ROULETTE AND BLACKJACK IN THE MOST ELEGANT QUARTER OF TOWN.

GOURMET CHEFS FROM NEW ORLEANS AND A FINE FRENCH RESTAURANT ON PREMISES. FULL BAR OPEN ALL NIGHT.

LADIES WELCOME; ONLY THE HIGHEST CLASS CLIENTELE, AND STRICT SECURITY FOR A SAFE AND PLEASANT EXPERIENCE.

PRESENT THIS HANDBILL FOR A TEN PER CENT SAVINGS ON YOUR FIRST SPORTING WAGER.

"Ain't it a dandy?" the man exclaimed. "I can't wait to go down there and see it. My brother-in-law works in Denver, and he says the building takes up a whole block. It's like a palace!"

"Hmm," Kate murmured. "But isn't it considered unwise to gamble, *monsieur*? Is there not a—criminal element, in such places?"

The man stared at her, nonplussed. "Oh—oh yes, ma'am," he mumbled. "Should've known better than to show this thing to a lady! I sure didn't mean to offend you."

"Oh, I am not offended; I understand perfectly! But one must be careful in a big city like Denver," she replied sagely. "There are many ways to lose one's principles. And one's money. I hear that not all the dealers in such places can be trusted."

"Is that a fact, ma'am?"

"Oh yes. I knew a man once who believed that he lost twenty-five thousand dollars to a suspect poker dealer."

"Twenty-five thousand dollars!"

"Yes. He was very inconvenienced." She handed the advertisement back to him. "A word to the wise, *monsieur*."

"Yes ma'am."

Kate nodded and made her way back up to her room, but once her face was turned away, she arched an eyebrow and curled her lips up just a *tiny* bit.

Chapter
Forty-Two

"What is it about that big blond man that you like so much, Kate?" Emil demanded with a frowning look. "I have considered it well, and I still cannot understand why you agree to marry him.

"True, he looks much better now that he no longer has whiskers like a goat. He has more respectable clothes. But he is not a man of fashion, and he has no money and no plantations."

Kate sat down in a little chair, smoothed out her dressing gown, and stared down at her son as he sat in the hotel tub, surrounded by clouds of soap bubbles.

She clasped her hands together and pursed her lips. "Well, let me see," she mused. "Doc is very handsome."

Emil frowned and conceded: "He looks much better now, than he did."

"Doc is very, very intelligent."

"Why then does he live in this rude place?"

"He has his reasons."

"You will have to buy his clothes and his food. He lives in a cabin."

Kate sighed. "Doc is very well off. He owns a nice

house, just out of town. We'll all go to see it when he comes back."

Emil turned his frank green eyes on her. "Perhaps you like him because he wears scent. Though it's astonishing that a man who lives at the end of the world should take thought for it."

Kate's mouth quivered, and she sputtered out a soft laugh. "Doc was wearing bay rum, from the barber's," she told her son. "It's customary for a man to have bay rum applied to his face after he receives a shave.

"But you may be right," Kate told him, her eyes twinkling. "It's easy to be bewitched by the scent of a man's aftershave. It is very pleasant."

"May I go to the barber's and also get aftershave?"

Kate shook her head. "No. You are far too young, and you are already quite enough of a temptation to women."

Emil considered this. "That is true." He nodded. "One must be responsible."

Kate reached for a basin of warm water and poured it carefully over his head. "Now be still while I wash your hair. I want to get your bath finished and get you dressed for bed. You should have been asleep an hour ago."

"I am not at all sleepy. Why should I go to bed so early? We never go to bed before midnight!"

Kate paused in the act of soaping up his hair. A pang of conscience pierced her heart.

"We're going to stop staying up so late," she murmured in a stricken tone.

"I don't mind at all," Emil assured her. "Gamblers stay up very late, *n'est-ce-pas?*"

"Yes. But you are a little boy, not a gambler, and little boys go to bed long before midnight."

***

After his bath, Kate bundled Emil up in his little pajamas and his housecoat and took him back to his room. She tucked him into bed and pulled up the covers.

"It's too early to go to bed," Emil told her. "You promised to show me how to cheat at cards!"

"I promised to show you how to *detect* a cheat!" Kate replied in a shocked tone. "I'm surprised at you, Emil! If I find out you've been using this to cheat at cards, I won't teach you anymore!"

"Very well," Emil sighed. "But I think it would be very amusing to cheat at cards! One would have to be bold and clever."

"One would have to be wicked and very foolish," Kate retorted briskly. "On the *Natchez Queen,* a cheat was thrown overboard and had to swim in the river to save his life—if he could."

"What if he couldn't swim?"

"Then it was very sad," Kate replied in a grave tone.

Emil digested this. "Very well," he said at last. "I shall not be a cheat at cards after all if I must be thrown into a river."

"You relieve me."

"Will you show me the trick now?"

Kate sighed, gave him a wry look, but reached for a deck of cards lying on the bedside table. She took the pack in her fingers and quickly dealt two hands.

"I am cheating. What am I doing?"

The little boy's bright eyes followed her hands as they flicked cards onto the table.

"Watch closely," Kate told him, and Emil followed her hands with his eyes. But even after three deals and reshuffles, he had to frown and shake his head.

"I can't see it."

Kate smiled, reshuffled the deck, and dealt a fourth time, slowing her hands as they moved back and forth.

Emil sat up straight and cried: "You're lifting the deck up off the table! I can see the edge of the cards!"

Kate smiled at him. "That's right. The dealer is allowing the players to see the cards. Do you know what this is called?"

Emil stared at her in fascination and shook his head.

"It's called rolling the deck. It can happen if the dealer is in league with one of the players or merely because he is careless."

"Show me another one!"

"All right." Kate shuffled the cards again and so quickly that the motion of her fingers was all but impossible to see. Then she set the squared deck neatly on the table.

"I just cheated. What did I do?"

Emil looked up at her face, smiled, and shook his

head.

"Watch again. This is called stacking the deck."

***

Kate showed Emil trick after trick until eventually his eyelids began to droop. Kate looked down at her little son in knowing love as he finally succumbed to sleep, and she put the pack of cards away.

She leaned over, kissed his brow, and rose to go to her own room. When she had closed the door behind her, she turned down the lamp and walked to the open window.

A cool evening breeze flowed in and ruffled the curtains, but Kate frowned as she stared out at the early stars burning in the sky.

Doc hadn't returned.

As long as she was busy with Emil, she could squash down her worry, but now that Emil was asleep, her worry came roaring back.

Doc had gone up the mountain to hunt a dangerous animal, one that might or might not have killed his daughter. Kate blinked back tears and shook her head.

She wanted to go to Doc so badly that her heart ached in her chest. If the worst had happened, he would need her.

But it was impossible for her to follow Doc. She had to stay with Emil, and she had no way to know where Doc and his friend had gone.

She didn't even know where Doc's cabin was.

Kate looked up into the sky again and questioned it with her eyes. She was tempted to pray, but instead, she turned her eyes to the black crags beyond the town and sent Doc her love—hoping that somehow, he would feel it and be comforted.

Chapter
Forty-Three

"To Lady Luck!"

Judge Carter lifted a glass of champagne, and a chorus of soft laughter filled the compartment of his private train car as his guests echoed:

"Lady Luck!"

Judge took a sip and set his glass down on the elegant poker table. "I'd like to extend my personal invitation to all my distinguished guests here"—he lifted the glass again, to more laughter—"to join me at the opening of the Lucky Seven this Friday evening. And as a token of my gratitude to the leaders of this beautiful and forward-looking city, you are all welcome to play and dine at the Seven as much as you like this weekend—on the house!"

This proclamation was greeted by more laughter and happy murmuring. Judge took another sip of champagne and tilted his head to listen as one of the most prominent businessmen in the city whispered:

"Any *entertainment* included in that invitation, Mr Carter?"

Judge nodded and murmured: "The Seven has a fifth floor, Mr Jenkins." He smiled. "I'll have one of my attendants give you a key."

"Thank you very much indeed, Mr Carter." The man returned the smile. "I'm sure I'll be a regular!"

The scenery outside the car gradually slowed and then came to a complete halt as the train pulled into its next stop, the tiny town of Indian Rock. The door to the car opened and a nattily-dressed young man walked in and whispered in Judge's ear.

Judge nodded, stood up, and told the room of partygoers: "Excuse me, friends. Duty calls!"

Laughter filled the room again as Judge and a knot of attendants stepped outside onto the little train platform. A reporter hurried down the steps and set up a bulky camera as the townsfolk watched in wonder.

Judge called down to the man impatiently.

"Hurry up! We have to be done here within twenty minutes!"

The young man lifted a stick with a long tray atop.

"Look this way, gentlemen!"

Judge adjusted his vest, and all the men looked down. There was a flash of light and a loud bang, and some of the bystanders gasped.

This seemed to be some sort of signal, and young men exited from the train car and quickly dispersed into the crowd, passing out handbills.

A small group of young men stood leaning against a fence, watching the train and the hubbub. Two of them were teenagers; one dark, and one fair. The third was in his early twenties, with a dark, serious look and a fringe of shining brown hair that fell over his eyes. As one of the attendants walked past, the brown-haired young man called to him.

"Let me see that."

He reached for a handbill and read it with a frowning expression. The two boys looked over his shoulder curiously.

"What does it say, Will?"

"It's an advertisement for a casino," the young man answered and tore the paper in two. He threw away the pieces, and they fluttered to the ground.

"Why'd you tear it up?" the blond boy asked. "Ain't you curious what it is?"

"I already know what it is," Will told him. "It's a place that'll help you throw a going-away party for your money. I've been to many-a place like it."

"But the paper said you get a discount!" Jeremy objected.

Will gave him a quick look. "Sucker bait."

He walked off on the words, and the darker boy leaned against the fencepost and laughed. "I could've told you that, Jeremy," he grinned and lifted his cleft chin mockingly. "But you couldn't win there even if it *was* on the up and up. You got the worst poker face in the world. A girl could skin you!"

This sparked a fight, and the two of them scuffled with one another, pushing each other's faces and taking an occasional swing.

"It's the truth!" the darker boy laughed and then took off running, followed hotly by his outraged companion.

After they left, Judge raised his hands and called to the people standing curiously on the street.

"Good afternoon, folks!" Judge called in his gargling

voice. "My name is Judge Carter, and I've come by today to invite you to my new casino down in Denver, the Lucky Seven. Our grand opening is this Friday, and to celebrate, the first five hundred people to come through the doors get a free meal at my brand new French restaurant, and free drinks at the bar!"

There as a surprised murmur as the townsfolk turned to one another, eyebrows raised, and arms crossed.

"Come on down and see us this weekend." Judge smiled. "Tell the doorman that Judge sent you and get a twenty dollar chip to spend at any table in the casino!"

A scowling grandmother watched him from far back in the crowd and yelled: "God'll judge you, all right, you card slicker! I had to raise my kids alone because my man gambled away all our money in a place like yours—and then shot himself when he sobered up and saw what he'd done! Them God-cursed gamblers didn't show him no mercy—they took him for everything we had, even when they saw he couldn't help himself! *Pah!*"

She spat on the ground and then turned and walked away, and the crowd watched her go in goggling silence.

Judge adjusted his shoulders and pasted on a smile. "Remember folks, tell the doorman Judge sent you, and get a free twenty dollar chip!"

He smiled, waved, and abruptly disappeared back into the train car.

But he slammed one of his attendants against the wall of the narrow corridor and ignored another when he tried to ask a question.

"Somebody should put that old hag out of her misery!" he growled and shot a resentful glance out through the car window.

As he stood there, a small, wizened man swam through the crowded corridor and took him by the arm. Judge gave the old man a freezing look, but the newcomer only smiled.

"Long time, no see, eh Judge?"

"I don't know you," Judge told him coldly and shook the older man off. "Get out of my way. I have to get back to my guests!"

"Why, of course you know me, Judge!" the man answered, undeterred. "I'm Broadway Bobby, remember? I used to be a regular on the *Natchez Queen*, back in the old days!"

Judge shouldered past him without a word, but the older man stopped him cold with the words:

"I saw Kate last month in Denver, Judge."

Judge turned towards him slowly, and his grey eyes narrowed.

"What did you say?"

The older man nodded. "You heard me. I saw Kate Dubois in Denver, big as life! She's got a son now, a little Creole who wears a high hat and an earring!

"We talked for a long time, about the old days on the *Queen*, and this thing and that." He smiled up into Judge's face, and a rapacious gleam flashed in his shrewd blue eyes.

"What would you give to know what she told me?" he whispered.

Judge's eyes hardened. "I don't know what you're talking about," he growled. "Now get out of my way, or I'll have my attendants throw you out on your head!"

He pushed past, and the old man watched him go with a keen, resentful look before reluctantly returning the way he'd come.

But when Judge reached the safety of his own private compartment and had shut the door behind him, he closed his eyes and leaned against it heavily. He bit his lips into a tight line and raged silently for a full fifteen minutes before he was able to compose himself enough to adjust his collar, straighten his jacket, open the door, and return to the party.

Chapter
Forty-Four

Clay grimaced, threw his clawing hands over the edge of the rock shelf, and then collapsed halfway over, panting. Doc was a dead weight dangling over his back, and Clay hung precariously twelve feet above the ground as he searched for a foothold on the rock face strong enough to push against.

Clay took a deep breath. One more solid push should get them all the way over the edge and onto the rock.

He moved his foot over the cliff face. He was putting all his weight on the other, and he scrabbled blindly for purchase.

Suddenly the wolves reappeared, charging the rock with a burst of slavering yips and howls. They stormed the rock and jumped up its sheer face in a bobbing line of hungry jaws, snapping for Clay's feet and Doc's dangling hands.

Clay suddenly screamed as searing pain branched through his left foot. They were almost out of reach, but a wolf had leaped up and nipped him in mid-air. It had to let go and fall back down again, but no sooner than it hit the ground, than it leapt again.

Clay panted and swayed, and pain branched up his left leg like a spear, but he gritted his teeth, inhaled, gripped the rock with his injured foot, and pushed up with all his strength. He dug against the rock face with both feet and summoned every ounce of strength in his back and shoulders, and inch by inch, he crawled over the edge.

He groaned and then screamed as he pushed Doc over the edge and onto the flat rock, and then collapsed onto it himself, gasping and shuddering in every muscle. He curled up into a twitching ball and lay there helpless for a moment or two, but the sound of eager yips and growls and scratching paws on the rock below made him sit up as soon as he could and sling the shotgun down from his shoulder.

"I'm going to blow you all to the moon, you God-cursed monsters," he growled and loaded both barrels with shaking hands. He knelt on the cliff edge, pointed the gun down into the wolves' bobbing jaws, and pulled the trigger.

The thunderous shotgun blast spattered the rocks and trees with hide and hair for twenty feet around, and the wolves that escaped fled into the night, but Clay scanned the creek bottom beneath them with wary eyes. It was fully dark under the cover of the trees, and he could see very little.

And that meant he had to stay awake and stand guard. The wolves might come back; and there were plenty of other things out hunting, besides wolves.

Clay put the shotgun down and glanced at Doc as he lay splayed out on the rock. The older man was unconscious and looked half-alive, and Clay's eyes moved from him to the creek bed far below.

His heel was throbbing, and he longed to wash it off in cool water. He weighed if it was worth the risk to go down for it, and the answer he got, at least for the moment, was *no*. So he sat down, leaned back against the rock, and closed his eyes.

He looked over at Doc. Doc was unconscious, and in the shape he was in, that was a good thing. There was nothing more he could do for him, and so Clay decided to rest and wait for daybreak.

He leaned his head back against the rock and turned all his mind to listening: the faint gurgle of the creek below, the hum of crickets in the grass, the small scufflings of night creatures in the underbrush, and the soft purr of owls out in the forest.

The sound of a low, throbbing yowl, eerily like a woman screaming, made Clay open his eyes and grab for the shotgun. What hair he had left prickled the length of his neck.

It was the cry of some kind of cat; could be a bobcat, or a—puma. It was soft and distant, but not distant enough, and there were hours yet to dawn.

Clay swallowed. A twelve-foot-high rock shelf was no protection against a puma if it chose to charge them.

Clay looked down at the creek bed again and a thrill of fear raced up his spine. The dead wolves were drawing predators to them.

The only question was—how many, and what kind?

A soft moan made him turn his head. Doc was swimming back up to consciousness.

Clay knelt down beside him. "Doc, be still," he said softly. "We're on the side of a cliff. If you roll over too hard, you'll roll off."

"Clay?"

"Right here."

Doc tried to raise his head off the ground. "Where are

273

we?"

"Still on the mountain, Doc. We're on the side of a cliff. Don't roll over, okay?"

Doc turned to look over the edge of the precipice. "We're on Sweetwater Creek."

"That's right. On the rock shelf above the trail crossing. Not far from your cabin."

Doc grimaced suddenly and writhed. "My back is on fire!" he groaned.

"I know," Clay told him. "I couldn't get us back to the cabin in time."

Doc opened his eyes and looked up at him. "I'm amazed we're here at all," he mumbled. "How in the world did you get me up this wall?"

Clay glanced at him and said nothing, and Doc passed a hand over his face. "Did I dream the part about wolves?" he groaned.

Clay shook his head and scanned the creek bottom.

"Are they gone?"

"I blasted them with the shotgun. They haven't come back."

Doc groaned again, but this time the sound was different—lower, softer. It was a sound wrung out of a deeper kind of misery, and Clay turned his face away. Doc had just remembered why they were there.

"Oh, my Dase," he groaned, in a barely perceptible murmur. "My Daisy!"

***

They stayed on the rock shelf for the rest of the night. Doc slipped in and out of consciousness, and Clay fought to stay awake as the moon climbed high overhead and began to slip westward towards its setting.

In the cold hour before dawn, Clay started and clutched the gun. He'd dropped off, and the sound of growls and grunts on the creek bed below them shocked him wide awake. A long, low howl left no doubt what it was, and Clay scrabbled in the shot bag for more shells.

But to his dismay, it was empty. They'd used them all.

Clay moved to the edge of the cliff. The wolves' heads were bobbing up less than a foot from where he was kneeling, and he took the butt of the gun and smashed them down. The wolves snarled and gnashed at the weapon with their teeth, and kept jumping.

A scrabbling sound to his left made Clay jerk around. One of the wolves had found a lower end of the cliff and was scrabbling to heave its back paws up on the shelf. Clay jumped up and swung the shotgun like a club, and the wolf spun into the air and crashed down onto the rocky creek bed with a horrible shriek.

But the others had seen it jump, and soon Clay was swinging the gun stock like a madman to keep them scrambling up on the rock.

The time crawled, and by the time the sky began to lighten, Clay was close to passing out himself. He could feel that he was reaching the end of his strength at last.

He slumped down onto the rock and clutched the gun. Something cold touched his foot, and he reached down for it. To his surprise, it was a shotgun shell. It must've rolled out of the bag while he was grabbing for the rest.

Clay loaded it into the gun. The sky was growing lighter, but the wolves hadn't gone. When he looked down, he could still see a dozen dark shapes slinking back and forth in the dim light.

He bit his lip and watched them. Maybe he could get them all in a single shot, and maybe not. If he didn't, he doubted he could continue to beat the rest off.

The decision was suddenly made for him. The wolves, following some signal between them, rushed the cliff all together with a storm of howls. Clay lifted the gun, pointed the gun right into the leaders' muzzle, and pulled the trigger. The thunderous blast echoed in the trees, and a half-dozen wolves went spinning out into the air.

Clay looked down into the creek bottom, panting. To his despair, there were still seven or eight survivors, and they loped off into the cover of the trees to wait and regroup.

But a sudden shotgun blast from his right made him turn his head in amazement and wild hope. A dark figure was outlined on the ridge above, and it reloaded the shotgun as he watched. The newcomer pulled the gun up and emptied another round of buck into the trees, and the stragglers of the wolf pack burst from cover and galloped over the hill in full retreat.

Clay raised up on his knees and waved. "Hey!" he shouted, "Hey, over here, up on the rock! We need help—I have an injured man!"

The dark silhouette swung the gun skyward and began to descend the hill. Clay watched in relief as the stranger picked his way down the zigzagging trail and crossed the creek bed. He stared down at the wolf carcasses, then up.

Clay frowned at the upturned face. He sat up suddenly.

"Who are you?" he demanded. The stranger slid the panel back on his lamp, and the light revealed his face.

"Who do you think, fool?" Daisy demanded, and to her utter amazement, Clay gave a shout worthy of a Pawnee chieftain and scrambled down from the rock.

The next thing she knew, she was being crushed against his chest.

"Be careful!" she yelped. "My ribs are cracked. I don't want 'em broken!"

But Clay wiped his wet eyes and laughed. "You're alive!"

"Last time I looked," Daisy told him, frowning, and Clay turned to the rock and shouted:

"Doc, Doc! Look! It's Daisy—Daisy's alive!"

Doc struggled up on one elbow and stared down at them; then put his hand over his eyes and wept like a child.

Chapter
Forty-Five

Together they lowered Doc down onto the sled and pulled him slowly back to the cabin. By that time, it was fully light, and the bright rays of dawn were streaming through the cabin window.

They laid Doc out on his bed, and Daisy cut him out of his shirt and washed his face and neck with warm water.

"Can't believe you brought that monster down," she muttered and turned her eyes away from the bruises and red weals covering her father's chest.

Doc's eyes opened a slit, and he looked up into her face. "That boy there saved my life a dozen times," he whispered, and Clay looked down at the floor. Daisy watched Doc with dark eyes as he explained how they'd come down off the mountain and been attacked by the wolves.

"I'm going for the doctor," she told her father and pulled a blanket up over his chest before turning for the door. Clay followed Daisy as she walked outside and untied one of the horses from the hitching post.

Daisy turned suddenly, looked at him and frowned.

"You said you wanted to impress me," she told him.

Clay met her eyes quickly but said nothing.

"Well, you just did."

The next thing he knew, Daisy had grabbed him by the ears and was planting a hard, crushing kiss on his lips, and in the next instant, she'd jumped on the horse and was already disappearing into the trees like a bat flying out of a cave.

But Clay stared after her long after she'd gone; he put his fingers to his tingling lips and murmured:

"Well I'll just be da—"

But a faint groan from inside the cabin made Clay turn his head and walk back inside. Doc wasn't out of the woods by a long way, and the shock of Daisy's kiss, in his weakened state, might just put him on the ground if he didn't find a chair quick.

***

Daisy came back an hour later with the doctor from Wolf Table. He was a young man in his twenties with pince-nez glasses and a ferocious moustache. He pulled a chair up to Doc's bedside, plugged two tubes into his ears, and pressed a small metal disc to Doc's chest.

Daisy's worried look deepened into a scowl. "What the fool is he doing?" she growled softly from the doorway.

"Don't fret, Dase," Clay told her. "Let the doctor do his job."

Daisy turned away and kicked savagely at a tuft of grass. Clay let her go and stayed in the doorway, watching as the young man unhooked the tubes from his ear and gently felt Doc's ribs.

Doc grimaced, then cried out sharply, and the sound yanked Daisy back to the door. She took one look at Doc's face and pushed in, but Clay took her by the shoulders and shoved her out again.

"What's wrong with you?" she scowled. "You saw what he did! I got ahold of the wrong man. That little green squirt don't know what he's doing. He's hurting Doc!"

Clay pulled the door shut and pushed her away. "You need to calm down," he told her. "That man can't do Doc any good if he has to fight you first."

"Get out of my way," she warned him.

Clay tilted his head and gave her an exasperated look. "You brought him up here to save your father's life, Dase. Let him do it!"

He caught a desperate gleam in her eyes and reached out to pull her to his chest, but Daisy wrestled out of his arms and staggered back a few paces.

"You needn't to think that just because I kissed you, I won't pop you in the jaw if I have to!" she cried. "Get out of my way!"

There was another loud cry from inside the cabin, and then a short, sharp scream.

Daisy dived under Clay's arms and burst through the cabin door to find Doc propped on his elbows, head rolled back and grimacing in pain.

"What the devil are you doing to him?" she cried.

The doctor turned to look at her. "Your father's ribs are broken," he told her. "He's lost movement in his legs as well. He may be paralyzed, but we won't know for sure for a week or so."

Daisy stared at him for a wide-eyed instant and then scrambled out into the yard. Clay turned to call after her, but she jumped on the horse and rode off in a frantic swirl of dust.

Clay watched her go with pity in his eyes, and then turned back to the doctor. "What should we do now?"

"He needs to be in town where I can tend him," the doctor replied. "I'm going to call in a specialist from Denver, as well."

He reached into his black bag and pulled out a small vial. Clay watched as the doctor squeezed out a few careful drops into a glass of water.

"Take this, Mr Dailey," he murmured and handed the cup to Doc. "It's laudanum. It'll make the pain more bearable."

Doc took the glass and quickly turned it up, and the doctor turned to Clay.

"He needs to be carried on a board," he instructed, "as flat as possible, and strapped down so he doesn't move."

"I think there are some boards out back."

"Do you think you'll be able to help me carry him down the mountain? I wouldn't want to trust him to a sled."

Clay sighed and pulled a hand over his mouth. "I'll do my best."

The doctor glanced at him with a sympathetic eye. "Do you need me to look at you, as well?"

Clay shook his head. "I'm okay."

"No you aren't. You're dead on your heels, boy."

Clay gave the doctor a weary look but said nothing, and the doctor sighed.

"I think I'm going to prescribe a few hours of sleep for the both of you. Mr Dailey is about as well off here as he would be in town, as long as I'm with him, and you have to get some rest or you'll collapse. I'm going to take this chair and sit here in the corner, and you can climb up into that loft and get some sleep."

Clay shot him a grateful look, climbed slowly into the loft, and collapsed on the soft sheets. He pressed his face into the pillow and inhaled the soft, clean scent of Daisy's hair and meadow grass, before exhaustion pulled him down into unconsciousness.

He slept dreamlessly, except for the memory of having his ears yanked almost off his head and being kissed hard on the lips, and this vivid event replayed itself over and over again in his mind until he sank down into complete forgetfulness.

Chapter Forty-Six

To Clay's surprise, he woke to the light of dawn on his face. He sat up on one elbow, shook his head, and rubbed his eyes.

"Why didn't you wake me?" he mumbled and threw off the covers. The doctor looked up at him.

"I didn't have the heart," he replied kindly. "But if you're rested up, we need to get going. I want to get Mr Dailey back down into town. I need to send a telegram to Denver, and I need to make sure Mr Dailey has someone present to provide the care he needs."

"I'm still here," Doc drawled, from the bed.

"Are you feeling well enough for us to carry you into town, Mr Dailey?" the doctor asked him.

"Certainly not," Doc replied dryly, "but I suppose I have no choice."

"The sooner I can get you settled, the better," the doctor told him.

Doc scanned the room. "Where's Daisy?"

Clay shrugged and looked down at the floor. "She was pretty upset last night. She took one of the horses and skunked out."

Doc sighed and lowered his head on the pillow. "Don't

go after her. She'll come back when she's ready."

"Well, if you're ready to go, gentlemen, I made a pot of coffee," the doctor told them. "It's all the breakfast I could find. Grab a cup, boy, and let's get going." He turned to Doc.

"Would you care for a cup, Mr Dailey?"

"Thank you," Doc replied, "but I'd like the laudanum more."

The doctor opened his black bag. "How much pain are you having?"

Doc looked up at him from half-closed eyes. "My spine is on fire from end to end," he murmured.

"Do you have any feeling in your legs?"

Doc's eyes glinted. "No."

The doctor nodded. He produced the little vial, pressed a few careful drops from a syringe into a glass of water, and handed it to Doc. Doc reached for it and gulped it down.

The doctor turned to Clay. "If you could bring those boards around front, we can get the pallet assembled."

"I'll do it," Clay told him. "You didn't get much sleep." He walked out of the cabin and was gone for about ten minutes; then he called to the doctor from the open doorway.

When the man walked out, he gestured to a pallet of five boards, lashed together with wire and fastened with nails.

"Will it hold him, do you think?" the doctor murmured, with his hands on his hips. "He's a tall man."

"The sled held together," Clay told him. "I used the same technique."

"Well then, let's get going," the doctor told him, and slapped his shoulder. Together they carried the pallet inside and slid it onto the bed next to Doc.

"Lift him up and over," the doctor instructed. "On three. One … two … three!"

Doc groaned as they lifted him and set him on the pallet. The doctor ripped some of the sheets into strips and tied him down to the boards at the shoulder, waist, and knees. The doctor pulled the strips tight and then knotted them.

He looked down at Doc through the golden pince-nez glasses. "Try not to move. Mr Dailey. It's very important to keep your spine as still as possible. If you're in too much pain, let me know, and I'll give you more laudanum." He took his black bag and set it on the foot of the pallet.

He nodded to Clay, and together they hoisted the pallet up on their shoulders, and carried it through the door and out.

***

They arrived in town two hours later, weary and walking slowly. They approached the main street from behind the row of shops on the west side of the road, and Doc turned his head.

"I'd appreciate it if you could get me to my house some other way than the main road. I don't want my fiancée to find out about this by seeing me carried through town."

They stopped just behind the buildings to rest, and Clay wiped his brow with his shirt sleeve. "I know a shortcut through the woods," he told them. "We'll have to go past the mercantile on the end of the row, but that's all."

The doctor knelt down beside the pallet. "How are you feeling, Mr Dailey?"

"I'm in considerable pain."

The doctor opened his bag and fished out the vial. He poured water out of a canteen into a little cup and counted a few careful drops of opium into it.

"There you are."

Doc turned the cup up and rolled his eyes up to the sky. It was late morning, and the early chill had given way to the warmth of a summer's day.

"We'll be at your home soon," the doctor assured him. "Where is it?"

"A mile down this road," Clay told him.

"Good. We'll be there by lunchtime."

***

They rested for a few minutes in the back yard of a milliner's shop, and then raised the pallet up again and carried it behind the Main Street mercantiles. They walked past the last shop on the row and were in the act of carrying it into the woods beyond when the doctor stumbled over a rock and almost dropped his end. The pallet swayed dangerously, and the doctor struggled to regain his grip.

"Hold on there. I'll help you!"

A blond boy jumped off the end of the wooden sidewalk and ran over to one corner of the long pallet. He was barely a teenager, but he was already taller than Clay, and lifted one corner easily.

"Thank you, son," the doctor wheezed. "We're carrying him down the road about a mile. Can you go with us that far?"

"Be proud to. My pa's in town all day, and he won't be back until this afternoon." He glanced back over his shoulder at Doc. "Ain't I seen you before, mister?"

"You might have," Doc replied weakly, and the boy's face lit up with recognition as they walked.

"Sure I do! Your daughter broke that big black horse in town that day!"

A weak smile dawned over Doc's face. "Almost broke me, too," he murmured, and the boy grinned.

"Beatenest thing I ever saw! She's a caution, all right!"

Clay gave the blond boy a quick look but said nothing to him, and Doc only replied, "That she is," and fell silent.

Chapter **Forty-Seven**

They arrived at the house thirty minutes later, carried Doc up to his bedroom, and carefully transferred him. Doc sank into the soft bed with a groan, and the doctor reached for the vial again and put a cup of laudanum to his patient's lips.

"Sure hope you get to feeling better, mister," the blond boy said.

"Thank you son," Doc murmured. "What's your name?"

"Jeremy McClary," the boy replied. "I live up at the Circle T in Indian Rock."

Doc had no reaction to this intelligence, but Clay looked up at Jeremy darkly.

"If there's anything I can do to help, just let me know, mister."

"I will, son, and thank you."

Jeremy nodded, walked down the stairs, and out of the house, and as he crossed the porch, he was startled to see Daisy loitering in the bushes by the side of the house.

"Hello Daisy!" Jeremy blurted in surprise.

"Howdy."

Jeremy bit his lip. "I'm sorry about your pa. Sure hope he gets to feeling better."

Daisy gave him a dark glance. "Kind of you," she mumbled but offered no other reply, and Jeremy looked down at his hands.

"Well—afternoon."

"Afternoon."

Jeremy straightened up and walked off with the slight swagger that young men adopt when they know a young woman is watching them go, but Daisy only glanced at him before fading back into the bushes.

Footsteps approached from inside the house, and soon the doctor and Clay stepped out onto the porch.

"If you don't mind, son, I'd appreciate it if you could come back into town with me. I need to bring some things back to this house, and I can't carry them alone."

Clay nodded, and they walked off through the yard and down the road. Daisy watched them go and then jumped up onto the porch and inside the house.

She paused in the doorway of Doc's bedroom, and Doc raised his eyes to look at her.

"How long have you been here?" he murmured.

"Since last night."

"Come and sit down beside me," Doc murmured and gestured towards a chair. Daisy pulled it up to his bedside and looked down at him in frowning silence.

"Clay said you were upset."

Daisy looked away and rubbed her nose.

Doc's eyes were full of a father's sympathy. "Now Daisy, I don't know what this is going to turn out to be. But no matter what it is, we'll get through it. Just like always."

Daisy nodded, still looking away.

"You were upset about Kate, too, weren't you, Dase? That's why you took off up the mountain in the first place," Doc went on quietly.

Daisy shrugged. "Figured you was getting hitched. Didn't need me in the way no more," she mumbled and wiped her nose again.

Doc frowned and took her hand. "You thought you were in the way?" he replied, in a tone of disbelief. "Dase, you're my daughter. You always will be. You know that, don't you?"

Daisy shrugged again and looked away, and Doc took her chin in her hand and turned her to face him.

"Daisy, I love you every bit as much as if you were born to me," Doc told her softly. "How could you think anything else? Don't you know that, after all these years?"

Daisy glanced at him gratefully but said nothing, and Doc set his mouth in exasperation and reached for her hand. Daisy took his and sniffed a little, and Doc gave her hand a kiss.

"I don't want to hear any more nonsense about you going away," Doc told her.

"All right."

"Have you told Kate what happened?"

Daisy shook her head.

"I want you to go into town and get Kate, Daisy. She's beside herself by now, and she's going to be hurt that nobody's told her anything."

Daisy looked down at him. "Doc, are you sure?"

"About what?"

"About that woman. About marrying her."

"I have never been more sure about anything in my life, Dase."

Daisy pulled her mouth down, and Doc squeezed her hand gently. "I'm surprised at you, Dase. It's not like you to be jealous."

At that, Daisy looked down at him. "I ain't jealous of Kate, Doc. If she makes you happy, I don't have no kick against her. It's just that—I'm afraid she's going to get you killed!"

Doc's eyebrows rushed together. "For heaven's sake, Daisy! What put such a wild idea in your head?"

Daisy frowned. "I went up to talk to the Prophet a few days after we came to town," she told him.

"That madman?" Doc demanded in exasperation. "How many times have I told you to stay away from him?"

"No, but Doc—he told me all about you. Things he shouldn't never have known! He told me your real name was Doc Dailey, and that you was a gambler, and that you was running from men who was trying to kill you!"

Doc's eyebrows shot up, and he rolled startled eyes to her face. "What?"

"That's right!" Daisy told him earnestly. "You hadn't told me none of that, but it all turned out true! And he said something else, too—he said that unless you was careful, you'd be dead by this time next year. He said that a woman would put you in danger, bad!"

Doc frowned at her in speechless amazement, and Daisy went on: "That's why I tried to run Kate off. I could see it was her, Doc. She was the one the Prophet warned me about, 'cause you love her, and you don't expect her to make trouble for you!"

"Good heavens," Doc murmured and pulled a hand over his face. "That's why you brought the gun to the café that day."

"Yep." Daisy nodded. "I didn't know which woman it was, then. But once Kate showed up, it was plain as day that it was her!"

Doc looked up at her with a bemused expression. "Daisy, I don't know what that old man told you, or why he knew what he did—but I want you to let go of the idea that I'm going to die, or that Kate is bad luck to me. And I don't want you to *ever* tell Kate that. It would break her heart."

"I won't if you don't want me to, Doc."

"That's my girl," Doc murmured softly and brushed his hand across her cheek. "Have I told you how overjoyed I am that you're all right?" he murmured.

Daisy sniffed and looked away. "Yep. Didn't think I was going to make it, there for a while.

"But that's another thing, Doc." She glanced over her shoulder at the bedroom doorway. When she saw that it was empty, she leaned forward and whispered:

"If I tell you something, will you promise never to tell anybody else—to keep it just between us?"

Doc stared at her in concern. "Of course."

Daisy met his eyes earnestly. "Old Crunchy had me on the ground, Doc," she told him. "He was standing right over me and had his mouth open so wide, I could count all his teeth! But then—then there was a flash like lightning, and I saw—"

She stopped and looked down at the floor. After a long silence, Doc prompted:

"Saw what, Dase?"

She looked back up at him and let go of his hand. "Never mind, Doc. But—that old mountain man is a whole lot more than he looks.

"Don't ask me how I know."

Chapter
Forty-Eight

Daisy walked back into Wolf Table thirty minutes later. She'd dragged her feet all the way to town because she still had a bad feeling about Kate, but nothing would do for Doc except she go and fetch that woman and bring her right into his house.

Daisy stopped, lifted one foot, and fished a rock out of her shoe. Doc sure had it bad. He wanted that French lady in spite of all the Prophet's warnings. It didn't even make no difference to Doc that he might *die* because of that woman.

Of course, Doc hadn't seen what she'd seen; and so he didn't pay the same heed to what the Prophet said.

Daisy stopped on the edge of town, leaned up against a tree, plucked a piece of grass out of the ground, and stuck it into her mouth. She had the feeling that maybe she should've told Doc everything.

Maybe he'd pay more attention to the Prophet if he knew that the old man had fought a bear right off of her.

But on the other hand, if she told Doc the crazy things she'd seen—or thought she'd seen—he might just think she'd gone loco.

And then he wouldn't pay no attention to anything else she said, or worse, he might sic that fidgety doctor on her.

Daisy hesitated just under the cover of the trees, debating whether to go get Kate, or to take off back to the house and try to reason with Doc again.

After a minute or two, she pulled the piece of grass out of her mouth, threw it on the ground, and sighed, "Blast it!" before emerging reluctantly from the cover of the trees and walking down the dusty clearing to the hotel.

***

When she entered the hotel, to her embarrassment, Kate was seated in the parlour and was watching the door with worried eyes. The elegantly-dressed woman rose in amazement as Daisy walked in.

"You're alive!"

Daisy glanced over at the curious hotel manager and looked down at the floor. "Yes, ma'am. Can I talk to you in private?"

Kate's quick eyes scanned her face anxiously. "Of course."

Kate led her up the stairs to her private room and closed the door behind them. She turned and questioned Daisy with her eyes.

"Where's Doc?"

Daisy looked down. "Doc is back at his house. He and a friend of mine went hunting Old Crunchy. That's a grizzly bear, ma'am."

Kate searched Daisy's grim face, and panic tinged her voice as she demanded: "What's happened to Doc?"

Daisy lifted sympathetic eyes to the older woman's face. "They killed the bear, but Old Crunchy—beat Doc up pretty bad."

Kate stepped in and took her by the shoulders. "*Is he hurt?*"

Daisy's blue eyes pooled with tears. "Yes ma'am. The doctor says he's got some busted ribs. He—he can't move his legs, neither. The doc says he might be paralyzed. We won't know for sure, for a week or two."

Kate's fingers fell from her shoulders. She turned away and put her hands to her mouth.

The silence stretched out, and finally Kate moaned: "Why didn't anyone tell me before now? I would have—" Her voice trailed off.

Daisy shook her head and kept her eyes on the floor. "That's my fault, ma'am. Doc would've wanted you there, but I skunked out to the woods, instead of coming down to tell you."

Kate turned and took Daisy into her arms. "It's all right, *cherie*," she murmured, and embraced her. "Of course you were devastated! I am happy that you will take me to Doc now."

She stepped back and smiled tearfully. "And I am not *ma'am*. You must call me Kate, like the rest of the world."

"Yes ma—I mean Kate. And"—Daisy adjusted her shoulders—"I'm right sorry I drew a gun on you. I shouldn't have, 'specially in front of your little boy. I'm sorry if I skeerd you."

Kate crossed her arms. "You terrified us both," she replied. "Emil may not be ready to befriend you quickly, but I forgive you. Come, let's go."

She picked up her bag and led Daisy out of the door.

When they descended the stairs and emerged onto the sidewalk outside the hotel, they discovered Emil, surrounded by a circle of little girls.

Kate extended a hand. "Come, Emil! We're going to Doc's house."

Emil turned back to his admirers and lifted his hat gallantly.

"*Au revoir, belles filles,*" he told them. "I am desolate to leave you."

"Ain't he elegant?"

"I love you, Emil!"

Emil reached out and kissed the hand of a giggling redheaded girl, and Kate pulled him away bodily.

"Come!"

***

They arrived at the house in the early afternoon, and by that time, the doctor and Clay had returned. A strange wicker chair with two big wheels on each side was sitting in the middle of the front room, and Clay was seated in it. He was rolling the chair idly back and forth as the doctor and his patient conferred together in the bedroom.

But Emil stopped dead in the doorway as they entered. His eyes were riveted to Clay's shaven head and his buckskin clothes, and he goggled in terror as he watched the Pawnee boy lounge in the wheeled chair.

"Oh, horrible!" Emil shrieked. "*Le sauvage a triomphé*! He has killed the invalid!"

Kate knelt down quickly and took Emil by the shoulders. "Hush, Emil!" she told him in a horrified whisper. "This young man is Doc's friend!"

Emil was still staring at Clay's shaven head, and when Clay met his eyes, he raised a dark eyebrow and smacked his lips; Emil screamed and fled. Kate watched him go with a look of pity but entered the house and paused momentarily to greet Clay.

"You must be Clay," she told him. "My name is Kate. I'm glad to make your acquaintance, and I must apologize for my son's rudeness," she murmured.

Clay stood up to greet her. "Pleased to meet you, ma'am," he replied quietly. "Don't worry about it."

"Is Doc's bedroom on the first floor?"

"Yes ma'am," Clay replied. "The first door to the left of the stairs."

"*Merci.*"

He watched as Kate gathered her silken skirts and passed, and when she knocked softly, and then disappeared inside the bedroom, he turned to Daisy, who was leaning against the front door.

"You better go get that kid. He looks like he could fall into the pond or something."

Daisy pulled her mouth to one side and disappeared, but when she was gone, Clay's placid expression darkened into a look of melancholy. He glanced down at his palms, slowly turned them over, and then rested them on the arms of the chair as he heard Daisy returning.

She walked back through the door, dragging Emil by his ear. "There you go, short stuff," she told him.

"Your mama will be back in a minute."

Emil rubbed his ear and glared up at her resentfully. "I do not forget that you showed us a gun!" he cried. "There will be a reckoning!"

Daisy's only reply was to turn and walk out onto the back porch. Clay, conscious of the little boy's wary eyes on him, sighed, got up from the chair, and followed her.

***

He found Daisy leaning over the back porch rail, and he leaned over it beside her. It was a beautiful afternoon; the sun slanted golden through the trees in the back yard, and a faint silver haze glimmered over the pond. Dragonflies flitted over the surface of the water, and a fish jumped silently in the shallows.

Clay turned to Daisy as she stared out into the trees. "I never got the chance to tell you how sorry I am about what happened to Doc," he said softly. "But I hope it's going to be all right, Dase."

Daisy shook her head. "Doc says it will be, but then, that's what he would say. I ain't so sure."

"No matter what happens, I'm here for you," Clay told her and turned his dark eyes to hers.

Daisy gave him a quick, unhappy glance. "Don't start up, Clay," she mumbled. "I hate to cry, and if you make me do it, I'll punch you."

"Don't want to get punched," Clay told her and gave her a teasing glance. "I'd a whole lot rather be kissed."

Daisy twisted, quick as a cat, her hands shot out, but Clay caught them halfway to his ears and held them fast.

"What I meant was—I'd like to kiss *you* this time, instead of you kissing me," he said carefully.

Daisy raised frowning blue eyes to his face. "What's the difference?"

Clay shook his head. "I'll show you."

He closed his hands over hers, leaned in, and kissed her softly on the lips. Daisy received this salute in silence, and when Clay stepped back again, she raised her brows and nodded judiciously.

"Okay, I kind of see it," she conceded. "But—"

Clay leaned in and kissed her again, and Daisy's hands slid out of his, worked the air momentarily, and then twined around his shoulders.

Clay smiled down at her. "See?" he murmured, but to his alarm, the gleam he'd just summoned up in Daisy's eye was one he'd seen before.

"No, no, wait Dase—"

But it was too late. Daisy had already grabbed his ears, and the next thing he knew, he was being kissed like a hard slap across the mouth.

Chapter
Forty-Nine

Kate closed the bedroom door and leaned against it. Doc was lying in the bed, but his eyes moved to hers at once, and she swept to his side and pushed right in between him and the doctor. Doc lifted his chin, and Kate leaned down to kiss him.

But to her surprise, the doctor put a hand on her arm. "I'm going to have to ask you not to touch him, ma'am," he said quietly. "It's very important that Mr Dailey lie absolutely still, at least for now."

Kate nodded, caressed Doc's face, and smiled down into his eyes. "I can't turn my back on you for an instant," she teased, and Doc smiled.

The doctor, seeing that he had been supplanted, turned and closed up his black bag. "I'll come back and check on you tomorrow, Mr Dailey," he said, and put his hat on his head, but neither of them paid the slightest attention to him, and so he sighed and walked out.

Kate sat in a chair by the bed and smoothed a twig of blond hair back from Doc's brow. "You've taken twenty years off my life in the last few days," she complained.

Doc looked up at her and reached for her hand. "I'm sorry, Kate."

"You know I forgive you anything when you look at me

with those beautiful eyes," she murmured, and her worried glance flicked down over the bruises and weals on his chest.

"I'll send for our things at the hotel. Emil and I are moving in," she told him. "I'm going to tend you while you recover."

Doc raised his brows. "What about the gossip?" he asked in mock surprise. "The scandal in a small town?"

Kate stripped off her lace gloves. "If any woman dares to say a word to me, I'll slap her until her head swivels."

"Why, Kate!"

"I will fight all comers with my knife."

Doc sputtered and burst out laughing, and Kate giggled and ran her pink finger over his lips. "Now lie and rest. I'll bring your dinner later. Where is your wine cellar?"

"Wine cellar?" Doc echoed and turned incredulous eyes to her face. "In Wolf Table?"

Kate's calm veneer suddenly cracked. Her face crumpled into grief. "*Pauvre chose!*" she cried, "to live in this savage place for ten years, without even wine! I will find our old champagne for you, if I have to send to New Orleans!"

Doc sighed wistfully. "I'd forgotten about that champagne."

"And I will engage a cook."

Doc closed his eyes in deep relief; then frowned and opened them again. "Not from here, I beg you, Kate."

"Of course not. From Denver. I'll hire a chef."

Doc looked at her again and squeezed her hand. "*Cherie*, we need to talk about what the doctor said. He told me that I might—that I might be paralyzed permanently."

Kate lifted his hand to her lips. "I know it, Doc."

"It might be a good idea to hold off on getting married, at least for a little while. Until we're sure."

"Sure of what, Doc?" she echoed softly. "You know very well that I'm mad for you. What is there to discuss? Unless you find you are no longer mad for me?"

Doc gazed at her fondly. "Kate," he murmured. "You know what I mean."

"I warn you, if you refuse to marry me, I will show you no mercy. I will denounce you as a cad, a man completely without honour, and you will never be received in any respectable home in New Orleans, ever again."

"I'm serious, Kate. I want you to think about it," Doc whispered. "You're emotional, I understand. I won't hold you to what you say right now."

The smile faded from Kate's face, and she frowned into his eyes. "Emotional, yes," she replied softly. "When you are hurt, I hurt too. But I am hardly a child," she reminded him. "Have I ever told you anything I didn't mean or made you a promise that I didn't keep?"

"No," Doc admitted, after a long pause. "No, you haven't, Kate."

She lifted her chin and raised a slender eyebrow. "Well then?"

"I'm sorry, darling," Doc replied softly. "You're right, I know you better. Please accept my deep apology."

Kate caressed his cheek and smiled softly. "I forgive you anything," she whispered, then kissed her fingertip and pressed it to his lips.

She turned on the words, stood up, and shook out her skirts. "Can you sit in the chair with the wheels?"

Doc sighed. "The doctor says it will be weeks before I can do it. And I confess to feeling just a little lazy."

"Very well," she told him. "Try to sleep. I will bring your dinner later, and you will eat it all."

A faint smile dawned over Doc's face, and he placed his hand on his chest and lowered his eyes.

"Ma'am. I hear and obey."

***

Kate dimpled at him, closed the bedroom door after her, and walked out into the house. Emil was sitting in a chair, looking very uncomfortable, and she went to sit beside him.

"I hope you're feeling calmer now," she told him. "No one has offered Doc any violence. We are all quite safe."

Emil set his mouth sceptically. "I am not convinced," he replied. "*Le sauvage* dreams of killing us all. And that barbarian girl attacked me in the yard and dragged me here by my ear, like a cat! If you wish to live with these wild people, I pity you, but I will be on my way."

Kate nodded gravely. "I'm very sorry to hear it, Emil. Where will you go?"

Emil lifted his chin. "Denver, I think," he mused. "I will go to the casinos and win at *vingt-et-un*."

"What of the little girls in town who love you?" Kate enquired. "You will break many hearts."

"I know it; it cannot be helped."

Kate nodded sadly. "Well, I was going to send to the hotel and have your things brought here so you could have your own bedroom, but since you are leaving, there will be no need." Kate extended her hand, and Emil shook it gravely.

"*Au revoir, Emil,*" she told him. "*Bonne chance.*"

Emil stood up, bowed stiffly, and kissed her hand. "*Au revoir, ma bonne amie,*" he told her. "I wish you every happiness, even though you are sadly bewitched and likely to go mad here." Kate bit her lip, looked down to keep from laughing, and watched as Emil straightened his hat and walked out onto the porch.

But if she thought Emil would hesitate, she was surprised: He sighed, adjusted his collar, and walked down the steps, across the yard, and out into the road.

Kate rose from her chair and hurried to the back porch, where Daisy and Clay were standing together at the rail. Kate paused on the threshold because Clay's arm was around Daisy's shoulder, and she hated to interrupt a tender moment, but Emil required supervision.

"I'm sorry to disturb you," she told them, as they turned, "but I would very much appreciate it, Daisy, if you could follow Emil into town and bring him back. He is running away."

Clay and Daisy exchanged a wordless look, and Clay dropped his arm from Daisy's shoulder. Daisy stuck her hands in her pants pockets.

"All right."

"And if you could give this to the hotel manager and tell him to have our trunks sent here, I would be very thankful." She reached into her bag and handed Daisy a crisp new bill.

"Is there food in the house?"

Daisy shrugged. "I could catch us a mess of fish from the pond," she offered.

"I won't put you to that trouble," Kate replied smoothly. "Here's some more money. Please bring back five dinners from the café, and a bag of coffee, and some bacon, and some eggs and bread for tomorrow morning."

"Yes ma—I mean Kate."

Kate leaned over and kissed her cheek. "You're an angel. And don't be offended if Emil is ... a little wary. He has had to adjust to many new things in a very short time."

Daisy received Kate's kiss in uncomfortable silence and glanced back at Clay before setting off. He nodded and smiled at Kate, and followed her out.

When they got to the front porch, he stopped her. "Want me to come with you, Dase?"

She raised her brows. "Think it'd be a good idea? That little shrimp thinks you're a killer." She chuckled. "But it *would* be fun to chase him a little way down the road."

"I'm serious," Clay retorted.

"So am I." Daisy grinned. "Did you hear him yell when I caught him in the yard? Ain't never heard such words!"

Clay sputtered and shook his head, and they walked off down the road together.

Chapter Fifty

The two of them found Emil sitting on the side of the road halfway into town. He rose warily at the sight of them, and Daisy extended her hand as they approached.

"We've come to get you, short stuff," she told him. "Your mama wants you to go back home."

"I am going to Denver," Emil informed her, and Daisy leaned against a tree and stared down at him.

"Got any Denver money?"

Emil scowled at her. "I have five dollars and forty-five cents of my own, and another twenty, also my own, for *vingt-et-un* in the casino," he replied haughtily.

"Well, a ticket to Denver costs thirty dollars," Daisy told him. "There's a rule on the train, too, that nobody shorter than four feet can ride, on account of they might fall out when the train goes over a bump and get scalped by Indians. All kinds of Indians hides in the bushes along the line. They like to wait for folks to fall off the train, and it's just good fun to them, to scalp the short ones. It's got to be kind of a tradition with 'em."

Emil's eyes rolled to Clay, who was standing beside her with his arms crossed. The older boy shot Daisy an exasperated look, but she continued:

"We've had a gracious plenty of scalpings along the

train line this summer. Why, look at Clay there. He got shook off a train car last month, and you see what they did to him. They got his hair, and would've got his head too if he hadn't fought like a wildcat."

"Daisy!"

"Bah, *ridicule!*" Emil replied scornfully, though his glance returned to Clay's shaved head. "Stand aside, or I will kick you!"

Clay glanced up at the sun. Stop playing around, Dase. It's past two," he reminded her. "You better get into town."

Daisy grinned and replied: "Yeah, go ahead and take the shrimp home. I've got to go to the hotel and get supplies. I can't lead him around by the nose, too. I only got two hands!"

Emil, seeing Clay's eyes turn to him, threw his hands up and ran away, but Clay scrambled after him and caught him. Emil kicked and screamed as Clay slung him under one arm and turned for home.

"Want me to come back and help you?" he asked as Daisy turned for town.

Daisy shook her head and then grinned at Emil as he thrashed under Clay's arm. "Settle down there, short stuff," she told him. "You're all right. Clay don't kill nobody in the daytime!"

"I demand satisfaction!" Emil shrieked. "I will meet you both at dawn!"

"Come on," Clay muttered, and carried him off down the road, as Emil struggled and shouted. Daisy watched them go with a grin and then turned for town.

***

It took Daisy the better part of an hour to settle up with the hotel manager because he took the opportunity to read her a long, stern lecture about teenagers who fell into a life of crime and went to jail before he finally closed Kate's account, and it took her another thirty minutes to buy all the groceries from the mercantile.

By the time she was finished, it was late afternoon, and when she stepped outside the store, she was surprised to find a crowd gathered in the dusty road. They were all listening to an old man who was shouting at the top of his lungs:

"What does God's word say?" he cried, "It says do not covet! It says that the love of money is the root of all evil! It says to be content with such things as you have!"

Daisy's eyes froze on him in terror because it was the Prophet. The wild fear seized her that he'd followed her into town because the old man only came down to Wolf Table once or twice a year. She shrank back against the wall of the store and watched in awe as he shouted:

"Why, why spend your money on that which is not bread, and your wages on that which does not satisfy? Only the faithless put their trust in the things of this world!"

"Aw, shut up, old man!" a teenaged boy laughed from the crowd. "It's no skin off your nose if I go down to that casino. If I get rich, I'll give you a twenty to buy you a decent set of clothes!"

The crowd laughed, and some of them walked away, and Daisy clutched the burlap grocery sack and slid along the building towards the end of the row, hoping that the old man wouldn't notice her.

But a couple of women in the crowd turned away, leaving a clear space, and the Prophet lifted his face and fixed Daisy with his bright eyes. To her horror, his appearance shifted like water, and for an instant, she saw his shimmering hair unfurl into the air and his eyes glow white before he shrank into an old man again. The sound of his voice swelled strangely and tamped down again like a dancing fire.

"Take no thought for your life, what ye shall eat," he roared, "or what ye shall drink; nor yet for your body, what ye shall put on. Is not the life more than meat, and the body than raiment?

"Behold the fowls of the air: for they sow not, neither do they reap, nor gather into barns; yet your heavenly Father feedeth them. Are ye not much better than they?

"And why take ye thought for raiment? Consider the lilies of the field, how they grow; they toil not, neither do they spin, and yet I say unto you, that even Solomon in all his glory was not arrayed like one of these.

"If God so clothe the grass of the field, which to day is, and tomorrow is cast into the oven, shall he not much more clothe you, O ye of little faith?

"But seek ye first the kingdom of God, and his righteousness, and all these things shall be added unto you!"

Daisy watched, hypnotized, as the old man stretched out his gnarled hands to the crowd, and she frowned in disbelief as a flurry of white, winged creatures burst from his fingers and shot up to the sky like sparks from a wildfire.

Daisy turned and streaked off into the woods as fast as she could run, and though she had to stop a dozen times to scoop up something that had fallen out of the sack, she didn't stop flying until she reached the house, and then she threw the bag down on the floor, disappeared into the woods beyond the pond, and didn't return even for dinner.

Chapter
Fifty-One

Judge Carter walked up to the huge main faro table on the first floor of the Lucky Seven, paused, and tapped his champagne glass with a fork. The game stopped momentarily as the dealer, the players, and many other bystanders looked up at him.

"Thank you, my friends, for making the Lucky Seven's first full month of operations such a success!"

Judge lifted his champagne glass. "To happy days!"

"Happy days!" the crowd of well-heeled onlookers echoed and lifted their glasses amid a widespread murmur of indulgent laughter.

The first floor of the Lucky Seven was a glittering palace of noise, light, and motion. Fifteen ponderous crystal chandeliers flashed above the heads of the elegant crowd, and rich Persian rugs adorned the marble floors. Each piece of casino furniture—from the roulette wheels to the pool tables—was brand new, custom made, and a gilded, rococo work of art.

The clatter of the roulette balls, the brisk announcements of smartly-dressed card dealers, and the cries of players—both winners and losers—filled the air. Uniformed waiters bobbed through the crowd with silver trays full of cocktail glasses and canapés, and others wheeled liquor carts up to the tables for the convenience of the casino's sporting clientele.

A five-piece band struck up in the corner, and the

men sang out lustily over the galloping beat of their banjos and guitars:

"*Lucky Seven, Lucky Seven,*

Send me straight to poker heaven,

Aces high and jokers wild

Mama tells me she's with child!

Kiss the dices, let 'em go,

Fifty dollars on the throw,

If you lose just throw again

And pray that Mama don't have twins!

That's a winner, buys my dinner,

Lord have mercy on this sinner,

Lady Luck come on and kiss me,

Can't afford the wife to miss me!

Lucky Seven, Lucky Seven,

Now I'm here in poker heaven.

Got my chips piled high and wide

Sure am glad I came inside!"

The band finished with a strumming flourish and

bowed to laughter and scattered clapping. Judge walked over and flipped a couple of red chips to the banjo player to more laughter and clapping, and then he worked his way slowly from the main entrance of the casino, past the roulette wheels and poker tables to the private elevator in the back that was the only way up to the fifth floor. The elevator was one of the first in Denver, and accessible only with a key.

Judge walked through a pair of swinging double doors that separated the main floor of the casino from the private, business end. He walked by a pair of very large men who nodded as he passed and moved through a narrow hallway to a small vestibule at the end.

The elevator door was small and tucked away from the stream of casino dealers, bouncers and waiters passing by outside. He unlocked the sliding cage door, stepped inside, and slid it closed again. The elevator rose with a clanking sound and slowly rose all the way up to the fifth floor.

When it stopped, Judge pulled the cage door aside and stepped out into a deeply carpeted and very quiet end of the building's top floor.

He walked to the end of the hall and unlocked a carved door. It swung out onto an opulent apartment overlooking downtown Denver. He walked across the huge, high-ceilinged room to the windows that made up most of the western wall. He could see out over the roofs of buildings, could see the train track from the stockyards stretching past his casino and east to Denver's Union Station, could see the sidewalks below filled with people moving in and out of the Lucky Seven.

Judge pulled a cigar out of his pocket and lit it with a

flick of his wrist. He stood smoking silently for a few minutes until a door to the right opened, and a beautiful auburn-haired woman glided out silently.

"You've taken your time," she pouted.

Judge glanced at her. A shining red-brown curl fell over the shoulder of her pink dressing gown, and her beautiful green eyes quizzed him.

"I'm busy, Renee. I have a casino to run."
"I've been bored to death," she complained and sidled up to him. She tickled his ear, and he pulled his head away impatiently.

"I'm paying you for your time, aren't I?"

She stepped back and pulled the gown down over one smooth shoulder. "I just thought that spending an evening with a casino owner would be ... a little more fun."
Judge looked up at her briefly and tossed her a roll of blue chips. She caught the roll, glanced at him in exasperation, and turned back to the bedroom.

"Be back by midnight," he called over his shoulder, but there was no reply.

***

Judge moved to a big desk facing the window and sat down in his leather chair. He opened a big ledger and made some quick entries, and then took another pull on the cigar.

There was a soft knock at the door of the suite, and Judge half-turned his head. "Who is it?"

"It's Davis, Mr Carter."

"Come in."

The door opened to admit his secretary, a young man with a sharp mind and, Judge suspected, the ambition of Cassius. Davis walked across the room to his side, opened a folder, and handed him a sheet of paper filled with neat rows of numbers.

"These are our first month's totals. Not bad at all, for a new casino."

"Maybe not. But I want to see twice these amounts." Judge threw the sheet onto the desk.

"I also need you to talk to the winner of the contest we ran at the opening. We promised to award a hundred dollars and a bottle of thirty-year-old whisky that you give the winner personally. I have the money and the bottle here in this case, and the man is waiting downstairs."

Judge shot Davis a green look. "I hope these promotions of yours are providing this casino some practical benefit," he growled. "They're bleeding me white, and I'm in hock up to my eyeballs. I've emptied my bank account and mortgaged my riverboat to raise cash for this place!"

"You shouldn't worry," the young man replied smoothly. "A casino is all about the long haul."

"Thank you Davis," Judge drawled coldly. "I would never have guessed that if you hadn't told me! Go down and get that fellow, and make it quick. I have to be at a private poker game in fifteen minutes."

Davis set the prize case down on the desk and left to obey, and shortly afterwards, the bedroom door opened and Renee walked out, buttoning the sleeve of her green velvet gown.

Judge let his gaze flick over her elegant figure and beautiful face, and a familiar pang stabbed him. He blew an impatient spout of smoke out into the air.

"Remember what I told you. Be back by midnight."

She tossed her head and walked out, and Judge turned back to his desk.

***

He let his gaze sweep out over Denver, all the way out to the far blue edge of the city, and his eyes roamed over row after row of clapboard houses and boxy brick buildings.

Kate was out there somewhere if that old weasel on the train could be believed. She was somewhere in Denver, with a little boy.

A little Creole boy with a top hat and an earring.

Judge sputtered, and smoke curled into the air. If that was true, the boy certainly wasn't Doc's, and that was a kind of revenge, in itself, though far short of what he'd wanted.

He'd hired the best bounty hunter in the nation to kill Doc Dailey, and paid out good money for it, too, but he hadn't heard from either Doc or the bounty hunter since, and he hadn't recovered a penny of the $25,000 that Doc and Kate had stolen from him.

It had been ten years, but that still rankled—especially when he thought of how much he could use that money now.

The door opened behind him, and to his annoyance, Renee had returned. She swept across the room and disappeared inside the bedroom again without saying a word to him. Soon after the front door opened again, and Davis returned, leading a scruffy-looking nobody who looked like he'd wandered in by mistake.

Davis led the man right up to his side, and Judge rose wearily.

"Mr Carter, I'd like to introduce Mr Abel Timmons, the winner of our opening day grand prize."

The man grinned at him and extended his hand, and Judge shook it limply.

"Do you remember me, Mr Carter?" he gushed. "You came to take a picture in the lobby of my hotel! You were going from town to town on the train."

Judge stared at him and pasted a smile on his face. "Oh, yes."

"It was in Wolf Table."

Davis caught his eye and glanced at the case sitting on the table, and Judge reached for it. "Congratulations on your win, Mr Timmons. Please accept this prize, a hundred dollars and a bottle of aged whisky, with the compliments of the Lucky Seven."

"I've never won anything this big in my life!" the man burbled, and Judge repressed the urge to roll his eyes.

The bedroom door opened again, and Renee swept across the room and out again without a word to any of them. Judge watched her go in irritation, but the rube goggled at her.

"Why—it just goes to show that everybody has a twin somewhere," he marvelled. "I've never seen that lady before in my life, but she's the spit and image of another woman who's been staying at my hotel!"

Judge's eyes moved to the man's face. "What?"

"If I didn't know better, I'd say they was the same woman," the man nodded. "Same height, same colour of hair, same eyes, same look! But the woman at my hotel talked French and was from New Orleans, she said."

Judge narrowed his eyes. "That's fascinating, Mr Timmons," he replied. "Do you know that lady's name?"

"Sure do. It was Kate De—oh, blast, I can't say it right, but it was De something, something French."

"Dubois?" Judge suggested gently.

"That's it! How'd you know?" the man exclaimed in surprise.

"It's a small world, Mr Timmons," Judge murmured and put the cigar to his mouth. "A small, small world. And did this Kate Dubois have a little boy with her?"

"That's right." The man smiled. "A little dandy, all dressed up like a swell!"

"Miss Dubois and I knew each other, once upon a time," Judge told him. "Miss Dubois worked on a riverboat casino that I own."

"Well, that must've been why she said it!"

"Said what, Mr Timmons?"

The man laughed and shook his head. "Oh, she was making a joke. She was pulling my leg, for sure! She told me not to come down to your casino because of the criminal element. She said she'd heard of a man once who said he lost $25,000 at poker, on account of his dealer." He chuckled.

Judge stared at him in stunned silence, and Davis, seeing his face, broke in quickly: "Mr Timmons, why don't you come down to the restaurant, and dine with us tonight, on the house?"

"Why, that's right kind of you!"

"Think nothing of it," Davis replied, put an arm around his shoulder and hustled him out as quickly as he dared.

But Judge glared at the door in thunderstruck silence for a full five minutes after it closed. He then sat down very carefully in his leather chair and stared out over the city in deep thought, for a long while.

Chapter
Fifty-Two

"Come, Emil!"

Kate held out a gloved hand and helped Emil debark from the train. They stepped out onto the platform of Union Station in Denver, and Emil drank in the elegant surroundings with an expression of deep relief.

"*Merci*," he sighed. "You have shown pity at last."

"I brought you here because we have things to buy," Kate told him. "I have to find wedding clothes for Doc, and for myself, and also for you and for Daisy."

"Take me to lunch," Emil begged. "I have forgotten the taste of food! Or at least, food meant for people."

"That reminds me. I must also engage a cook and arrange for at least two water closets to be installed at Doc's house before the wedding. That dreadful shack in the back yard—*horrible!*"

She pulled a dark veil down over her face, and Emil looked up in frowning disapproval.

"Why do you wear such a heavy veil, and on such a warm day?"

Kate glanced down at him. "Do you remember the man I pointed out to you at the hotel? The one who came to town on the train?"

"*Certainement.*"

"Well, he is here in Denver," Kate murmured, scanning the crowd. "He knows me, and I do not wish to be seen."

"What is his name?" Emil demanded.

"He is called Judge Carter, and he is our wicked enemy. He is even now trying to murder Doc, though Doc has done nothing wrong."

Emil digested this. "Why then does your friend not challenge him to a duel? The beast has offered him an insult!"

"No one fights duels anymore," Kate told him, with a look of amusement.

"Oh, but they do," Emil objected. "When I was only a child, I saw many!"
Kate's smile faded. "You are still a child, and that's impossible. Surely no one would be mad enough to expose you to violence!"
"I saw Monsieur Talleyrand, the owner of our plantation, shoot three other men to defend his honour," Emil insisted and pointed his finger towards the far end of the station like the barrel of a gun. "I carried his gun case and stood as a witness alongside his friends!"

Kate stared at him in speechless horror.

"And I say, let your friend find his enemy, and give him the glove. I will certainly stand as his second!"

Kate's mouth crumpled up in pity, and she knelt down quickly and took Emil in her arms right in the middle of the station. She lifted her veil and kissed his cheek tearfully; then she wiped her eyes and murmured: *"Pauvre petite chose! Le monstre!"*

But Emil adjusted his crooked hat and cried: "Control yourself, I beg you! I am a man of the world—not a *petit garçon!*"

Kate laughed and kissed and embraced Emil again, despite his complaints, and told him:

"Never mind, *cherie*—you're safe now, and we'll have a happy time, and put all thought of—of *Monsieur Talleyrand* behind us! We'll have lunch at the best restaurant in Denver. You may have all the cake and pie you like, and a whole pot of coffee, if you want it."

Emil allowed himself to be mollified and straightened his vest and his dignity. When he was satisfied that Kate would not embrace him again, he extended his arm.

"*Fais-moi l'honneur, madame.*"

Kate smiled down at him and took his arm. "*Avec plaisir—mon petit chevalier.*"

***

They dined at one of the few French restaurants in Denver, and to Kate's relief, the sight of cream-filled pastries and coffee put Emil in high spirits. He became brighter and more animated than she'd seen him in weeks.

"Why don't you ask Doc to buy a house in Denver?" Emil asked as he munched a blackberry tart. "We die of boredom in that place where he lives now, and why when we could just as easily live here, where there is amusement all around? Then, too, in that rough camp we are in constant danger of bears and *sauvages.*"

"You forget, Emil—the man we wish to avoid lives here in Denver. We are taking a little chance even to be here today, you and I." She smiled at him over her coffee cup and was amused to see his eyes kindle.

"And I forbid you to call that nice boy *le sauvage*. His name is Clay, and he is always perfectly polite."

"He attacked me in the road as I was leaving," Emil replied indignantly. "He laid hands on me and dragged me back against my will! There will be a reckoning between us!"

"I asked him to bring you back," Kate told him softly. "He was very kind to do it."

"Bah!"

"Don't you want to go on living with us, Emil?"

Emil tilted his head. "I consider it. But the matter is far from settled."

***

They finished their lunch in a leisurely fashion, and when they were done, Kate walked out to the curb and waved for a cab. A gleaming hansom rolled up, and it soon whisked them to the elegant street where Denver's finest couturiers created expensive custom clothing.

The cabman helped Kate down, and a smiling young man opened the front door of a neat brownstone for them. They discovered that the inside of the establishment was wood panelled, richly upholstered, deeply carpeted, and very discreet.

An impeccably dressed older man met Kate and bowed slightly. "Good afternoon, madame. Welcome to Monsieur Girard Couturiers. My name is Edward. How may I help you?"

Kate opened a small velvet handbag and pulled out a tiny piece of paper. "I wish to order five suits of clothes, and matching shoes and hats, for my fiancé. We will be married soon, but he suffered an injury and is unable to come in himself. I have his measurements here."

"Allow me to wish you and your fiancé every happiness, madame."

"*Merci*," Kate smiled and handed the paper to the man who perused it with a nod.

"We have a large catalogue of the latest styles from Paris and London; also fabric swatches and colour palettes. Please follow me."

Kate took Emil's hand and followed the man through the elegant drawing room through a polished door. It opened onto what looked like a salon, with a couch and upholstered chairs.

"Please have a seat. I'll be back momentarily. Would you like a cup of coffee, or perhaps a glass of wine?"

"Oh, no thank you. We just dined."

The man nodded towards Emil. "Perhaps your son would like a sweet?"

Kate turned to Emil, who was scowling. "I do not care for a *sweet*," he replied severely, and the man raised an eyebrow and left.

After he left, Kate turned to Emil. "That wasn't very polite, Emil," she told him.

"Sweets! They are what I offer my *copines*," Emil told her scornfully. "I will ask him for a cigarette instead."

"You will certainly not get one," Kate told him.

The man returned in a few minutes, carrying several large catalogues and rings of cloth samples. He took a seat to one side of Kate and passed a catalogue to her. He pointed to an illustration of two young men in evening clothes.

"Madame will notice that this year, for formal wear, the gentleman's full-dress tailcoat is *de rigueur*, and is made of fine black wool with satin lapels. The matching waistcoat is cut quite low, and the shirt has a plain front with a high collar and white silk bow tie. The trousers are also of fine black wool with a narrow, slightly tapering leg."

Kate tilted her head and murmured: "What do you think, Emil? The full-dress suit, or the tuxedo for Doc?"

Emil glanced at the pictures. "The full-dress suit looks much better," he replied decisively. "The tuxedo jacket is too loose."

"I agree." She raised her eyes to the salesman and added, "We will take the full-dress suit with the white tie, the black leather shoes, and the silk top hat."

"Madame has impeccable taste," the man murmured, and produced a different catalogue.

"Here we have selections for less formal attire, for business occasions, sporting events, and lounge wear. What would madame prefer to see first?"

Kate smiled and pressed a pink finger to the picture of an elegant young man. "Sporting events," she murmured.

***

By the time Kate and Emil emerged from the

brownstone, Kate had purchased a wedding suit for Doc, followed by three complete changes of clothes suitable for a casino evening, another for a hunting party, a half dozen velvet smoking jackets, silk and linen pyjamas, and a few other mysterious garments that made Emil frown in puzzlement.

She had also added to Emil's collection of fine brocade waistcoats and purchased two new pairs of custom trousers for him, plus three silk ties, a new silk hat, new shoes, and a beautiful full-dress suit of his own for the wedding.

The grand total, which the abashed salesman had whispered into her ear, came to more than a thousand dollars, but she paid it instantly, in cash, and without the slightest sign of distress.

"It has been a great pleasure to serve you, madame," the man told her with a smile. "Your purchases will be ready on Tuesday of next week. Will you return for them, or shall I have them shipped to your address?"

Kate smiled at Emil. "I think we will return for them," she replied. "That will give my son and I another excuse to have a pleasant time."

"Very good, madame."

The salesman escorted them to the door of the shop, hailed a cab for them, and opened the door of the cab as they climbed in.

"Good afternoon."

Kate and Emil settled into the plush seat of the cab, and the man closed the door. The cabman whipped up the horse, and the hansom rolled away.

But as soon as it disappeared, a man in a bowler hat

and a brown suit stepped out of a small alley nearby, threw his smouldering cigarillo down on the street, and hailed another cab. As soon as he jumped up into the door opening, he leaned over to whisper in the cabman's ear, and the rig clattered down the street after the previous vehicle at a slow, deliberate pace.

Chapter Fifty-Three

Doc raised himself on one elbow and struggled up to a sitting position in his bed. The house was empty, and there was no one to see if he shook off his enforced confinement. Kate had taken Emil into Denver to do some shopping, and Daisy and Clay had gone into Wolf Table to buy groceries.

Doc flung the bedcovers off. Over the last month, the searing pain in his chest had slowly subsided, and he was beginning to feel almost human again. He had the full use of his arms and upper body, but his legs had remained stubbornly wooden. He'd regained patchy areas of sensation in them, and he could move his feet a little, but his legs refused to hold him up.

The doctor had said that time was the only thing that would heal him, if he was going to be healed, but he'd been lying in bed for a month, and he was reaching the limits of his patience.

Or, if he was really honest with himself—he was beginning to fear that there would be no more change in his condition.

The doctor wanted him to use the wheeled chair, and he knew the doctor was right, but he'd refused. It was true that the rolling chair would help him get out of bed and move around the house; but he hated it.

Instead, he'd been secretly practicing with an elegant black cane that Kate had bought him. It was not a cane for invalids, but a gentleman's accessory for an evening out—and as such, acceptable to him.

He pulled it out from behind his pillow and set it firmly on the floor in front of him. The cane was stout and had a long, flat silver head that he could press under one armpit and use to support his weight until he could grasp the bedside chair with his other hand, and pull himself over into it, and back again.

It was hard to do because without just the right balance, the cane would go clattering onto the floor, and he'd fall back heavily on the bed.

Doc set his mouth, took a deep breath, and pressed the cane underneath his arm. He strained with all his strength, grabbed the seat of the chair, and swung himself over into the seat.

He fell heavily into the chair and overbalanced to one side before he could grasp the sides and right himself again, but it was the biggest improvement he'd made since the day he was brought back—moving from the bed, to a chair, and back again.

Doc leaned back into the chair, breathing hard. It had been exhausting at first, but the more he practiced, the more skilled he became. He was hoping that other things that he couldn't do at the moment would also come in time.

But he'd gone long enough without improvement, that he'd begun to wonder how he'd cope if he'd reached the end of his recovery.

If he never got his legs back.

Doc set his mouth into a hard, tight line. Until now, he hadn't allowed himself to face the worst. He'd been active all his life, and for the last ten years, he'd lived in the wilderness and relied on his physical strength for everything: food, shelter, defence.

But now he might have to ask Kate for help to go to town, or to ride on the train, or even to dress himself.

Doc closed his eyes. Kate had been an angel, but she was still young and beautiful, and he couldn't make her his nursemaid for the rest of her life. If things didn't change for him, he was going to cancel the wedding.

Kate would be hurt, but better she should be hurt now, and for a short time, than to be burdened with a hopeless invalid for the rest of her life.

***

Doc shook his head and bitter frustration burned his eyes. It was unimaginable to be bound to a chair for the rest of his life. He'd always been a thinking man and usually four thoughts ahead of everyone else in the room. But his mind couldn't save him this time.

Nothing could save him if his body didn't heal itself.

The sound of the front door opening, and Daisy's cheerful voice in the front room, made Doc grab the cane, press it under his arm, and swing his body back to the bed. He fell over, face down into the blanket, and had to pull himself upright, and lift his legs back into bed with his hands.

The effort exhausted him, and he fell back onto his pillow and closed his eyes. A moment later, Daisy walked in with Clay at her heels.

"Well, we're back, Doc. I got you some cigars from the mercantile, but what you want with 'em, I don't know. They so high-smellin', they stunk up everything else in the bag."

Doc glanced at the box. It was all they had in Wolf Table, and Daisy was right: they were cheap cigars.

"Thanks, Dase," he murmured and gave her a smile.

"I'm going back home," Clay told her and nodded to Doc. "I'll be back down in a day or two."

"Stay to dinner," Doc suggested, but Clay shook his head.

"Thanks, Doc, but I have to get back. Lots of stuff around my cabin needs doing."

Daisy followed him out and paused by the bedroom door. "Anything you need, Doc?"

"Not right now," he told her and smiled reassurance. "Do me a favour, Dase, and close the door on your way out. I'd like to rest for a while."

"I'll be quiet," Daisy told him and closed the door softly behind her.

***

Doc sighed, stared down at the box of cigars, and placed them on the bedside table. He glanced out the window. The afternoon sun was sifting through the branches of the big oak outside and painting the glass with white light and leafy shadows.

Doc watched the shadows dance and wondered if there was a God, and if so, if that God could be persuaded to help a man who'd never had the faintest knowledge of him or impulse towards him.

His visit to the church in Wolf Table had been the only time since his baptism that he'd attended any worship service. And he remembered the sermon that day only vaguely.

Something about a man running into the wilderness because he was in danger.

Something about him finding God there.

A wave of exhaustion swept over him, and he closed his eyes. Sleep slowly pulled him down into unconsciousness, and the last thought he had, before he dropped off, was a strange vision of a tall ladder stretching up into the sky, and a fiery creature descending to the earth from its unguessable heights. And a voice crying:

Surely the Lord is in this place; and I knew it not. How dreadful is this place! This is none other but the house of God, and this is the gate of heaven.

Chapter
Fifty-Four

Daisy poked her head under the table in the living room and frowned. She'd put her mother's Bible on that table a month ago, and it had laid there ever since, but it was gone now, and she couldn't figure where it went.

She knew she hadn't moved it, and the little shrimp was too small to tote such a heavy book. She'd asked Kate about it, and Kate had only laughed, and Doc was stove up in bed, and so he couldn't have taken it.

But she couldn't find it, no matter where she looked. That only left Clay, but he was strict about stuff like that; he never touched anything that didn't belong to him.

Daisy frowned, walked back to her bedroom and flopped down on the bed. She kicked her shoes off, crossed one knee over the other, and stared up at the ceiling.

Kate had finally talked her into sleeping in her own bedroom at night, instead of out in the hammock on the porch, but she'd only agreed because it was September, and the nights were getting cold.

They'd given her a bedroom with a soft bed, and a couple of bedside tables and a lamp, and a big wardrobe to keep her dresses in that she never wore.

It was a nice bedroom, with fancy wallpaper and a nice lamp with a painted shade, but sometimes it still made her feel so boxed in that she had to open the windows, and if the night was warm, sometimes she just snuck out and spent the night in the hammock anyway, and nobody the wiser.

Clay had laughed at her when she told him about it and teased her that she was getting citified, and it made her so mad that she hadn't talked to him for days. Mostly because it was true, and she didn't like it.

Kate had just kind of taken over at the house and didn't ask nobody no odds; she'd slapped Doc in that old wheeled chair and made him go around in it, even though it was plain as drums and bells that Doc hated the thing.

It was true that the chair helped him get around, but she would've let Doc make that decision if it was up to her.

Kate had hired a woman to come and cook for them, too, and that part she liked because nobody else at the house could cook worth a flip, but the old woman had started telling Kate that her daughter needed to wear a dress, and stirred Kate up against her, and the next thing she knew, Kate had bought her a corset and tried to truss her up in it like a Thanksgiving turkey, and had pulled them laces so tight she almost blacked out. She'd had to take her pocket knife and cut the strings loose, and Kate had shrieked out something in French and thrown her hands in the air; and when Doc heard about it, he got mad at her.

But nobody had peeped to her about a corset since then, and that suited her down to the ground.

A soft knock at the bedroom door made Daisy lift her head. "Come on in."

The door opened, and Kate appeared in it. "Your young man is here, Daisy," she said with a smile, and Daisy made a face.

Kate always made it sound like some big lovey-dovey thing, when the truth was that she liked Clay, and he liked her, and once in a while they kissed each other. It was as natural as breathing, and why Kate always smirked her lips when she saw Clay was beyond her.

"Thanks."

Daisy bounded up out of the bed, stuck her feet in her moccasins, and walked out to meet Clay. But to her thunderstruck amazement, when she walked out into the living room, Clay was standing there all slicked up in a white cowboy shirt, a pair of jeans, and a belt with a big buckle on it, and—a cowboy hat.

Daisy rolled her eyes to Kate, and the smile on the older woman's face confirmed it: she'd gotten ahold of Clay, all right.

Daisy put her hands on her hips, but there was something in Clay's eyes that warned her not to laugh. So she nodded and bit her lip.

"Fancy!" She walked all around him, nodding her head. "Real fancy! You look—"

"*Very* handsome," Kate suggested, smiling. "Doesn't he, Daisy?"

"Yep," Daisy nodded and swallowed a laugh. "Real nice!"

Clay straightened up, hooked his thumbs in his belt, and looked pleased. Kate rubbed her mouth with her hand and smiled: "Why don't the two of you go outside and pick some flowers for the dinner table tonight? It will be cheerful."

Daisy looked at Clay and shrugged, and they walked out across the back porch and across the sleepy back lawn, all the way down to the pond. Daisy flopped down on the ground, kicked her shoes off, and stuck her feet into the water, but Clay remained standing.

She squinted up at him. "Sit down, grandma," she scoffed. "What's wrong with you?"

Clay crouched down beside her but didn't sit on the grass. "I don't want to mess up my clothes," he told her.

Daisy looked up at him, and a soft smile dawned over her face. Clay was tickled pink about his new duds; she could see that. And it surprised her: as well as she knew him, she'd never have guessed he cared about them kind of things.

"You look good."

"I feel good. Never thought I'd bother with slicking up, but—it's nice, Dase."

Daisy smiled up into his face, and on an impulse, stood on her knees, walked over, and reached for his ears: but Clay caught her hands and put them on his face instead.

***

They stayed out by the pond for a while, and when they finally returned, carrying a handful of scraggly pond irises, they paused at the back door because Doc had come out into the living room and was sitting in the wheeled chair.

To Daisy's surprise, they seemed to have caught Doc and Kate—*flirting* with one another. Doc and Kate were well past their prime, in their mid-thirties at least, and Daisy watched in horrified fascination as her elderly father cavorted with his fiancé.

Kate flounced past playfully as Doc half-turned his head to follow her. She ran her fingers across his broad shoulders, tugged his ear, and bent down to peek into his face with laughing eyes as she sang:

"Catch me if you can

You're just the gentleman

To make a lady quite misplace her wits;

It's scandalous and shocking

But I'll show my ankle stocking

To see what kind of mischievous you get.

Oh! You naughty fellow,

I'm just a poor marsh mellow

When your moustache tickles underneath my ear;

Don't you dare dismiss me,

Pucker up and kiss me

And take me in your arms again, my dear!"

Daisy leaned one elbow against the doorframe and put her other hand on her hip, and Clay sputtered with silent laughter as he watched Kate whirl flirtatiously around Doc's chair.

"Come on, Dase," Clay told her and turned to go. "This is a private party."

Daisy shot them a wry look and turned to follow, but she noticed that Doc was laughing for the first time since he'd come down off the mountain, and she was just in time to see him grab Kate's hands and pull her to his lips.

Daisy shook her head and followed. Kate had made a lot of changes around the place, all right, and she wasn't sure she liked all of them: but one thing was plain as day—Kate was *good* for Doc.

And in her book, that made up for all the rest.

Chapter
Fifty-Five

Emil turned in his little bed and murmured in his sleep. It was almost three in the morning, and even though his pajamas were made of fine linen, and his pillow of goose down, he frowned and tossed.

He was having a nightmare. He dreamed that the little redheaded boy in town had stolen three of his *copines,* and in a town as small as Wolf Table, that was a catastrophic loss.

He was considering whether he could win them back with candy, or if he would be obliged to fight, when a scraping sound made him open his eyes sleepily.

The next thing he knew, a big, dirty hand clapped over his mouth, and he was pulled roughly from his bed and slung over a man's shoulder like a sack of salt. He cried out, but the sound was hopelessly muffled by the man's beefy palm; and the fellow sat down in his open window and stepped outside, just as he had stepped in.

Emil beat the man's chest with his fists, but the man growled: "Be still, or I'll break your neck!"

Emil's curly head bobbed up and down as the man jogged across the dark yard and out to the road. He was handed up to another man sitting in a closed carriage. The man pulled Emil inside and slammed the door shut, and then the driver whipped up the horses, and the carriage bounced away down the road. The other man jumped up onto his horse and followed at a gallop.

It was over within ten minutes.

The silence of deep night settled down again over the house, and the only sound to trouble the sleep of the occupants was the hum of crickets and the occasional purr of owls.

But Emil straightened up on the carriage seat, adjusted his rumpled pyjamas, and glared at the men sitting opposite him. They were swine—low, vile *poltrons*, men of the kind that Monsieur Talleyrand had once said were not worth a bullet.

"How dare you lay hands on me!" he cried. "Who are you, and where are you taking me, dogs?"

One of them, a short, thick-set man, glanced at him. "Shut up, or I'll make you shut up."

Emil's eyes flashed. "You offer me a low insult? I demand satisfaction!"

"I'll give you satisfaction," the man growled and grabbed for Emil's head, but his companion, a taller, well-dressed man, shoved him to one side.

"He said to bring him in alive and in one piece. I don't want to have to explain to him."

The other man adjusted his shoulder and looked away

angrily. "Just keep the little monkey quiet, then, or I'll smash his mouth."

The taller man turned his eyes to Emil's outraged face. "You hear that, kid? You better settle down if you know what's good for you."

Emil glared at him but subsided into fuming silence, and the carriage rattled down the dark road at a breakneck pace.

An hour later, the carriage rattled into Denver and turned into a broad alleyway, and then another until it stopped just behind the Lucky Seven Casino. The tall man grabbed Emil and hustled him out of the carriage, across the alley, and through a small door.

They came out into a larger passage, and the man clapped his hand over Emil's mouth as they walked to its end. The casino was closed and empty except for a cleaning crew in the main hall, and they moved unseen to the little elevator. The shorter man produced a key, unlocked the cage, and held the door open as they stepped inside.

Soon they were moving up, and Emil's eyes widened in wonder as floor after floor glided past, just like they were flying through space.

The car stopped at the fifth floor, and the shorter man pulled the cage door aside again. The taller man took his hand off Emil's mouth, and they walked down to an ornate door at the end of the hall.

It opened out onto a huge room with a western wall that was made almost totally of glass. A thickset, redheaded man was seated at a desk at the far end, and Emil's face gathered darkness.

"Swine!" he cried, pointing at the man, "Murderer! Kidnapper! There will be a reckoning between us!"

An auburn-haired woman, lounging in a chair to one side, laughed and turned to the man. "He forgot *exciting host*," she drawled and rose lazily. She walked over to where Emil stood and played idly with his hair, but Emil pulled away in outrage.

"You are not my mother!"

"No, she isn't," Judge agreed, and the woman turned angry eyes to his face, drew herself up haughtily, and swept out of the room.

Judge nodded to the two men. "Take him down the hall, and keep him quiet," he growled. "And I better not see any marks on him. If he gets hurt, I'll throw you two to the sheriff."

The taller man gave the shorter one a significant glance and took Emil by the arm, and he was hustled out of the big apartment and down the hall to another, smaller apartment.

There were two women lounging in it. They were wearing long dressing gowns, and their flowing hair fell loose over their shoulders. The oldest was in her thirties, and she walked over and knelt down in front of Emil.

"Why hello, honey." She laughed, and tickled his chin. "What's your name?" She looked up at the tall man and giggled. "He belong to one of you?"

"No, thank God," the heavyset man retorted and sat down heavily on a tufted sofa.

"Look at his little silk pyjamas, Ruby," she called to the other woman. "He's dressed like a little prince!"

The other girl rose curiously and came to kneel down in front of Emil. "He's a purty thing, ain't he?" She smiled. "How old are you, honey?"

"In six years," Emil replied coldly, "I have already seen this country, and have witnessed duels, and played poker and faro in many gambling houses. I have six *copines*, and I am not a child."

"He talks like a prince, too." The first girl giggled. "And look, Opal—he's got a little gold earring in one ear!"

"What are you getting paid to do?" the heavy man demanded. "Crazy women paying more attention to a kid, than to us!"

"You jealous?" the older woman teased and stood up.

"We're supposed to be watching this kid," the taller man reminded him. "Not those girls. Come on."

He took Emil by the hand and led him through another door in the suite, and the heavy man followed reluctantly as the two women shook their skirts at him and laughed.

Chapter **Fifty-Six**

Kate stretched luxuriantly in her bed, yawned, and reached for her lacy dressing gown. She pulled it on, placed her long braid over one shoulder, and rose to greet the day.

Golden morning light was streaming through her bedroom window, and the smell of coffee wafted in from the kitchen, where Mrs Hawkins had been toiling since seven o'clock.

It was now a little past eight, and a beautiful fall morning for a nice breakfast on the back porch. Kate slid her feet into her slippers and walked out into the living room.

She drifted into the kitchen, where a metal tray holding two steaming coffee cups awaited her. She lifted one to her lips with an expression of deep appreciation.

"Morning, ma'am."

"Good morning, Mrs Hawkins," Kate replied pleasantly. "I think we will have our breakfast on the porch this morning."

"If you like. I'll have it ready in about ten minutes."

"*Merci.*"

Kate carried the tray to Doc's bedroom door and knocked softly with her foot. "*Bon matin!*" she called softly. "Wake up, sleepyhead."

She pushed the door open and peeped inside. Doc had thrown one elbow over his face, and he groaned incoherently.

Kate dimpled and pushed in. She set the tray down on his bedside table and let the scent of steaming coffee work its magic. Doc opened an eye and lowered his arm.

"Is that coffee?"

"Black, and piping hot," she told him and handed the cup to him carefully. Doc pulled himself up to a sitting position and took it.

"I think we will have breakfast on the porch this morning," Kate told him. "It's lovely out, and not too cold."

"Are the kids up?"

"Not yet," Kate murmured, and put the cup to her lips. "Or at least, I didn't see them. Emil never rises before nine, and Daisy may be outside. She sometimes sleeps in the hammock."

Doc sighed but reached for Kate's hand, and she took it and laughed. "Don't scold her. She will soon be married, and it will be her husband's challenge, not yours."

Doc paused in the act of lifting the cup to his lips. "I hope you're wrong," he murmured. "I don't want Dase to get married right away."

"No? But why?" Kate asked. "She and her young *copain* are so sweet together."

Doc raised pained eyes to her face. "I'd feel better about it if Clay could offer her something besides a cabin in the woods. He's barely surviving up there."

"Perhaps you could give him a job."

"I've tried. He's too proud. He won't take anything he thinks is charity."

"What can he do?"

"Hunt and fish. Track. Ride."

"He could work on a ranch, then."

Doc nodded. "Maybe. But that would take him out of town. The nearest big ranch is the Circle T, and that's in Indian Rock."

"We'll have to enquire."

The sound of Mrs Hawkins' voice made Kate smile and turn her head. "Breakfast is ready! I'll bring your chair in a moment."

Kate set her cup down on the table and walked out to the back porch, where the cook had plates and cups already set on the wicker tables.

"Oh, Mrs Hawkins, did you drop this?" Kate bent

down to retrieve a large white envelope on the porch floor.

The older woman glanced at it. "No. It ain't mine."

Kate turned away and flipped the heavy envelope over. On the opposite side, the words KATE DUBOIS were scrawled in ugly black letters.

Kate took a few steps down the porch and opened the envelope. A big, crumpled piece of paper was inside, and she unfolded it, frowning. To her horror, the paper read:

KATE DUBOIS. WE GOT YOUR KID. IF YOU CALL THE LAW, WE'LL KILL HIM.

Kate put a hand to her mouth, and she whirled on her heel and rushed back into the house.

"Emil!"

She burst into her son's room. To Kate's dismay, Emil's pillow and bedcovers were on the floor, and there was no sign of him, but the window was open, and the curtain rod had been knocked askew.

Kate looked down at the paper through swimming eyes.

COME TO THE LUCKY SEVEN. YOU KNOW WHY.

Kate put a hand to her mouth to stifle a sob and closed her eyes in misery.

Doc's voice wafted in from his bedroom. "Kate, is that you? I thought I heard your voice. Is something wrong?"

Kate turned instantly. "No, nothing's wrong," she called and tried to put a smile into her voice. "I just remembered, I need a—a bottle of cream, from town. I'll go and get it. It won't take a minute!"

There was a heavy silence, and Doc finally replied: "You sound upset."

"No, I swear it!" she called and laughed. "I may even bring back a bottle of wine, for later. I'll tell Mrs Hawkins to bring your chair."

Kate put a hand to her cheek and wiped away the tears; then she hurried to her bedroom and dressed faster than she'd ever done in her life.

Ten minutes later, she emerged from her bedroom in a tailored black dress, black boots, black gloves, black hat, and a black revolver, tucked into a hidden pocket in her skirt.

Kate paused on the threshold of the house to carefully secure her hat with a pair of long, heavy pins, and to fumble with her bag.

As she stepped out of the house, the crumpled paper fell out of her bag and onto the porch, but she was in too much of a hurry to look back.

Chapter Fifty-Seven

Daisy walked back into the house at ten o'clock, after having spent the morning fishing in the pond. She left a pail of fish on the back porch and walked into the house looking for food.

Mrs Hawkins looked at her with a disapproving eye. "Where have you been all morning, girl?" she asked. "Miss Dubois was asking for you, and you missed breakfast."

Daisy looked over her shoulder. "Got any left?"

The older woman dried her hands on her apron. "I saved you a plate." She took a plate off the counter and handed it to Daisy, who took it to the front porch, and sat down on the steps and ate.

She gobbled up the eggs and bacon and toast within ten minutes, and the sound of the wheeled chair rolling over the floor made her look back over her shoulder.

Doc sat there in the doorway with a worried look on his face. "Have you seen Kate, Dase?"

Daisy shook her head and mumbled: "Not since last night. Why, is she gone?"

"She left for town two hours ago, and she hasn't come back. I'm starting to get worried."

Daisy slapped her hands clean, then picked a crumpled piece of paper up off the porch. "Throw that away, would you Doc? I've gotta go clean my fish." She tossed the paper onto Doc's lap and breezed past him.

Doc glanced towards Wolf Table with a worried frown, but there was no sign of Kate. He stayed on the porch and watched the road for thirty minutes, but there was no movement on the narrow dirt track running past his front door—not even a solitary rider.

He sighed in frustration and glanced down at the paper. It was wrinkled and dirty, and he was about to wad it up and toss it into a trash basket when he saw thick black letters partially bleeding through from the opposite side. He flipped the paper over, and his brows slowly lowered over his eyes.

KATE DUBOIS. I GOT YOUR KID. IF YOU CALL THE LAW, I'LL KILL HIM.

COME TO THE LUCKY SEVEN. YOU KNOW WHY.

YOU'RE GOING TO MAKE IT ALL UP TO ME.

Doc swore softly, threw the paper down, and turned the chair sharply back into the house. He sent it flying to the back door and called:

"Dase, I want you to go up to the cabin today. Go and get the rest of our stuff and bring it down. I want all of it back down here."

Daisy looked up at him in mild surprise as she skinned the fish. "Ain't much left up there to get," she told him. "Just a few blankets, and pails and such."

"It's sentimental to me, Dase."

Daisy looked up at him and grinned. "All right. It'll give me a chance to talk to Clay. He's been up there for a week now, and it's only fair that I go see him, now and again."

"Run on now."

Daisy shrugged, wiped her hands, and stood up. "All right, Doc. Just don't let my fish spoil."

"I won't."

Daisy grabbed a glass of water off the sink, took a deep pull, and sauntered out of the house, out across the lawn, and away. Doc watched her go, and as soon as she was gone, he sent the chair back into his bedroom.

***

It took him thirty minutes to pull on his clothes, and as he was dressing, he tried to cobble everything together in his mind.

Emil had been kidnapped last night and taken down to the Lucky Seven. Judge was holding him; it couldn't be anyone but Judge, and he'd done it to bring Kate to heel.

To bring her under his control again.

To get revenge against the woman who'd rejected him.

Doc rolled the chair to his bedside table, opened the drawer. He pulled his pistols out, loaded them expertly, and put one in his jacket and the other in his boot.

Kate had gotten the letter earlier that morning, and that explained the frantic note in her voice, the sound that had made him call out to her. She'd lied to him and gone to Denver alone because she didn't want to frustrate him, didn't want to make him feel useless.

Doc took hold of the black cane, braced it against the floor, and slowly lifted himself out of the chair. He swayed on his feet, grasped the back of the chair, and slowly got his balance.

He'd been practicing secretly for weeks, and no one had seen him stand. He hadn't wanted to get their hopes raised until he was sure he could walk.

He didn't know how far he could walk without falling down, but he was about to find out.

Doc moved slowly to a chest of drawers and pulled out the second drawer. He flipped the false back, and pulled out bundle after bundle of cash and threw them into a small leather valise.

Then he took the black cane in one hand, and the valise in the other, and walked slowly out of the bedroom and across the living room floor.

Mrs Hawkins came to the door of the kitchen, shrieked, and dropped a plate of biscuits when she saw him. But he only turned to her and said:

"I'm going down to Denver. If I'm not back by tomorrow morning, I want you to go for the sheriff and tell him to arrest Judge Carter of the Lucky Seven Casino for my murder."

The woman goggled at him, and he walked out to the barn to saddle the wretched mule and beat him to the train depot. But Ezekiel was almost the only animal he could ride because the brute was shorter than a horse and easier to mount.

Doc managed to saddle the mule and then pull himself slowly onto its back, and once he was there, he kicked it savagely. The beast took off down the road, and Doc found himself praying as he went.

Oh God, hear me now. Hear me please.

I've never been a religious man, and I've never cared for you. But I need your help. I'll do anything you want.

I read in that book that you want me to repent; so I'll repent. I'll give up anything, do anything.

Anything you want.

Just help me get Kate and Emil back alive.

Give me the strength to protect them. Help me get there in time!

He kicked the mule again, and it screamed in protest but took off flying down the road at a flat gallop, and he drove it as hard as it would run, all the way into town.

Chapter Fifty-Eight

"I'm beat."

Daisy threw a pile of old blankets down on the front porch of the house and flopped down on the floor. She'd spent most of the day up on the mountain, and it was late afternoon.

"What Doc wants with all them ratty things, I don't know. Wouldn't have figured he cared anything for 'em."

Clay sat down beside her and set down a bag of pots and pans. "Well, at least the cabin's cleaned out."

Daisy turned her head and called back into the house. "We're back, Doc!" she called. "Come and get all these blankets you're sentimental about."

But instead of Doc, the frazzled cook appeared in the doorway, wringing her hands. "Where have you been, girl!" she cried. "I've been beside myself!"

Daisy frowned at her. "What's wrong?"

"What's wrong! Miss Dubois went into town this morning and never came back, the little boy is gone, and Mr Dailey came walking out of his bedroom and out of this house—"

Daisy and Clay whooped together, and Daisy jumped up and grabbed the woman by the shoulders.

"*Walking*! You saw Doc walking?"

Mrs Hawkins nodded in distress. "Yes. But he was so strange! He told me that if he wasn't back by tomorrow, to go get the sheriff and tell him to arrest someone down at the Lucky Seven Casino in Denver. For his—his murder!"

Her mouth crumpled up, and she stared fearfully into Daisy's eyes. "You don't suppose that Mr Dailey's ordeal has affected his *mind*?"

Clay stood up, frowning. "Doc went down into Denver?"

"Yes, I tell you! And I'm worried about Miss Dubois. She only meant to go shopping for a little while, but she's been gone all day. The little boy is missing, too!"

Daisy frowned at her. "Doc didn't tell you nothing else?"

The woman shook her head. "He just got that mule and rode him off towards town."

Daisy looked up at Clay, and he shook his head. "Doc sent you up the mountain to get you out of the way, Dase," he told her. "Something bad's happened. Does Doc have any enemies?"

Daisy scowled. "The Prophet told me that a man was trying to kill Doc. Probably had to do with his gambling, but I'm not sure."

"That would make the most sense," Clay mused. "But it's crazy for Doc to go down there when he can hardly walk. There had to be some real strong reason for him to go."

"It all started this morning when Miss Dubois picked up that letter on the back porch," Mrs Hawkins fretted. "I don't know what it said, but she ran out right after, and she hasn't come back!"

"Letter? What letter?" Daisy demanded.

"I tell you; I don't know. But whatever it was, she left right after she read it."

Clay stepped into the living room and bent down to pick a crumpled piece of paper off the floor. He handed it to Daisy.

"Could this be it?" he asked grimly.

Daisy read it in frowning silence and looked up at Clay. "The devil who sent this, whoever he is, grabbed Kate's little shrimp, and she must've skunked out to Denver to get him back. But they ain't no talk of money in this thing, and I don't like the way it sounds."

"Doc didn't either, and that's why he left," Clay murmured.

"I can't let Doc go down there alone," Daisy told him with a worried look. "He's still half crippled, and if he's not careful, he'll—he'll be dead before tomorrow," she finished, in a small, shaken voice.

"We need to go get the sheriff, Dase," Clay told her. "Let him handle it. You got no business going down to that casino. There's nothing you can do there except get hurt!"

"The devil you say!" Daisy cried, eyes flashing. "You don't have to come with me if you don't want to!"

Clay stared at her in desperate appeal. "Dase, for once in your life be reasonable! If you go down there, you'll be putting Doc and Kate in danger, not helping them!"

"If you can't stand with me, then get out of my way!" Daisy retorted and pushed him aside.

"Where are you going?"

"To get Doc's shotgun!"

Clay grabbed her by the shoulders. "If you go down there and start waving a shotgun around, they'll shoot you!"

"I ain't afraid of it! Let me go!"

Clay held her still and stared into her face desperately. "Daisy, if—if you promise to leave the gun here, I'll come with you. I'll help you get in."

Daisy searched his eyes. "Why would I even go without a gun?" she demanded. "Ain't nothing left to talk about. They grabbed the shrimp, and they want to kill Doc!"

"We'll think of something. I'll help you. But only if you leave the gun here!"

"Blast you, come on then!" Daisy told him bitterly. "We're wasting time arguing about it!"

Clay's expression lightened, and he took her arm. "We can make the last train down if we hurry," he told her, and together they ran out the front door and out into the road.

"Wait!" Mrs Hawkins called after them. "This is madness! What about the sheriff?"

But to her dismay, there was no answer.

Chapter
Fifty-Nine

Kate slipped into the little service hall at the back end of the Lucky Seven. It was still morning, and the place was dark and empty. There was no sign of life on the first floor, except for the distant sound of a lone employee setting out glassware.

Kate moved silently to the end of the hall, to the little vestibule that housed the elevator. The cage was locked tight, and there was no sign of a key.

Kate glanced back over her shoulder, and seeing no one, reached up and pulled two steel pins from her hat. The first was thick and straight and had a flat elbow at one end, and she pushed it against the bottom of the lock and held it down. Then she pushed the second pin into the lock and began to move it carefully.

It took her five tries, but on the fifth, the lock clicked softly, and Kate opened the door and stepped inside.

She pressed the button for the fifth floor, and as the car ascended, she carefully placed the pins back into her hat and smoothed her hair.

***

Kate stepped out into the deeply carpeted hall holding

a black revolver in one gloved hand. The sight of the ornately-carved door at the end of the hall made her arch an eyebrow in contempt, and she moved towards it silently.

She put her hand on the knob and tested it gently. To her surprise, it wasn't locked, but she didn't walk in immediately.

She drew herself up, took a deep breath, and the frowning, troubled look on her face slowly vanished. It was replaced by an expression as serene and untroubled as dawn.

Kate concealed her pistol hand behind the folds of her skirt and opened the door with the other. It swung open on a cavernous room with a wall of huge windows overlooking the city.

Judge was seated at a desk at the far end, looking down at something, and she moved quickly and silently towards him. A quick glance right and left told her that they were alone, and she raised the pistol and aimed it at the back of his head.

Judge didn't turn around, but his dragon-voice greeted her calmly.

"Hello, Kate."

She stopped in the middle of the room, still holding the gun. "Where's my son?"

Judge turned then, and his smiling eyes raked over her. "I'm surprised at you, Kate. A pistol? Really? We're old friends here."

Kate kept the gun on him as he pressed a button, and a moment later a tall man appeared in a doorway to the left. To her joy, he was dragging Emil by one arm.

"*Maman!*" Emil shrieked, and Kate fought to maintain her poker face as she gobbled him up with her eyes.

Judge turned to her with a wry expression. "Put that pistol down, Kate. I don't have any plans to hurt your little boy. For the love of all that's holy—have a seat, and let us behave like civilized people." He gestured towards a seat, but Kate's green eyes narrowed.

"Give me my son back, or I'll blow your head off," she said softly and cocked the trigger.

Judge laced his fingers together on the desk and sighed. "Put down that gun, or I'll tell Cecil there to break his neck."

They stared at one another for a pregnant moment, and then Judge nodded towards the man. He grabbed Emil like a doll and closed his hands on his neck.

"No, no!" Kate shrieked and threw out an imploring hand. "Don't hurt him!"

Judge smiled at her and held out his hand for the gun. "I knew you'd see reason, Kate."

Kate slowly handed it to him without taking her eyes from Emil, but the man slammed the door shut, and she could hear Emil's voice crying as he was dragged away.

She turned burning eyes to Judge's smug face and

whispered: "If any harm comes to Emil, I'll kill you."

"No harm will come to Emil, if you're reasonable Kate."

"What do you want?"

"Please—sit down."

Kate lowered herself into the chair facing his desk, and Judge turned and stood up. He came out from behind the desk and walked over beside her, and Kate watched him, her eyes glittering with contempt.

"If this is about the money Doc won from you, I can put your mind at rest," she told him scornfully. "He won it fairly. But if it still rankles—after ten *years*—I'll gladly write you a check for twenty-five thousand dollars."

Judge walked up behind her and put his hands lightly on her shoulders. "It's not about the money, Kate. It was never about the money." He leaned down and whispered in her ear:

"I propose we play a few rounds of poker. Just you and I."

She turned her face away, but Judge took her chin in one hand and compelled her to look at him. "A tournament, Kate. Winner take all. And you get your son back, either way.

"If you win, you and your little boy leave here, and no hard feelings.

"If you lose, you and your little boy leave here, the same way.

"But if you lose, you satisfy my curiosity, Kate. And not reluctantly," Judge murmured, and ran his thick fingers across her neck. "Willingly. Enthusiastically. For a long, long time."

Kate glared at him but said nothing.

"Then—and *only* then—we'll be even, you and I."

Chapter Sixty

The last train into Union Station arrived a little after eight o'clock. The sun had set, and gas lamps flickered along the Denver streets as Daisy and Clay hurried towards the Lucky Seven.

"You still ain't told me no great ideas," Daisy told Clay reproachfully. "How are we going to get the shrimp, or protect Doc, without any guns?"

Clay glanced at his own cowboy shirt and jeans, and Daisy's loose boy's shirt and pants. "We'll stand out like a sore thumb if we try to get in," he mused. "Everybody else is slicked up, and we ain't."

"If we had shotguns, that part wouldn't matter!"

They rounded the corner, and the Lucky Seven suddenly appeared in all its glory. The windows in all five floors glowed golden, and music and laughter streamed from its ornate double doors. The sidewalks and streets outside were packed with people.

But the railroad track temporarily blocked their way. A train was parked on the tracks, and they had to walk far around to get to the other side.

Clay studied it as they walked past. The train was carrying freight, mostly livestock, and he suddenly ran up and jumped up on a wooden slat in the ventilated car.

Daisy stared at him. "What're you doing?"

Clay climbed up the slats and poked his head over the top of the car. "These are roofless cars, Dase."

"Well, hoo-ray."

"I can get inside!"

Daisy put her hands on her hips. "Why the fool would you *want* to?"

Clay's smiling face stared down at her. "There's ten cars of cattle sitting right here in front of the Lucky Seven."

"So?"

"If Doc and Kate are inside the casino, trying to get Emil, wouldn't it be good if something pulled everybody's attention away from what was going on inside?"

A sneaking grin dawned across Daisy's face, and she put her hands on her hips.

"If I can climb down inside this car, I can open the door and throw down the ramp." Clay smiled.

Daisy was already on her way to the car behind him. "You open that one, and I'll get this!"

Clay grinned and climbed over the top of the car, and Daisy's cackling laugh drifted back to him in the darkness.

***

But inside the Lucky Seven, Emil sat in the corner of the small room where he was being held, nursing a red nose and a pouting lip. The two swine who were holding him were playing poker to amuse themselves, and no one had given him a crumb of food or a swallow of water in all the time he'd been there.

What was even more outrageous, his *Maman* was in the other room, being held by their wicked enemy.

Emil rolled resentful eyes to the two men as they played cards. The pigs had offered him unforgiveable insult, and he had reached the limits of his endurance.

It was, in fact, time for action.

Emil scrambled down from the sofa where he was sitting and stood at the side of the poker table. He watched with keen eyes as the stocky man dealt cards.

Suddenly Emil jerked ramrod-straight and shrieked: "Aha! He's stacking the deck! Watch his hands—he's cheating!"

The dealer growled: "Shut up, you little mongrel!"

"I saw it! You stacked the deck!"

The man threw down the deck and snatched at him. "You're nothing but Mama's little *café au lait bâtard*! We'll sell you down to Mexico, and then we'll see what happens to that smart mouth!"

"Leave him alone!" the other man cried and pulled Emil out of his grasp. "And the game is over. I want to see that deck!"

The heavyset man scowled at him. "Are you calling me a cheat?"

"I wondered why I was losing every game! I'm taking my money back!"

"Oh no, you *ain't*!"

Emil scrambled out of the tall man's arms as the heavy one surged across the table. The two of them fell on the card table, and it collapsed with a crash, and they began to roll on the floor.

Emil ran to the chair where the heavyset man had been sitting and pulled a pistol out of the gun holster hanging over the back. Emil checked the gun for bullets, found it fully loaded, and scampered out of the room as the men thrashed back and forth.

He ran through the larger salon and out to the hallway. When he opened the door, he found the passage empty, and walked out boldly.

There was no sign of life, but a faint sound from the end of the hall drew him like a magnet.

His mother's soft voice.

Emil walked to the carved door and opened it a crack. There was a card table set up in the middle of a big room, and his mother and the redheaded man were playing poker. Outside, the lights of Denver flickered in the darkness through huge windows.

"That's four games for me, and four for you," the man's gravelly voice rumbled. "This will be the tiebreaker, Kate!"

She glanced at him in distaste and made no reply.

Sounds from the hall behind made Emil turn his head. The sound of pursuit was approaching, and he opened the door quickly and slipped inside the apartment. The heavy footsteps pounded off down the hall in the other direction, and neither of the poker players lifted their heads.

Emil moved behind a potted plant and watched as Kate took the deck and shuffled it expertly. But as he watched, his eyes widened in recognition as her hands flashed back and forth—almost too quick to follow.

Chapter
Sixty-One

Daisy flung the ramp down from the sixth cattle car, and Clay's voice called her from the darkened street.

"Hurry up, Dase!"

She scampered down the ramp, and Clay took her hand. They ran back to the last car, and Clay left her on the sidewalk. "Stay here, Dase. And watch!"

He ran to the car, jumped up onto the lowest slat, and yelled: "Yeahh! Go, go, go!"

Daisy put her fingers to her lips and blew a piercing whistle, and the cattle in the last car shifted, bellowed, and then began to pour down the ramp and out into the street.

"*Yee-ahh*! Go, go!" Clay ran towards them, whooping and waving his hat, and the cows turned away from him and fled down the street. As they ran, the cattle in the other cars came stumbling down the ramps and into the flowing stream, and Daisy laughed to see swells lose their high hats and ladies their bags as they scattered into the safety of shops and restaurants.

Daisy and Clay followed on the run, whistling and

whooping, and drove hundreds of cattle down the road. The street was clear and empty straight ahead as it ran past the north side of the Lucky Seven. But as they watched, the lead cows floundered, bellowed, rolled their white eyes, and veered sharply to the right, stumbling over each other in terror as if a wall of fire blocked the empty road ahead.

The stampede poured right, and veered again, sharply left—and right through the front doors of the Lucky Seven.

The flying cattle scattered the people on the sidewalk, smashed through the open front doors of the Lucky Seven and poured in, trampling furniture and sliding across the marble floors. The sound of screams and breaking glass issued from the depths of the casino, and soon bedraggled patrons came climbing out, dodging away from the cows still pouring into the building.

***

On the fifth floor, Emil watched from behind the potted plant as his mother shuffled the deck of cards. But suddenly Judge's big hand shot out and grabbed her wrist. His gray eyes narrowed in fury.

"Why, you cheating little witch!" he cried, and Kate rose from the table in alarm. "I've been sitting at this table all day, watching your hands, and only just now—"

Kate jerked her hand free and backed away as he rose and strode towards her. "I gave you a chance," he fumed. "I played fair. But you've cheated me from the first day we met!"

Kate screamed and turned to flee, but Judge caught her by the arm and threw her down across the desk. He leaned over her, and with a lightning fast swipe, ripped the neck of her dress open as she screamed and thrashed.

Emil stepped out from behind the plant, tucked his left hand behind his back, and called out loudly: "*En garde*! Defend yourself, brute—or be shot down like a dog!"

Kate lifted her head and shrieked, "Run, run Emil!"

Emil lifted the pistol, touched it to his nose, and then pointed it slowly at Judge's broad back.

"This is your last warning!"

But Judge frowned and looked up from Kate's anguished face. An ominous sound from the street below made him suddenly release her and hurry to the window. The floor trembled faintly, and screams began to rise up from the sidewalk outside the building.

Judge looked down into the street, and to his horror, hundreds of cattle came pouring from the rail line, thundering towards the entrance of the Lucky Seven.

He swore savagely and turned towards the door just in time to be shot. Emil's pistol cracked loudly, and Judge staggered back with a bleeding arm.

"Why you little devil!" he snarled and yanked the desk drawer open in fury. Kate twisted over on the desktop and clawed at his hands.

"No, no!" she sobbed, and fought frantically for the gun Judge had in his hand. "Run, Emil, run!"

But Emil stood calmly with one hand tucked behind his back and his pistol raised skyward as he waited for his dueling opponent to fire.

Judge swore and backhanded Kate's jaw, and she was sent rolling over the desk and onto the floor. The sight made Emil shout:

"Bah, I am done with you—swine! Dog without honour!"

Emil lifted the pistol and fired again, and Judge dove for the floor as the window shattered behind him. The pistol spun across the desk and fell onto the floor at its massive base.

But the sound of gunfire drew a new arrival from the hall outside. The big carved door swung open, and Doc walked through it.

He took the scene in at one glance: Emil, standing ramrod straight with a smoking pistol in his hand; Judge Carter, rising slowly from behind his desk, and Kate, lying face down on the floor with her dress torn and her hair falling around her shoulders.

Doc's cold blue eyes narrowed on Judge. "Emil, give me that gun."

"Do it, Emil!" Kate shrieked. Emil considered, then bowed slightly, and handed the pistol to Doc.

Doc leaned on the black cane and trained the gun on Judge, and Kate scrambled up from the floor and ran to her son. Doc half-turned his head as she passed.

"Did he hurt you, Kate?"

She glanced at him gratefully. "No. No, Doc."

Emil's eyes blazed. "He struck her with his fist!" he cried.

Kate unceremoniously pushed him out the door and down the hall to the elevator, but Doc stayed behind.

He pushed the door shut behind him and limped towards the desk. "Kick that gun over here," he said, in a cold, quiet voice.

His rival's face contorted with fury, but Judge extended his foot and sent the pistol skittering across the wooden floor.

Doc knocked it into the corner with his boot and advanced on the other man, holding the gun in front of him.

"How about it, Judge? Should I kill you?" Doc enquired. He cocked the pistol and pointed it at Judge's head. "You certainly tried to kill me."

Judge raised wary eyes to his face and squared his shoulders, but Doc laughed softly.

"No, I don't think so. I'm not like you, you

contemptible little man." He set the pistol down on a table and shifted his weight off the cane.

"But I am going to do something I've dreamed of for ten years.

"I'm going to beat your tiny little ears together, you thick-skulled, pea-brained brute!"

He lifted the cane on the words and brought it down across Judge's head with a mighty *crack*. Judge went staggering back a pace, then pulled back and threw his fist at Doc's jaw.

Doc blocked the blow with the metal cane and sent his right fist across Judge's chin in a dark blur. Judge spun backwards and fell on the floor, and Doc rolled his eyes to the ceiling, planted the cane on the ground, and leaned on it heavily.

Judge pulled himself up off the floor, pulling his hand across his jaw. "You're winded, aren't you?" he marvelled. "Yes, I can see it! You're dragging that right leg. Did you come up here thinking that you could pound me, Dailey, when you're leaning on a *cane*?"

Judge walked up boldly and kicked the black cane out from under him. It went clattering out across the floor, and Doc staggered back.

"Why, I don't even have to hit you, Doc." Judge smiled in frowning wonder. "You're about to fall down all by yourself!"

Judge pulled his arm back on the words and smashed his fist into Doc's ribs. Doc groaned and doubled up, holding his midsection, and Judge smashed his fist across Doc's jaw.

Doc staggered against the wall and lifted his arm to block another blow to the jaw. He backed away, panting, as Judge advanced.

"You always were a cocky one," Judge told him. "The pretty boy who always won. The man that everybody liked, even though you were nothing but a God-cursed thief! Well, you're not going to steal from me this time," Judge's gravelly voice growled. "I'm going to throw you out that window, Doc, and then I'm going downstairs to bring Kate back up here where she belongs. You stole her from me once. You aren't going to do it again!"

Doc's eyes narrowed to two icy slits, and he drew himself up, panting. He adjusted his shoulders, clenched his fists, and screamed like a madman. To Judge's stunned amazement, Doc's civilized personality suddenly vanished, and he grabbed Judge Carter with both hands, and by his sharp lapels.

***

Thirty minutes later, Judge Carter staggered out of his penthouse apartment. His fine linen shirt was torn open, his mouth was swollen and bloody, and one arm hung limp.

He made his way down the hall to the gilded elevator and leaned heavily against its back wall as it slowly descended.

He pulled the cage door back with a *bang,* staggered

out into the service hall, and onto the main floor of the casino. But when he reached its threshold, he stopped dead, staring in disbelief.

The place was desolate and empty. Doc was gone, Kate was gone, and all his customers had vanished. Even the cattle had swept through and gone. But every stick of furniture in the Lucky Seven had been smashed to splinters; shattered glass covered the marble floors; huge potted plants and statues were overturned and broken, and a small fire was burning in the doorway to the restaurant.

And as he stood there, a strange old man with long gray hair and bushy eyebrows appeared in the doorway. The old man leaned against the twisted frame, and the two of them stared at one another for a pregnant moment; then the old man dusted his hands clean and walked out again without a word.

Chapter Sixty-Two

Kate tucked Emil into his little bed and gazed at him tenderly as he closed his eyes and sighed. She leaned down, kissed his smooth cheek, and walked out of the room softly.

Doc was standing just outside and took her arm. The two of them walked to the back porch of the house and sat down on a wicker sofa. The midnight air was soft and pleasantly cool, and the last crickets of summer hummed in the grass.

Kate reached for Doc's hand and caressed it. "My knight," she murmured. "My hero!"

Doc smiled, but the smile didn't reach his eyes. They were still smouldering.

"It frightens me how much I enjoyed thrashing that fool," he drawled. "I think I could be a killer someday, if I'm diligent."

Kate laughed and kissed his hand. "Never!"

The dark look in Doc's eyes faded. He smiled and looked over at her. "Well, maybe not. But we're going to have to watch little Emil."

"He made my heart stop a dozen times tonight!" Kate

shook her head, and seeing her tears, Doc sputtered and reached for her.

"Now, now," he soothed, and folded her to his chest. "Emil's safe now. We're all fine."

Kate lifted her sparkling eyes to Doc's and smiled. "Yes, we're all fine," she said softly. "I came back to life when I saw you standing straight and tall in the doorway! How do you feel?"

"Sore," he sighed. "Tired. Daisy was right. I'm past my prime."

"Oh, I don't believe that for an instant," Kate teased and twined her arms around his neck, and Doc laughed and leaned down to kiss her.

***

The next morning, Daisy and Clay were summoned to the little office Doc had made for himself in the parlour of his house. The two of them stood in front of Doc and Kate, hands clasped and guilty eyes lowered.

"Your intentions were good," Doc began with a sigh, "but neither of you gave the slightest thought to the consequences of releasing a hundred cows into the streets of Denver. And it is only a matter of time before the owner of the Circle T Ranch presents me with a bill for every one of them. I shudder to think of how much money that will be."

"People could have been killed!" Kate added reproachfully.

"There are also an untold number of shop and café

owners who will hunting us up," Doc continued. "The bills will be breathtaking!"

Clay rubbed the back of his neck with his hand. "It's my fault, Doc," he murmured. "I was the one who thought of it. Daisy just went along."

Daisy grimaced up at Doc. "It was a better plan than mine," she confessed ruefully. "I was going to take your shotgun to the Lucky Seven and blow that polecat's head off, but Clay talked me out of it."

Doc straightened in alarm and reached for Kate's hand. Seeing that he was speechless, Kate replied:

"It's a miracle that the two of you weren't trampled—climbing around in cattle cars and stirring the beasts up to rage through the streets!"

"Yes, it was," Doc murmured unexpectedly. "It was a miracle." He raised his blue eyes and announced:

"This Sunday, all of us are going down to that little church in Wolf Table and thank God that we're still alive. You will wear your dress, your hat, and your boots, Daisy Dailey, and you will sit quietly while the preacher admonishes the wicked."

Daisy opened her mouth to protest, but Doc added severely: "That, or face the sheriff!"

Daisy closed her mouth with a snap, and Doc nodded grimly. "Now Daisy, you are restricted to this house, and Wolf Table, until Christmas—longer if you complain. And Clay"—he turned his light eyes to Clay's dark ones—"if you want to see Daisy again, you must find a job. I don't care what kind of job it is, but it will have to be here in town, or close by.

"I might help you find a job on a ranch if you think you might like that line of work. Though if you want to work at the Circle T, I suggest you don't mention my name."

Clay sputtered with laughter, then bit his lip. "I'd be grateful for that, Doc," he replied quietly.

"Very well then. You may go."

Clay looked at Daisy and whistled soundlessly; then the two of them clasped hands and walked out of the room and into the back yard.

Kate watched them go and then turned to Doc with a puzzled look. "Church, Doc? That isn't like you."

Doc met her eyes. "No. But when I read that letter and came down to Denver not knowing if you or Emil were alive, I prayed to God. I'm not sure, but I think I gave him my soul."

Kate raised her brows in surprise. "You, Doc?"

"I'll have to enquire more particularly about it, but I think that's what happened." He reached for a thick book on his desk and patted the cover.

Kate reached for his hand. "Very well, Doc," she replied softly. "I don't understand anything about God, but if it's important to you—I'll learn."

Doc squeezed her hand. "We'll learn together, Kate."

Epilogue

Emil adjusted his silk top hat and leaned casually against the sidewalk railing outside Hiram Heller's Mercantile.

"I was surrounded by murderers," he told his audience dramatically, "big evil beasts! My life, and my mother's life, dangled by a thread!"

"Oh, Emil!" came a chorus of girlish voices.

"So I stole a gun from the ugliest of the two and escaped to rescue my helpless mother, who was being held captive by the biggest brute of all—a swine without honour. He offered her violence right before my eyes!"

"What did you *do*, Emil?"

Emil raised his brows and straightened the cuffs of his velvet jacket. "What any man of honour would do. I challenged him to defend his life or be shot down like a dog!"

There was a collective gasp, and then a breathless:

"Did you really shoot him, Emil?"

"I shot him immediately," Emil replied, to another gasp.

"*Dead*, Emil?"

"Alas, no. The coward fled me. I shot again, and then my father arrived to finish him off. Together we rescued my mother from his clutches, and the beast is now in jail for kidnapping me."

Six pairs of adoring eyes fastened themselves on Emil's face. "You're the bravest boy in the whole world, Emil!"

"Never heard anything like it!"

"I love you, Emil!"

Kate emerged from the mercantile moments after and found Emil at the centre of a circle of little bonnets. She walked over and smiled:

"Are you ready to come home, Emil?"

A scowling little boy standing a few yards away demanded: "You his ma, lady?"

Kate turned towards him with a smile. "Yes, I'm Emil's mother."

"Any of that big pack true?"

Kate smiled more deeply and put a gloved hand on Emil's shoulder. "Every word of it," she replied proudly. "Emil is my brave knight. He saved my life and my honour from a wicked man. It truly happened, just as he has said."

Emil gained an inch in height as the little girls around him *oohed* and *aahed*, and the little boy stomped off in disgust.

But as Kate took his hand, and they walked out of earshot, Emil told her: "It is now time that I should have a gun to wear like all other men of the world. I prefer an ivory or pearl handled revolver."

Kate glanced at him. "You will never touch another

gun in your life," she informed him grimly. "If I find you have touched one, I will beat you with sticks and without mercy. Then I will tell Doc, and he will beat you again."

Emil looked up at her in frowning shock. "This is an outrage!" he gasped.

But Kate met his eyes. "This is a promise," she assured him and slapped his seat.

***

When they arrived home, Emil scampered away to play in the yard, and Kate set down the package she had retrieved from the post office. She untied the strings, opened the elegant box, and smiled in delight at the sight of the shimmering wedding gown hidden beneath the delicate layers of rice paper.

She lifted it to her shoulders and let its silken folds ripple to her feet like flowing water. The gown had been specially designed for her by the most exclusive couturier in New Orleans and was the last word in elegance. A lacework of tiny crystals fell from the sleeves and down the bodice like layered ruffles, and the skirts were intricately worked with seed pearls, more crystals, and metallic silver thread in tiny, even stitches.

Doc happened to walk in on her as she turned back and forth, and Kate shrieked and laughed in dismay. "Oh no, close your eyes! It's bad luck for the groom to see the bride's dress before the wedding!"

Doc smiled but refused to look away. He shook his head and came and took Kate in his arms. "You know, I don't think I believe in luck anymore," he told her.

Kate stared up at him in scandalized astonishment.

"You must be joking!"

"I believe that some things are meant to be," he told her. "And that they're going to happen, no matter what stands in the way.

"And the devil fly away with the *luck*."

Kate let the dress fall back down into its box and curled her arms around his neck, but her smile faded. She searched Doc's eyes with a serious look and nodded.

"So do I, Doc," she murmured and stood on tiptoe to kiss him. When they parted, Doc sighed and played with a tendril of her red-brown hair.

"Are you going to be all right in this little town?" he asked softly.

"Are you, Doc?"

The end of Doc's mouth curled up. "We'll see. Now that Judge is gone, there's nothing to keep us from getting a place in Denver. Nice restaurants, plenty of entertainment, a handy rail hub."

"There's nothing to keep us from going back to New Orleans, either."

Doc raised an eyebrow. "That's true, isn't it? I miss the old town. But—I wonder if a big city is the best place to raise our children. It was fine for us, but I wonder what New Orleans would do to Daisy and Emil."

Kate fell silent. "Emil will be difficult when he is older; I know it. And there are many ways a boy can come to grief in New Orleans!"

"And Daisy—well, she'd probably just hate it there.

She loves these mountains."

Doc smiled and lifted an eyebrow. "Let's stay here then, for now," he suggested. "Maybe I can tame you if I keep you here long enough—you gambling hall hussy!"

Kate burst into trills of laughter, and Doc bent down to nuzzle her neck, and Daisy walked in on them and put her hands on her hips.

She looked over her shoulder and called back to Clay:

"They're at it again. I swear, Clay, if I ever get this mushy, you can kick me in the shins."

She glared at her parents in disgust and turned to go back out into the yard.

***

A week later, on a bright September morning, sunshine flooded through the peaked windows of the Friendship Church of Wolf Table. The church was packed because an event was happening that everyone wanted to see: against all odds, the grizzled mountain man from the wilds of Pine Ridge was marrying the fancy French lady from New Orleans, Louisiana.

Bets had been placed in town, both for and against it, and everyone wanted to see it proved beyond doubt.

The townsfolk craned their necks to look as the smiling minister beamed at the bride and groom. The elegant couple were dressed as if they were in Paris—the groom in his spotless black full-dress suit, top hat, and cane, and the bride in her delicate crystal-fringed gown, bouffant hairdo, diamond-encrusted hair barrettes, and sheer, snowy veil.

"Dearly beloved, we are gathered together here in the sight of God, and in the face of this congregation, to join together this man and this woman in holy matrimony; which is an honourable estate, instituted of God in the time of man's innocency, signifying unto us the mystical union that is betwixt Christ and his church."

The preacher paused, turned the page of his prayer book, and went on reading, but almost no one in the little chapel seemed to be attending. Kate, whose rich red-brown hair, angelic face, and glittering wedding gown commanded Doc's whole attention, was looking love into her groom's eyes and had been since she reached his side and took his offered arm.

Clay, who was standing to Doc's right, was staring steadfastly at Daisy, whose expression alternated between fleeting happiness and intense discomfort. She looked very slim and elegant in her gown of pale blue silk, bouquet of blue irises, and tiny boots. But she kept tilting her head under the voluminous and extremely expensive blonde wig that Doc had insisted she wear to spare the guests the shock of her chopped-off hair, and every now and then, she lifted one boot and scratched her other leg with it.

Emil stood ramrod-straight at Doc's side and held the ring pillow perfectly still. He had marched down the aisle to the sighs of the little girls and the soft laughter of the adults since he was dressed like a little bridegroom in his silk top hat, full-dress tailcoat, waistcoat, and spotless black trousers.

Most of Wolf Table had turned out for the wedding, as was the local custom, and the little church was full to overflowing. There were even a few visitors from out of town. Among them was a tall blond boy with bright blue eyes who stood at the back of the chapel with his arms crossed. Although he was in attendance, he seemed not to hear what was being said, and he never took his eyes from Daisy's pert profile, elegant gown, and beautiful, if artificial hair.

"Marriage was ordained for the mutual society, help, and comfort, that the one ought to have of the other, both in prosperity and adversity," the minister intoned. "Into which holy estate these two persons present come now to be joined.

"Therefore if any man can show any just cause, why they may not lawfully be joined together, let him now speak, or else hereafter forever hold his peace."

Daisy glanced back over her shoulder and gave the assembled guests a warning glare, but no one offered opposition, and the minister smiled: "I now pronounce you man and wife. You may kiss the bride."

Doc reached over, lifted the glittering veil from Kate's face, and leaned down to give his bride a lingering kiss, and the guests laughed softly.

The pianist, none other than the longsuffering Mrs Taylor, threw her hands down onto the piano keys and pounded out the notes to The Wedding March, and Doc and Kate ran out of the church in a hail of rice and laughter.

The couple had made it clear, and it was known to the guests ahead of time, that they would leave the church immediately after the wedding. The two of them climbed into a carriage waiting on the lawn, and Daisy, Clay, and Emil walked out onto the church steps to watch as Doc waved and whipped up the horse. The horse danced across the lawn and into the road at a brisk trot, and Daisy watched wistfully as it rolled away.

Clay turned to her with a smile. "Well, that's that, Dase," he told her. "We got 'em hitched."

"And thank the Lord," Daisy retorted and yanked the trailing wig off her head. "I couldn't-a stood another second under this sweaty mess!"

To Emil's horror, she threw the wig down on the church steps and took Clay's hand, and the two of them fled down the road at a run.

"Barbarians!" he cried, "Will you leave me here to entertain our guests alone?"

But there was no reply, and Emil huffed, drew himself up, and marched back to the front of the church, where he held up his hands for attention. The wedding guests laughed to see him, standing stiff and flustered in his elegant clothes, and he announced:

"*Mesdames et monsieurs*, it is my unfortunate duty to tell you that my sister and her *copain* have been unavoidably diverted and are desolate to be so suddenly deprived of the pleasure of your company."

He took a deep breath and continued: "But if you will follow me, my parents have arranged two private train cars to take their guests to the Silver Swan in Denver, where we will continue our celebration in the utmost pleasure and comfort."

There was a murmur of astonishment, followed by laughter and clapping, and Emil bowed again and came down from the dais.

As he did, six little girls rushed to his side, and Emil bowed deeply.

"*Bonjour, mes belles copines*," he greeted them, and a chorus of adoring voices greeted him.

"You look like a bandbox beau, Emil!"

"Never saw a boy look so good in clothes!"

"I love you, Emil!"

***

An hour later, Kate emerged from the luxurious private compartment she and Doc shared, wearing a diaphanous dressing gown fringed in lace. Doc had rented a whole train car for their honeymoon, with a bedroom suite, a salon, and a private dining room all its own. The train was speeding east, carrying them back to New Orleans for a month-long honeymoon.

Doc walked out of the bedroom wearing a burgundy smoking jacket and carrying a bottle of champagne. He opened it with a loud *pop*, and Kate laughed as he filled their glasses.

Doc put the bottle onto a table and lifted his glass to Kate's. The glasses touched with a faint *ting*, and they took a sip of champagne.

Doc closed his eyes and sighed deeply. "Oh, how I have missed a fine glass of wine," he moaned and took another sip. "It makes me feel faint, to think that we'll soon be dining in New Orleans."

Kate laughed indulgently. "Are you sure you don't want to go back for good, Doc?"

Doc was silent for a moment. "I dreamed of it for years," he murmured. "I've missed everything about it. But it's not home, Kate. Not anymore. Heaven help me, I've gotten used to Colorado."

Kate laughed musically and ran her fingers along the satin lapels of his jacket. "Who would have dreamed it?" she teased. "Doc Dailey, the riverboat gambler—the man who broke the bank on the *Natchez Queen*—settling down at last!"

Doc's bright eyes gleamed, and he tilted his head. "Are you sure I won that money fair and square, Kate?" he asked softly. "Was that Lady Luck—or was that you?

"Come on, now, tell me the truth."

"I will tell you what I told Judge. I am an honest dealer, and the play was perfectly fair."

Doc nodded and set his champagne glass down on the table; then he reached for Kate and pulled her to his chest. "All right, Kate. I believe you.

"Now, as I was saying, before we were so rudely interrupted—"

But Kate only laughed and threw her arms around him, and Doc crushed her to his lips.

(turn the page)

Thank you!

Thank you for reading my Christian Romance Novel, "The Frontier Gambler's Lady"! It means a lot to me!

The core soul of the book you just read was influenced by thousands of readers who became part of my "family" before you! The title, the cover, the essence of the book as a whole was affected by them!

I personally want to thank them for their support on my journey! I devote this book to them!

If you are not a member yet, **click this link to join**: https://chloecarley.com/ccbbsd

After you sign-up, you will receive as a BONUS my Full-Length Novella, "Boston Bride Salvation! With more than 140+ positive GoodReads reviews it's a safe choice, you don't want to miss:

FREE EXCLUSIVE GIFT
(available only to my subscribers)

Visit my webpage below to get the FREE BONUS:

https://chloecarley.com/ccbbsd

Made in the USA
Lexington, KY
15 August 2018